KILL FOR ME

Karen looked on, transfixed and disbelieving. The figure glanced at her and behind the black mask Karen saw two eyes and a mouth, the eyes boring into her with what felt like pure hatred.

The assailant walked up to Dianne and stood above her, pointing the gun with both hands, taking very deliberate and careful aim at her chest.

"No, don't!" Dianne screamed, trying to crawl away on her back. "It hurts so bad!"

Karen yelled too.

The attacker slowly cocked the pistol, pulling the hammer all the way back with a soft, dull clicking sound—one, two, three, four distinct clicks. Then it fired, a dull flat pop, just eighteen inches away from Dianne, who was still screaming.

Other Avon Books by
Stephen Singular

A KILLING IN THE FAMILY

Sweet
EVIL

STEPHEN SINGULAR

AVON BOOKS ◆ NEW YORK

SWEET EVIL is an original publication of Avon Books. This work has never before appeared in book form.

AVON BOOKS
A division of
The Hearst Corporation
1350 Avenue of the Americas
New York, New York 10019

Copyright © 1994 by Stephen Singular
Published by arrangement with the author
Library of Congress Catalog Card Number: 93-90913
ISBN: 0-380-76795-3

First Avon Books Printing: June 1994

AVON TRADEMARK REG. U.S. PAT. OFF. AND IN OTHER COUNTRIES, MARCA REGISTRADA, HECHO EN U.S.A.

Printed in the U.S.A.

RA   10 9 8 7 6 5 4 3 2 1

To Nancy

part one

TWO FULL DAYS

One

One cold November morning in 1806, an adventurous spirit named Zebulon Pike was exploring in Colorado when he looked up and saw a mountain floating in the sky, mistaking it for an azure cloud. Centuries earlier the Ute Indians who had hunted in the southwestern United States had called this bald upthrusting of rock "The Long One." Pike tried to name it Grand Peak and then Blue Peak but the only name that stuck was his own. In the mid-1800s the mountain gained national notoriety when a gold rush caused thousands of fortune seekers to head west in Conestoga wagons with "Pikes Peak or Bust" painted on their sides. In 1893 Katharine Lee Bates composed "America the Beautiful" while studying its majestic purple face.

Pikes Peak stands 14,110 feet above sea level and dominates the landscape around Colorado Springs. Snow-covered well into summer, it rises from the foothills on the western edge of town and loses itself in the scudding clouds. When storms hit the mountain, they drop sudden violent showers on the city, rain or sleet or bits of hail that are quickly replaced by shafts of light so brilliant they hurt the eye. In late afternoon, Pikes Peak can be stunning—pink stripes of fire riding the ridgetops; a dusting of snow beneath the flames; black clouds churning and blowing apart; golden swirls shooting down from the heavens; red rocks caught out by the sun; barren patches of dirt; holes of blue sky; a clear hard wind, like a great blast of music exploding into new creations. In one hour Pikes Peak can generate a week of fantastic weather.

The mountain, more spectacular than any skyline, is very close to town, intimate and hovering, hanging above the city and looking down on the population as if it were a judge, capable of being lenient and life-giving or brutal and harsh. You can't escape its face—visible from everywhere. Occasionally, while walking along the pavement or conversing on a street corner, a citizen of the Springs will glance over his shoulder and see it in the distance, floating and drifting, a mass of dust, grave and imposing, reminding him of the grandeur of the Rockies and of the great and strange forces moving in the air.

At eight-twenty on a clear mid-September evening Sheila Gillen stepped out of the Otis Park Community Center to be alone with her cigarette and away from those who disapproved of her nicotine habit. She struck a match and inhaled, taking in the dimly lit grounds. North and east of downtown Colorado Springs, Otis Park is a modest neighborhood of small houses built of wood, stucco, or brick. The soil has a reddish tinge and lilacs are abundant, coloring the alleys and decorating the lawns. The park occupies a square city block and holds, in addition to the community center, a basketball court, a swing set, a tennis court, an asphalt parking lot, a green synthetic-surfaced track that senior citizens enjoy walking around, a baseball diamond, and a playground with an elaborate structure that children like to climb. At night adults meet in the center to discuss local issues or personal matters. A low gray building fronted by heavy lodgepoles and a latticework awning, the center is built into the side of a hill. Concrete planters ring the facade and a sidewalk curls around the eastern edge.

Sheila rested against a planter, taking another drag. For the past two hours, she had been attending a meeting of thirty people suffering from systemic lupus erythematosus, known informally as "lupus." On the second Wednesday of each month, the group came together to discuss the illness, an inflammatory disorder of the connective tissue that binds together the internal organs. The disease, which afflicts women nine times more often than men and usually during their childbearing years, affects the joints, skin, kidneys, lung covering, heart covering, lymph nodes, and spleen, leaving most people in pain or exhausted and a few dead. Its cause is unknown. Lupus is triggered when the body's immune system, instead of attacking invading viruses, bacteria, or fungi, attacks the healthy tissue within. Sometimes the disease leaves ulcerating lesions on the face and is called *noli-me-tangere*—"Do not touch me." For no apparent reason lupus flares up or goes into remission and then, years later, may suddenly and mysteriously return, visitations that are not only frightening but incomprehensible.

"Lupus," Sheila once said, "doesn't always show on you and it bothers you when people come up and say, 'How can you be so sick and look so good?' Every day I have pain and you can't measure pain. You lose a lot with the disease. I can't work anymore. I don't have the energy. Sometimes you have depression and you just wanna give up. The support group at Otis Park helps me deal with all this. It's a bitch session. You're around your own kind. You can't complain too much about the illness to family members. They're scared of you, at least at the start."

Sheila blew smoke into the warm, late-summer air, into the lamps above the patio in front of the community center. Something behind her moved. It was just to her left— something startling—like a shadow walking fast. She turned and saw a figure wearing a black ski mask over its head and green army fatigues—someone marching with shoulders hunched, coat collar up over the ears, hands in pockets, marching toward the parking lot as if the night were cold. Sheila stared and the figure stared back, their eyes locking, as if they might have known each other. A shiver passed down the length of Sheila's body and she felt a chill. Dropping the cigarette, she crushed it out with her heel and went back into the building, anxious to be with the others in the group. Although she said nothing to the women, who were drinking coffee, eating cookies, and talking, she was spooked, and she wasn't alone. Earlier in the evening, another lupus victim had excused herself from the meeting and left Otis Park, walking quickly to her car and driving away with the windows rolled up and the doors locked. "I just felt that something was wrong," she said.

By eight-thirty the group had begun to disperse and two other women walked outside. Karen Johnson was frail-looking and bespectacled—she had had lupus since the age of eight—but her companion, Leilani Capps, had only lately been diagnosed as having the disease and appeared more robust. Tonight was her first lupus gathering. The women stood by the planters and chatted, Karen smoking a cigarette and Leilani noticing something just to the east of the building. A figure moved in the grass and looked at her; a puffy figure in odd clothing tiptoed closer and peered right at her. She was so uncomfortable she glanced down, trying to ignore what she'd seen. She thought it must be the gardener who cared for the center's grounds. When she looked up, he'd vanished.

Dianne Hood walked outside and joined the women on the patio. Thirty-two years old and the mother of three small children, Dianne had frosted blond hair and a pretty smile, which had helped her get modeling work in the late 1970s, when she was a college student in San Angelo, Texas. In those days she was very attractive and considerably thinner. Lupus had added flesh to her cheeks and torso, while taking away her strength. Since being diagnosed with the illness eighteen months earlier, in the spring of 1989, she had endured severe headaches, bad mood swings, skin rashes, memory lapses, chest pains, weight fluctuations—up to 160, down to 138, up again to 146—irritability, a significant loss of energy, welts when she was exposed to sunlight, side effects from taking a variety of drugs, exhaustion in her lungs and aching joints. There were times when she had feared for her life. In recent years Dianne had gone through a born-again Christian conversion and in March of 1990, in a prayer book near her bedside, she had even outlined the songs for her funeral, the verses she wanted read, and where she desired to be buried. She carried handwritten copies of those verses everywhere.

By mid-September of 1990 her concerns about dying had begun to fade and she was unquestionably better. At this evening's meeting, Marty Wood, the president of the lupus group, thought Dianne was "bubbly. She grinned at me and winked. I noticed a drastic improvement in her." Sheila Gillen observed that Dianne was "always with a smile now," unlike the depressed woman who had first come to Otis Park the previous winter. Delrece Moore, who conducted self-help classes and had been Dianne's teacher at earlier gatherings, found her "very upbeat and starting to help others with their lupus. I hadn't seen her for a couple of months and was struck by how much better she looked. She told us that her only problem now was potty training her two-year-old."

Tonight Dianne had been a "greeter"—she had worn a pink corsage and stood at the center's front door, welcoming others in her warm west Texas drawl which made people feel at home. During the meeting, she'd told the group how much their support meant to her and how she'd finally learned to interact with doctors so she could get the medication and treatment she needed (her physician, Dr. Austin Corbett, did not believe her illness was ever life-threatening and had lately described his patient as "almost normal"). Dianne confessed her difficulty in finding the right prescriptions—she'd tried the steroid Prednisone, Flurazepam, the pain reliever Lorcet Plus, Salicylsalic, Aralen, the sleeping pill Dalmane, Voltaren, the anti-inflammatory Losec, Plaquenil, and Prozac. The drugs had left her weak and dizzy, but now she was on reduced dosages and regaining her strength. Gradually she had taught herself to cope with the disease and had even begun to hope that the lupus might be going into remission. Just this morning, she had attended a Bible study session with her best friend, Darla Blue, and confided to her that she was finally at peace with her life.

As Dianne, Leilani, and Karen lingered in front of the center, Leilani was struck by Dianne's good humor and her whimsical outfit: a white stretch top painted with purple irises, a denim skirt, and white tennis shoes painted to match the top. Under her right arm Dianne carried a purple-and-straw-colored handbag, its long leather strap hanging at her side. Leilani said good night to the women and turned to go back inside the building, glancing into the darkness once more but seeing no trace of the phantom she had seen earlier. In the twilight, Karen finished her cigarette and Dianne talked of her children. She enjoyed these meetings and would have liked to stay longer, but her husband, Brian Hood, also thirty-two and an insurance salesman with the Prudential, was home with the kids. He always asked her to be back by nine and she always was. Moving away from the center and onto the small asphalt parking lot, the women walked toward the Hoods' 1980 green Honda Accord, Karen in the thick grass that bordered the lot and Dianne in the concrete gutter.

As they passed two wooden posts holding signs that reserved parking spaces for the handicapped, footsteps slapped behind them, getting louder. They turned to look. Someone wearing a pulled-down black ski mask, gloves, an army jacket, and camouflage pants was right behind them, reaching out for Dianne's handbag. The women stared at the figure—Karen thinking it must have been a gag the other members of the group were playing on them and if it wasn't a gag, then it was a vagrant, a bum, a thief dressed in old army clothes. Dianne, as if sensing it wasn't a joke, instantly held out the bag.

"Take it!" she said. "It's yours!"

The figure grabbed the bag and grabbed Dianne's arm, swinging her around and dragging her across the parking lot toward the center, ten feet, fifteen, twenty feet, until she was on the patio in front of the building. Karen froze, knowing the situation was serious and Dianne needed help, and then she whirled and sprinted toward the center—running smack into one of the wooden posts and knocking her glasses askew. She righted herself and saw Dianne being flung toward the concrete, a large black handgun suddenly emerging from the army jacket and firing with a dull flat pop.

"I've been shot!" Dianne yelled as she hit the pavement, her leg bleeding where it had scraped the cement. She lay on her side, staring upward. She pulled her knees up to her chin, her arms crossed on her chest, assuming a fetal position.

The attacker bent over her.

"No!" Dianne writhed backward on the concrete, ripping her shirt, trying to squirm away. "No! Please, don't!"

Karen looked on, transfixed and disbelieving. The figure glanced at her and behind the black mask Karen saw two eyes and a mouth, the eyes boring into her with what felt like pure hatred.

With the bag draped over one arm, the assailant walked up to Dianne and stood above her, pointing the gun with both hands, one hand supporting the other for a firmer grip, taking very deliberate and careful aim at her chest.

"No, don't!" Dianne screamed, trying to crawl away on her back. "It hurts so bad."

Karen yelled too.

The attacker slowly cocked the pistol, pulling the hammer back with a soft, dull clicking sound, all the way back—one, two, three, four distinct clicks—until the gun was in firing position. It popped again, just eighteen inches away from Dianne, who was still screaming.

Two

Jennifer Reali parked her burgundy Jeep Cherokee in front of the home of Kay Everett, who ran a small day-care business in a northern suburb of Colorado Springs. The Reali girls—Tineke was three and Natasha one—stayed at the Everett residence while their mother worked Mondays, Wednesdays, and Fridays in a floral shop on the south side of town. Jennifer was twenty-eight, a lithe attractive woman with shoulder-length brunette hair and a very changeable face. In the right mood, her features were striking: good teeth, a full, flat upper lip, intelligent hazel eyes, a straight jawline, and a dimple in her chin. In the wrong mood, she was plain and pale, her face devoid of color and her expression harsh. She resembled the English actress Glenda Jackson, although she was generally softer and prettier than Jackson, with a more feminine air. Jennifer was five feet five inches tall, weighed 128 pounds, often wore glasses and looked deceptively fragile. In years past, she had been a good soccer player and an exceptional oar on her high school rowing crew in Seattle, winning a silver medal at the national championships. Her arms held considerable strength and her legs were trim and hard, as she liked jogging and exercising at a local health club.

If Jennifer was picking up her daughters after dark she usually called ahead, but on this occasion she had failed to do so. Brittany Eagan, a curly-haired teenager who lived with the Everetts, was watching the girls this evening. Through the day-care operation, she'd become acquainted with Jennifer and liked her—the young mother was friendly and outgoing and polite, always interested in what Brittany was studying in school and in her grades. Jennifer treated her like an adult, an equal, taking the time to pay attention to her. Even tonight, when she arrived at a few minutes before nine and looked somewhat weary, she had exchanged a few words with Brittany before asking about her children. The Reali girls were already in bed and had to be awakened and escorted out to the Cherokee. As they were standing in the driveway, Jennifer thanked her for watching them and then, with gentle and precise movements, she strapped her daughters into their car seats, waved to the teenager, and said good night.

She drove to 2645 Canton Lane in the suburb of Briargate, a relatively new development in the northeast end of town. Few mature trees grew on these streets and most of the houses were like the Realis'—spacious split-level brick affairs with double garages, a basketball hoop in the driveway, scattered toys, and a young pine or two in the front yard. Everything looked open, unsettled, unfinished. Jennifer wasn't intimate with her neighbors but occasionally talked to Mary Garren, an older woman who lived across the street. Mary had secretly dubbed her "Supermom," the kind of young wife and mother who was always in motion—cleaning her house or rolling on the grass with her children or washing the car or mowing the lawn or performing other domestic chores, a whirlwind of activity, running in one door and out the other. Mary had once told her to relax and take some time for herself, because there was more to life than being perfect.

Jennifer liked Mary's company but felt that many Briargate residents looked down on army renters, viewed them as transients, and she resented that notion. Her family was well established in Seattle and had been for decades—her father, Keith Vaughan, was a prominent architect in that city—but she had to admit that her husband, Captain Benjamin Reali, who had a military background, came closer to fitting that description. His father, Ben senior, had been a career sergeant and the boy had

spent part of his youth in Germany, on an army base near
Berlin. Ben junior was as used to moving around as his
wife was to staying in the same place, one of many differences between them. On numerous occasions he had tried
to introduce Jennifer to military wives at the various
places where the couple had been stationed, but the friendships never took. Jennifer felt no more comfortable with
these women than she did in Briargate and, sometimes, her
discomfort showed. When she and Ben were living off
base in Europe, a group of army spouses had jokingly
nicknamed her "The General" because she liked giving orders.

Bordering the north end of Otis Park is Iowa Street and
one block north of that is Cache La Poudre, the two streets
connected by a narrow red dirt alley. Dawn Palma lived on
the alley's east side and just after 8:30 P.M. she had heard
screams and run to her bedroom window, gazing into the
faint light and watching someone dash up the alley. Moving away from Otis Park, the figure wore a ski mask and
what looked like a sweatshirt, one hand held under the garment, the other raised in the air and waving free. Dawn
left her bedroom and told her mother about what she had
glimpsed in the shadows.

"Call the police," the woman said.

While Dawn was dialing 911, Karen Johnson, who was
no longer transfixed by the shouting, ran over to Dianne,
who was lying on her left side and moaning, bleeding onto
the cement patio in front of the community center.

"So bad," she kept saying. "It hurts so bad."

Karen ran into the center, arriving just as someone was
coming out. The automatic glass doors swung toward her,
hitting her and knocking her down. She got up and walked
unsteadily into the building.

"Dianne's been shot!" she said. "She's been shot!"

For an instant nothing happened, the room growing perfectly silent, the women holding their coffee cups and

turning and staring at her. Then everyone moved, as if they already knew what to do in an emergency.

Sarah Troup, the vice president of the support group and a registered nurse, ran through the front door and out onto the patio. She knelt over Dianne, touching the woman's wrist for a pulse. Sheila Gillen also went outside and stood over Dianne, who remained on her left side with her left arm extended on the concrete and her eyes fixed open, her lips gasping. Sarah rolled her onto her back, thinking the worst, and when she felt for a jugular pulse, nothing was there.

"Can anyone do CPR?" she said. Sarah didn't believe that cardiopulmonary resuscitation would accomplish much, but she knew it couldn't be harmful and thought it might be of some emotional benefit to those in the lupus group, because they could later tell themselves that at least they'd tried to help.

"I do," Sheila said, kneeling down and quickly beginning the chest compressions, blowing into Dianne's mouth and holding a towel on the prone woman's left side, now pouring blood. Dianne's breath was growing more and more faint.

Karen Johnson had come outside and was sitting next to Dianne, talking to her and crying, watching her friend's eyes grow dim. In the confusion, someone pushed Karen aside and she wandered back into the building, dazed and disoriented by all the activity—people running in and out the glass doors, looking for blankets, searching for phone numbers, shouting instructions, and cursing. Ron Brinkmeier, the Otis Park custodian who was working at the center that evening, dialed 911 and Connie Arms, a dispatcher with the Colorado Springs Police Department, answered the call, immediately relaying it to the ambulance corps, the paramedics, and the fire engine crews that worked with local law enforcement. The call also went into an eight-foot-by-four-foot tape-recording machine that operates twenty-four hours a day and can document forty telephone conversations at once.

"We have a shooting at 731 North Iowa at Otis Park," Brinkmeier said into the receiver.

"Who was it?" asked Connie Arms, typing the information onto her computer screen as Brinkmeier spoke.

"A young lady at the meeting. She's bleeding very heavily and needs help."

"Are there any witnesses?"

"I'm not sure."

"Is she still down?"

"Yes. He shot her and took her bag. He took off."

"What direction?"

"He just took off running."

"A man did?"

Brinkmeier looked confused and handed the phone to the woman standing next to him, who was weeping.

"This is Karen Johnson," she told Arms. "A man did it."

"Tell me what he looks like. We'll try to find him."

"He was short. He had on a black stocking mask. He came up behind us. We tried to get away. He pushed her on the ground and shot her."

"Which way did he go?"

"I can't tell directions."

"I gotta know, babe."

"He went east around the park."

"How many shots?"

"He shot her twice and ran away."

"Is her family there with her, babe?"

"No," Karen lost control and wailed into the phone. "Oh, God! Oh, God! Oh, no!"

"Karen?"

"Yes."

"Are you with her?"

"No, I'm inside."

"Is a fire truck there?"

She looked out the window. "Yes."

"Does her family know?"

"I have her home address. Someone will call her husband."

"Did she say anything to this guy to tell you that she knew who he was?"

"No. He came up behind us and I thought it was someone from the meeting, but Dianne turned around and knew right away what was going on."

"What kind of gun was it, babe? Blue or black?"

"Black. A revolver. He had on a fatigue jacket and military pants."

"Did he talk?"

"He didn't say anything. He was about five-foot-seven, five-eight."

"You're doing a great job of remembering, babe. Is Dianne still there?"

"They're taking her away," Karen sobbed, glancing through the window again. "I was with her and she told me it hurt really bad and I said I was coming in . . ."

"You've been great, babe. Thank you. Good-bye."

"Good-bye."

Jennifer put her children to bed and went into the backyard, sitting in the darkness, glad to be out of the house. It was too large tonight, too quiet, and it felt cold. She lit a cigarette and took a long drag, the smoke slowly burning her lungs, wishing as she exhaled that she had never taken up the habit, but it was only temporary, she told herself, and she wasn't really a smoker and she could quit whenever she wanted to. She took another drag and thought about her husband; she didn't like being separated. She thought about going inside and calling Ben but then changed her mind. They'd already spoken several times today and would probably talk again tomorrow. They were going to see the therapist soon and that would definitely help them with their marital problems. She didn't want to need Ben but she was lonely tonight, very lonely, and something in the thick night air made her want to cry.

She snuffed out the cigarette, stood, and walked inside.

She awakened her older daughter, Tineke, and the two of them went upstairs to the master bedroom and lay on the mattress, the young mother stroking her three-year-old's soft hair and cheeks, whispering to her words and phrases she said without thinking, small comforting sounds. She put an arm around her daughter and kept muttering, relieved to be talking to someone, even if there was no response. She reached for the phone, picking up the receiver but then putting it down. She grabbed it again and dialed a familiar number but then dropped it back onto its cradle before the first ring. Breathing deeply, she closed her eyes and felt her daughter's silky hair, gently pulling the little strands, turning them on her fingers. She spoke the girl's name. She suddenly opened her eyes, picked up the receiver once more, and called Ben, who was supposed to be working late at his office at the Fort Carson Military Reservation, five miles south of Colorado Springs. Was he still there, she wondered as she dialed the number, or had he gone out with a friend? When they'd spoken at five-thirty this evening, Ben had invited her to dinner at the Officers Club but she'd declined, saying that she planned to go shopping at the nearby Citadel Mall and then jog in Dublin Park, not far from their residence.

Captain Reali answered the phone crisply, the way he did everything at the base.

Jennifer felt better just hearing his voice. "You're still there," she said.

"Yeah, I'm still here. What's up?"

"Will you come back?"

"What?"

"Will you come home?"

"When?"

"Tonight."

He glanced toward the receiver, his mouth bending downward into a surprised expression. Just four days earlier she'd asked him to leave the house—not really asked so much as told him to go. She'd needed some time alone, she said, to sort through their marriage and she'd needed some distance so she could think clearly about the future. Even though Ben had been sleeping on the couch in recent weeks, her request had shaken him. He'd reluctantly packed a sleeping bag, toiletries, and a few civilian clothes, and taken them to the home of an army buddy, First Sergeant Dave Roper, who lived in Security, just outside the Springs. Since leaving home, Ben had phoned his wife every day, often more than once, to see how she and the children were doing. He missed all of them and he missed his house. He had also made some calls seeking professional psychiatric help, and this coming Saturday, September 15, he and Jennifer were finally, after much discussion and hesitation on his part, going to see a marriage counselor.

"I don't know if it's a good idea for me to come home right now," he said.

"Why not?"

"Because you wanted me to move out."

"I want you to come back, Ben."

"Do you want me there permanently? If I come home, I don't want to leave again."

"I want you to stay with us, be with us."

"Let's wait three more days, Jen. Let's talk to the counselor and see what he says. Then we'll know more and I'll come back if that's the best thing to do. Okay?"

She was disappointed but thought he might have been right. "Okay."

They hung up and she continued stroking her daughter's fine hair.

Jennifer dialed the number of her parents, Gail and Keith Vaughan, in Seattle. She had called them earlier in the day just to chat, and when the phone rang now the Vaughans were spending an uneventful evening at home. Gail answered and Jennifer confessed that she was struggling with her recent separation from Ben. The mother and daughter spoke about this for several minutes and then said good-bye, but the call left a disconcerting residue on the Seattle end of the line. Gail thought her daughter sounded terribly lonely. After mentioning this to her husband, she decided to call back, and this time she told Jennifer that if she felt this bad, she should drop her pretensions of strength or indifference, drop her anger and pride, phone her husband, tell him that she and the girls needed him, and ask him to come home—now. As Jennifer lay on the bed and listened to her mother, she held Tineke against her side and stroked her hair and face, still muttering to her, three generations of females connected by touch and sound over a thousand miles of darkness.

Marty Wood, the head of the lupus gathering, had located Dianne's home number among her records and was dialing it inside the community center. She'd decided, in the interest of kindness and trying to avoid panic, not to tell Dianne's husband the whole truth.

When a man answered, she said, "Is this Mr. Hood?"

"Yes," Brian said.

"This is Marty Wood, with the lupus group. Your wife has been hurt in an accident and you need to come down here."

"I can't. The children are asleep."

"One of us can come to your house or you can get a neighbor to watch them."

"Is this a joke?"

Marty, a stocky woman with frizzy orange hair and some fire in her manner, was taken aback by the remark. "No," she said forcefully, "this is not a joke."

She glanced sideways at Delrece Moore, the featured speaker at tonight's meeting, and made a strange face.

"The children," Brian repeated, "are asleep."

"Look, dammit," Marty said, "your wife's been shot and she needs you down here."

"She's gonna be all right, isn't she?"

"I have no idea. You need to get your butt down here."

Across the room a voice shouted that the paramedics had arrived and were taking Dianne to Memorial Hospital. Without hanging up, Marty set the receiver on a table, then started for the door. She turned to Delrece, pointed at the phone and said, "Tell that asshole to get down to Memorial Hospital."

In gentler language and with more patience, Delrece passed along the order and was surprised when Brian asked where the hospital was located, for it was only a few blocks south and east of the Hood residence. After getting the address the young insurance salesman, wearing blue thongs, red shorts, and a white long-sleeved pullover with "Sun Valley" on the chest and "Prudential" on the left arm, went next door and enlisted a neighbor to watch his three young children. Then he drove quickly to the hospital, which is seven blocks from Otis Park and very near the United States Olympic Committee headquarters and training center, a Colorado Springs landmark. Before he arrived, Dianne had been taken to Memorial's first-floor trauma room. Dr. Oscar Arguello-Rudin, a vascular surgery specialist, had already examined the woman and found her to be in full arrest—no pulse, her pupils fixed and dilated—so it was too late for the physician to open her chest and pump her heart. At 8:52 P.M. he officially pronounced her dead and soon after this he informed her husband that there was nothing more he could do. When he received the news, Brian leaned against a wall of the trauma room and began to cry, swearing loudly and pulling at his hair. He bit his nails, ripped them off and spit them out, his face gone pale and his body limp. Police escorted him out into the hallway.

Patrolman Creston Shields stayed in the trauma room with the corpse until it could be transported to the refrigeration chambers at the El Paso County Coroner's office. John Amundson, also of the C.S.P.D., took Dianne's blood-soaked clothes to an evidence room downtown and hung them up to dry. A third officer approached the grieving husband in the hallway at Memorial and, to Brian's disbelief and outrage, tested his hands for gunshot residue, a standard procedure which produced negative results. Brian was still weeping, his torso was giving in to spasms and he was asking anyone who would listen how God could have allowed such a thing to happen to his wife.

He begged the authorities to let him sit with Dianne's body in the trauma room but they said no, they were already conducting a homicide investigation and she had become off-limits. When he tried to force his way in to see her they physically restrained him, a formidable task because Brian stood well over six feet tall, weighed more than two hundred pounds, and had been a college football player. He wondered aloud how he was going to explain their mother's death to his three young children—Jarrod, age nine, Lesley, seven, and Joshua, two—and when he had composed himself enough to use the telephone, he began calling friends and relatives, telling them that his wife had just been murdered and if he got his hands on the man who did this for just two minutes, he would . . . exact revenge.

Three

The Major Crimes/Homicide Unit of the Colorado Springs Police Department had been called to Otis Park and Detective Brian Ritz was overseeing the murder scene investigation, while Detectives Charles Lucht, Michael Lux, and Tim Hogan interviewed those who had attended the lupus meeting. Other police gathered in the parking lot, spoke to people in the neighborhood, encircled the area in order to contain a suspect on foot, and scoured several blocks for evidence connected with the shooting. Near one of the concrete planters in front of the center they found a coin, a key, and a fragment of a lead bullet. After passing through Dianne's back and right shoulder, the slug had made an impact on some nearby cement. Another bullet remained inside the victim. This round, the fatal one, had entered her right arm before piercing her chest and heart, eventually coming to rest in her left arm. She had bled to death, from seven different wounds. Once the fatal bullet had been removed from Dianne, it would be taken to the local ballistics lab where Dr. Larry Howard would fire similar rounds into water tanks and cotton boxes to determine the caliber of the ammunition.

Officer David York, working containment north of Otis Park, talked with half a dozen people on the fringe of the center, including three young women inside a vehicle, but they had seen or heard nothing unusual. York continued cruising the neighborhood, until a man waved him over to the curb. Julian Medina introduced himself and said that he lived at 2115 East Cache La Poudre, one block north of

Otis Park, and that his home bordered the red dirt alley that joined Iowa Street with Cache La Poudre. Each Wednesday morning he carried his full green plastic trash cans out to the alley and each Wednesday evening, after the garbage had been collected, he brought them in. Tonight, he had finished watching "Doogie Howser, M.D.," then turned off the television and walked outside to retrieve the cans.

On the lip of one of them, Medina had found a drab olive army jacket, a pair of forest green camouflage pants with the cuffs rolled up, a gray sweatshirt with white fleece lining, two green wool glove liners, and a black knit ski mask. Thinking that sanitation workers had left the garments behind, he carried them into his backyard and draped them over a wooden bench. When Medina's wife had returned home from a church meeting and told him about the commotion at Otis Park—the sirens, shining lights, and patrol cars—she had suggested he find a policeman. Medina described the clothing to Officer York, who came to his backyard and guarded the potential evidence, supervising the activity until other officers arrived, along with some trained dogs who sniffed the clothes in order to trace the scent of the shooter. They lost it where the alley ended.

Dianne's handbag was found on the sidewalk just east of the center; nothing had been removed, its contents weren't even rifled. As the police cordoned off the murder scene with yellow tape and went about their work, full night descended on Colorado Springs and, in response to the darkness, a timer on the Otis Park sprinkler system was triggered, spraying water on the center's foliage and the grass and trees and shrubs near the front door, and washing some of Dianne's blood off the pavement.

In the small town of Security, First Sergeant David Roper was sitting with Ben Reali in his backyard. The smell of grilled marinated steak moved around them and filled the air with the promise of a good and long-delayed dinner. The men had been sipping beers and talking about the possibility of America going to war in the Persian Gulf against Iraq and its leader, Saddam Hussein, who had recently invaded the tiny Mideast country of Kuwait.

"What were you doing tonight?" Roper asked, changing the subject.

"Working at the base," Ben said.

"All night?"

"Yeah. Where else would I have been? There's so much paperwork in the army. I get tired of it."

Roper took another drink. "You think we're going over there—to Saudi Arabia?"

Ben shrugged and leaned forward. Even when he was sitting down, there was eagerness in his movements and the aggressiveness of a born soldier. "If we have to go," he said, "I'm ready."

The captain was thirty years old, handsome, stocky, dark-haired, and barrel-chested. He served in the Fourth Infantry Division at Fort Carson, in the 104th Military Intelligence Battalion, and he had a high-level security clearance (he'd long feared that going into therapy with his wife might cause him to lose that clearance). In his intelligence work, he was often gone from the base on secret maneuvers for weeks at a time: either "down range" to army camps in Colorado or shipped off to California's Mojave Desert. He was always prepared to go anywhere for anything related to his job; he loved the army and being promoted. Succeeding in his chosen field and "getting more stars on my uniform," as he put it, meant being willing to move, and in the past half dozen years the Realis had changed addresses six times: from Seattle to Fort Benning, Georgia, to West Germany to Italy to Fort Huachucha, Arizona, and then, in the summer of 1989, to Colorado Springs, where he had promised his wife, who was weary of being uprooted, they would stay for several years. The young man had lately been thinking about making another move but this one would only be temporary.

Six weeks earlier, when Saddam Hussein invaded Ku-

wait in early August of 1990, the United States government began deploying troops to Saudi Arabia. Combat between American and Iraqi soldiers seemed imminent and
few places in the U.S. were more affected by this news
than Colorado Springs, which is surrounded by retired military personnel and those on active duty. East of town is
Peterson Air Force Base, to the south is Fort Carson, to
the north is the U.S. Air Force Academy, and to the south-
west is the most impressive and forbidding installation of
all—NORAD, the North American Aerospace Defense
Command, headquarters for America's nuclear arsenal,
hidden in the belly of Cheyenne Mountain. In the summer
of 1990, these four military compounds employed thirty-
one thousand people. When Saddam marched his troops
across the Kuwaiti border, this part of Colorado began preparing for war. Ben knew that at any moment he could be
called away from his family and sent to the Persian Gulf.

Roper turned the steak over and glanced at his friend.
"How are you, Captain?" he said.

"Fine," Ben laughed a little sourly, as if he were laughing at himself.

"You look worried. Is something bothering you?"

"Jennifer called tonight. She calls a lot. She sounded
upset. Being separated isn't easy, Dave. She's . . ."

"What?"

"I don't know. It's a good thing we're going to see that
counselor on Saturday. Maybe he knows something we
don't. Is that meat done?"

"Yeah."

"I'm really hungry."

Roper laid out the meal and Ben finished his beer, opening another and preparing to devour his steak. As he
picked up his utensils and began to carve, the phone rang
inside. Roper answered it and Ben wasn't surprised that
the call was for him or that it was his wife. He'd felt that
she would try to reach him again tonight and as he laid
down his knife and fork and took the receiver, he sensed

that something in her mood had changed from an hour before.

"I want you home now, Ben," she said, "and I don't want you to leave me again. Ever."

"I'm eating," he replied.

"I want you home now."

Her tone of voice told him that it was time to go home but, because he was ravenous, he took a few more bites of steak, apologized to Roper for interrupting their dinner, got into his military-style Jeep, and drove straight to Briargate. Jennifer greeted him at the door, makeup highlighting her cheekbones and her hair braided in the way he especially liked, but the braids, he noticed, weren't as tight as usual. When she kissed him, she felt cold, clammy, and he was aware that she had been smoking, which was unusual because of her recent commitment to exercising at the health club. He saw some empty beer bottles in a trash can and glanced at a nearly drained liter-and-a-half bottle of red wine on the counter, surprised at how much she had drunk since he had left the house.

"It's late," she said. "Let's go to bed."

They went upstairs, and while undressing, they discussed having another child, a son this time, and they talked about taking a vacation in Europe. They slipped into bed and began making love. But their rhythm was off, jerky and robotic; neither of them said anything, not wanting to spoil their reunion. Later on, when they were lying in the dark, she asked Ben to hold her, just hold her, and he did, but her skin was so damp that he eventually slid a bedsheet between them so he could fall asleep.

It was quite late when Mark Ramey, who worked at the Prudential with Brian Hood, drove to Memorial Hospital and took his colleague home. Ramey was dumbstruck by his friend's appearance. Brian had long, curly, light brown hair, worn in a permanent, and he always made a point of being well coiffed and well dressed, but tonight he looked ghastly—chalky and tearful and he kept grabbing at his hair, yanking out strands.

"I feel so guilty, Mark," he said on the ride home, "so bad for all the things I said about Dianne and for all the thoughts I had about her."

Ramey tried to comfort him but without any success.

"I just feel so awful," Brian told him.

When they reached the Hood residence, the house was filled with people who had heard the news and who, like Ramey, attempted to soothe the young father but could not. Brian's closest friend, David Blue, soon arrived from Glenwood Springs, Colorado, where he'd gone on a business trip. Blue, who owned an orthopedic company in town and regularly attended a Bible study group with the Hoods, had learned of Dianne's death four hours earlier and driven straight through to Colorado Springs. When he saw his friend, he was also struck by the man's distraught manner and his angry words. "Some jerk killed my wife," Brian kept saying, as he sat on the couch and sobbed. Blue tried to console him but he seemed beyond consolation, repeating the same questions about God's role in the murder and asking how he was going to explain their mother's absence to his children.

Blue spent the night at the Hood address and in the morning he told a reporter for the Colorado Springs *Gazette Telegraph* that Dianne's husband had "served her," especially since she'd become ill with lupus eighteen months earlier. "Brian took days off from work so that she could get out of the house. He was the type of guy who was so thoughtful and he was not afraid to share his innermost thoughts and feelings with you."

Four

On Thursday morning, when Jennifer and her daughters arrived at Rich Designs flower shop, she asked her boss, Rich Schell, for an early paycheck and a trim. Ben liked her hair long, but for once she was determined to have it her way. Rich handed her the check and said he would be glad to cut her hair, as he had once done that for a living. Since those days, Schell, a redheaded, red-bearded and red-faced young man of fastidious taste, had gone on to create one of the most successful and unusual floral stores in the area. Decorated with colorful stuffed dolls, porcelain rabbits, jars of chutney, elaborate and handsome bird cages, gift and card displays, sachets of potpourri and dried flowers hanging from the ceiling, Rich Designs looked like the bedroom of a wealthy and highly imaginative child, a kind of exotic wonderland.

Schell was exceptionally proud of the store and did not like anyone or anything interfering with his business. Four months earlier, when Jennifer had shown up seeking a job, he had asked her to try her hand at a particular floral design, then stood back and watched her with a critical eye. She had once arranged flowers at the open-air Pike Place Market in Seattle, but that was long ago and now she was nervous, wondering if she had lost her talent or forgotten her technique. When she finished, she glanced at the man with an uncertain expression and apologized for the results. Schell said nothing immediately, carefully examining her handiwork. He has arched brows and an intense manner but as he studied the flowers, his features gradually softened into a smile. He pronounced the arrangement "sensational." He had hired her that day and had had no regrets.

Jennifer was personable with customers and efficient on the telephone (some of his employees stayed on the line too long once an order had been taken). She came to work on time, was intelligent and cheerful, and was a good conversationalist with a sharp sense of humor. She had a kind of sensitivity that Schell associated with artistic people. Rich liked discussing national or world events around the shop and his new hire was better at that than anyone who had been in his employ. She was attractive, articulate, an excellent representative for Rich Designs and, her boss quickly decided, the best worker he had ever had.

While Rich cut a few inches off Jennifer's hair and commented on the morning's headlines, Natasha and Tineke played in the shop, causing their mother to worry about the valuables that could be toppled or broken. Alaine Kuestersteffen, another employee, came into the store and joined the conversation. A little sheepishly, and without regard for the truth, Jennifer admitted to her coworkers that she'd been "a sucker" the evening before when Ben had called wanting to come home and she had given in. Her friends congratulated her on the reunion.

"Did you hear about the murder last night at Otis Park?" Schell asked.

Both women shook their heads.

"Where is Otis Park?" he said.

Jennifer and Alaine looked at one another and neither of them had an answer.

Rich couldn't remember the name of the person who had been killed and the conversation flagged, then moved on to other things. When he had finished cutting Jennifer's hair, he French-braided it to her specifications and she left with the girls.

Brian and Dianne's relatives began arriving in Colorado Springs on Thursday for the funeral that would be held two days later. The family's grief was compounded by the fact that Dianne had been struggling with lupus for more than a year but in recent weeks her health had definitely improved. John Hood, Brian's older brother and an architect in the San Francisco Bay area, called her murder "a tragic event for all of us." David Moore, Dianne's brother and a lawyer in San Antonio, said, "She was really a fighter. She wouldn't tell me the true story of hurting when I would call her. I had to talk to Brian to find out how she was really doing. She was real tough. A good person, but a tough person." Moore had made plans to phone his sister on Wednesday but got busy with a case and never made the call. "It's a crying shame," he said. "I just love her."

Dianne and David Moore were natives of the west Texas oil town of Midland, where they had been raised by their mother after their father left when Dianne was four. They had grown up poor but determined to leave the poverty behind, get an education, and create a good life for themselves. For Dianne, however, tragedy was always near. When she was fifteen, her best friend in high school was killed when a desert sand cave collapsed and suffocated the girl. In her freshman year at Angelo State University, in San Angelo, Texas, her boyfriend was killed in a car wreck on his way to a homecoming weekend at the college. Despite these losses, or because of them, Dianne became known as a battler, someone who did not give up easily at anything and who tried to retain a bright outlook no matter what. In San Angelo she worked as a short-order cook to raise money for school. Then she took up modeling and became popular when her enlarged photograph was used in a local promotional campaign. She studied history and envisioned herself as a museum curator.

Brian was in her chemistry class at Angelo State. A psychology major and a defensive tackle on the varsity football team that won a Division II national championship, he was a campus hero. Six feet four inches tall and weighing 235 pounds, he looked and moved like an athlete, strong and light on his feet, with a certain grace to his walk. He was broad-shouldered and good-looking, with a large well-shaped head, high cheekbones, and a sweeping quartermoon jaw. If anything, his head was almost too large, creating the impression that he was an even bigger man than he was. Something boyish did remain in his features, a kind of mischievousness or a look of pure happiness when he smiled, but there was also something serious. From one moment to the next he could be an overgrown kid or a stern and imposing adult. His cheeks were pockmarked. Except for that he had the stature and the good looks of a leading man.

Throughout Thursday, friends and mourners came by the Hood residence at 1015 Custer Street, just north of downtown, to express their sympathy to Brian and the children and to offer what assistance they could. Flowers, cards, and food were delivered. Visitors sat on the couch and hugged the bereft man, trying to find something appropriate to say. Pastor Steve Thurman, the Hoods' minister at Fellowship Bible Church in the Springs, was present when Brian attempted to explain to his two oldest children, Jarrod and Lesley, that their mother was in Heaven. The children, unfortunately, could not absorb the information and began screaming at their father and crying, asking questions that had no simple or comforting answers. Brian had not stopped biting his nails and by now his fingertips were raw and bleeding.

The Thursday headline of the *Gazette Telegraph* read, "MASKED MAN SLAYS WOMAN IN PARKING LOT: Police Believe Robbery May Have Been Motive." When Detectives Ritz, Lucht, Lux, and Hogan assembled at the downtown investigations bureau that morning, however, they all agreed that money was a poor motive for such a crime. People simply did not carry much cash to meetings at the Otis Park Community Center. A thief might strike at a suburban shopping mall or an expensive store on Main Street but not at a lupus gathering in a working-class neighborhood. And why would a robber stand over his victim and fire a second shot—yet not harm an eyewitness who was several feet away and also holding a handbag? And why did he drop Dianne's purse? And why would anyone shed his clothes so near the shooting?

The killing had been heavily publicized on the TV news Wednesday night, and on Thursday the police station received a dozen calls from people who reported seeing unsavory characters in combat uniforms. The only thing surprising about this was that the number was so small. At any time of day or night one could spot soldiers in fatigues walking along the streets of Colorado Springs or driving their cars and more or less blending in with the civilian population. Most were young men and many of them looked a bit rough around the edges—longish hair, faces that had been scarred in fights, and aggressive walks. Their presence gave the town an underlying feel of transience and a sense that violence could explode at any time. Wherever one looked, young men and women were preparing themselves for war, and occasionally, the city felt occupied.

The four detectives followed up the calls about dangerous people in camouflage, but none led anywhere. They spent the rest of the day pursuing vague trails and learning nothing of substance. Dr. Larry Howard, the manager of the crime laboratory, examined the fragmented lead-nosed bullet that had passed through Dianne's back and shoulder, looking at it under a microscope and weighing the slug. It was so "mutilated" that he could not determine its precise identity, but its weight, 250 grains, indicated that it might have been fired from a Colt .45 (caliber reflects the diameter of a gun barrel—.45 is $45/100$ths of an inch). After Dr. Howard had studied the bands and grooves on the bullet, he couldn't locate any such markings in a current firearms identification book, and he was anxious to receive the second, less-fragmented bullet, which the coroner was now extracting from Dianne.

Barbara Ray, an agent with the Colorado Bureau of Investigation in Pueblo, forty miles south of the Springs, was in charge of examining the clothing recovered from Julian Medina's trash can. In the ski mask, she found a brown hair, belonging to a Caucasian, and a red synthetic carpet fiber. In the camouflage pants she found a light brown hair, possibly from a dog. These things were helpful but only if connected with a suspect. Detectives often say that if they do not get any good information in the first forty-eight hours of a murder investigation, the case becomes much more difficult to solve. By mid-afternoon of their first full day of work, they had no reasonable leads and the job ahead appeared both time-consuming and tedious.

As was his custom every working day, Ben arose very early on Thursday and left the house at 6:00 A.M., but when he arrived at Fort Carson he did something unusual. He asked Sergeant Patrick Judy, a unit supply specialist at the base, to log in one of his guns at the armory. Sergeant Judy, who was in charge of maintaining a record of all personal weapons that entered the compound, performed this task and wrote down that at 6:45 A.M. on September 13 he had received a firearm from Captain Reali. The gun, a reissue of one of the most famous revolvers in the Old West and sometimes known as the Peacemaker, or a "long Colt," had been a gift from Ben's father. Ben owned a firearms collection of which he was exceptionally proud—he called his guns pieces, spent many hours in the garage cleaning his rifles and pistols, and built from scratch the rounds he planned to shoot.

Until the past few weeks Ben had left most of his guns at home, always keeping the Peacemaker loaded and under the mattress he and Jennifer slept on. However, when the U.S. government started shipping troops to Saudi Arabia and Ben believed his own departure was imminent, he had taken some weapons down to the base. If he went into combat, he wanted a personal gun nearby, in addition to the government issue firearms. He had a number to choose from: a Colt Series 80 handgun, an automatic pistol, a

Smith & Wesson revolver, three single-barrel shotguns, two double-barrel shotguns, an 1887 Winchester pump, a 30.06 rifle, a Browning 1885 hunting rifle, a 1903 Springfield, and a few others.

On the way to work that morning, Ben's Jeep faltered and when he got to Fort Carson, it died; the catalytic converter would have to be replaced. He called Jennifer, asking her to drive down in her Cherokee and bring him home for lunch. Ben had been casually acquainted with Brian and Dianne Hood at the health club where he and Jennifer were members, and before hanging up he mentioned a radio report he had heard on the ride to the base.

"Did you know that Dianne Hood was murdered last night?" he said.

"Yes," his wife replied. "I can't believe it."

"I can't either. This doesn't sound like your standard 'Hawaii Five-O' case."

"What do you mean?"

"The whole thing stinks. I don't think it's a robbery. You don't get robbed at a place where you wouldn't be carrying any money. I really liked Dianne. Remember when she was at our house last spring?"

"At the birthday party?"

"Yeah. Tineke's third."

"That was fun," Jennifer said. "I liked her too."

"What do you think happened?"

"I don't know." She hesitated before saying, "You don't think Brian was involved, do you?"

"Well . . . I don't know what to think."

That afternoon Jennifer called the flower shop and told her boss that the Otis Park murder victim had been Dianne Hood, a woman she had known personally and had befriended this past summer. She was shocked that someone would lie in wait and gun down a good person like Dianne, a wife and mother of three small children.

The sound of the victim's name sent an immediate and uncomfortable rush through Schell and later, after he had hung up and was going about his tasks at the store, he could not dismiss what he had just heard. He knew that Jennifer had met Brian Hood last spring at U.S. Swim and Fitness, a health club on the north end of town, and over the summer Brian had paid several visits to the floral shop. Schell had found the man disturbing, in part because it was hard to conceive of a more unlikely setting than Rich Designs in which to find the strapping Hood. With his overall bigness, his athletic movements, and his cocksure attitude, he was not the sort of person who conjured up stuffed dolls, sachets of potpourri, and porcelain rabbits. Something about him was too aggressively masculine. He had a quality—a sexual aura about him—that people felt and immediately liked or disliked. To Schell, he was "a gross individual."

As Rich thought about the events of the past twenty-four hours, his mind moved in several opposing directions but the pressure in his stomach was consistent and uncomfortable. He was engaged in a fierce inner debate about his favorite employee, and he was thinking and feeling things he did not want to. Should he phone Lieutenant Rich Resling, an acquaintance of his at the Colorado Springs Police Department, or should he put all these questions aside and just go on about his business? He did not want to harm anyone and he did not want anyone to harm his beloved shop. After an hour or so, he made the call.

Five

Brian had always been known as a complainer. In high school in Dallas he had regularly groused about doing his homework and the chores he took on around the house. In college, after breaking a bone in his lower leg, he bitched to his father, Andy Hood, a prominent executive with the Prudential, about playing football. He said he hated the sport and was tired of being pushed around by overzealous coaches, tired of them slapping his helmet, tired of them grabbing his face mask, so tired that he wanted to quit the team, even though he was a star. Andy gave his son a pep talk about commitment and ignoring pain, about enduring hardship and finishing what he had started. That is what men did. Brian stayed with football but sometimes he still felt like quitting.

The first time Brian got Dianne pregnant, they were both in college, and she got an abortion. In her senior year she became pregnant again and the young couple, following her desires and some more persuasion by Andy Hood, were married in Midland in December of 1980. After the wedding Brian began pulling two shifts: one at a local health club and one on the oil rigs near San Angelo. His wife would later tell her friends that during this second pregnancy her husband had an affair with a woman at the club—one reason Dianne demanded they leave Texas. Brian knew some people in Colorado Springs and the Hoods soon moved to the city, where he found a job driving a beer truck.

The young man, lately a campus demigod, was now struggling to establish himself as father, husband, and provider for his new family. He became a liquor salesman with a reputation as a drinker and a flirt who was not averse to marijuana or cocaine. He was trying hard to adjust to domesticity, but this did not come naturally to Brian. He loved being around women, looking at them, talking with them, teasing them, touching them, and looking some more. He liked joking with bank tellers, waitresses, saleswomen, and total strangers. He liked making shocking remarks about their clothes or their bodies—comments about how he was really the father of their children. These dalliances were exciting and stimulating. They made him feel alive and attractive. Right away he told women they were beautiful and he was drawn to them. Many found him brash and off-putting, but some were flattered and a few were interested.

In the mid-eighties Brian began a transition that permanently altered his life. It started with a discussion about religion with his grandmother on a flight back to Colorado from Texas and it grew from there, a kind of spiritual search that developed slowly and without much direction, a search for help and guidance, for something to assist him in his struggles with drinking, with fulfilling his domestic responsibilities and with his creeping, vagrant need for other women. What could he do about his lust? How could he stop always feeling like a sinner? He was looking for something beyond the speeches of his father and the platitudes about manhood, something of his own. More than once he had tried to ignore the pain and be happy but his conflicting desires, inner difficulties, and complexities had not vanished. Being a man, it seemed, was simpler for some men than for others. Or maybe it was simpler in his father's time. Or maybe he was just too different from his dad. Being satisfied with what one had was easier for certain people than others. Wanting more was annoying and troublesome, yet for Brian it was real. He was groping for something elusive, something that might never have occurred to his father.

By the mid-eighties Andy Hood, a handsome, well-dressed man with a soft voice and a gentle smile that made most anyone comfortable buying insurance from him, had become the head of regional marketing for the Prudential in Houston. He looked and acted successful. There was a graciousness in his eyes and face that was very appealing; you immediately wanted to like him. In 1984, when he realized that his son was discontent with being a liquor salesman, he suggested that Brian apply for a job with the Prudential office in Colorado Springs; it was several steps up from peddling booze and a position with a future. Brian took his advice and the general manager at the Colorado Springs headquarters, William Bramley, interviewed him and gave him some tests but didn't think the young man had the right qualifications. In Bramley's eyes, Brian was immature and had one other disturbing trait: he wasn't a Christian. Bramley liked to hire and promote those who not only shared his religious beliefs but felt about them as he did—passionately. His office was full of Christian employees and some attended his place of worship, Village 7 Presbyterian Church, in the north end of town.

Inside the Prudential corporate hierarchy, Andy Hood was Bramley's superior but when Hood asked the general manager if his son was a good candidate for the Prudential, Bramley was candid: Brian did not fit the image his office wanted to project and should look for work elsewhere.

Early in 1986, two years after Bramley had refused to hire him, Brian returned to the older man to ask if he would be his spiritual mentor. Bramley was flattered; there was nothing he would rather do than help young people who were searching for faith. Using a program called the Timothy Study, geared specifically to Christian businessmen, Bramley and his pupil met several times a week in his office at 6:30 A.M. for an hour of perusing the Bible. This lasted for nine months and in that time the Hoods also joined Village 7 Presbyterian Church. The general manager's Christianity was based upon a very literal interpretation of the Scriptures. Every phrase came from God

Himself and was a specific commandment. To Bramley, memorizing passages was important and he was quickly impressed with Brian's ability to pull verses from anywhere in the Bible and quote them verbatim. At the end of nine months, the older man had changed his mind and the younger one became a Prudential employee.

"There was definitely a bonding between Brian and myself at that time," Bramley has said. "After the Timothy Study there was a remarkable change in him. He showed a high degree of respect for me and my wife. He was very familiar with the Bible and I had no reason to doubt the sincerity of his faith."

Brian stopped taking drugs and drank much less. He talked a lot about Christianity and on occasion he proselytized: if religion had helped him this much, it could surely help others. He also talked a lot about his children, telling people that he wanted them to be raised in a home with strong Christian values and bringing the same verve to his faith that he brought to most things. Although he joined the Prudential as a novice insurance salesman in a highly competitive industry, four years later he won an award for being in the top ten percent of their salesmen nationwide. He was known as "a closer"—when he got someone interested in a policy, he found a way to make the deal. By the late eighties, he was forever calling up friends or near-friends to ask if they wanted to attend his church or needed more insurance. People either found him charming or boorish, but he was hard to ignore.

On Friday morning Jennifer dropped her children off at Kay Everett's day-care service and then drove to work at Rich Designs, arriving at 8:15 A.M., fifteen minutes earlier than usual. Her boss had called a staff meeting this morning and purchased sweet rolls for the occasion, trying to soften what he had to say. Schell did not like confronting others with uncomfortable facts but today he felt he had no choice. Once he and Jennifer and Alaine Kuestersteffen had assembled in the rear of the shop, he brought out the rolls and said the time had come to face a delicate issue: the women were using the office phone too much for matters unrelated to selling flowers. Both Jennifer and Alaine had been taking an unusually high number of personal calls, which tied up the lines, wasted time, and hurt the business. He scolded Jennifer for being late the previous Wednesday (she'd acknowledged her tardiness by bringing in a dozen donuts for everyone, but then consumed eight of them herself). The women apologized to Rich, promising to do better, and Jennifer went about her regular chores of taking phone orders, putting together floral arrangements, and making deliveries.

In mid-morning, Captain Reali received a call from the Colorado Springs Police Department, asking if they could send two detectives out to Fort Carson at four this afternoon to speak to him about a criminal matter. He said yes, unsurprised by the request. Young soldiers worked for him and some were bound to be rowdy, especially if they believed they were going to war. When he mentioned this to the police officer on the phone, the man replied that they did not want to question him about military personnel but about himself. Ben was taken aback.

"What are you talking about?" he asked.

"I can't tell you," the officer said.

"Why not?"

"Just be in your office at four and you'll find out."

Ben spent the rest of the day thinking about this appointment and at three-thirty he picked up the telephone and dialed Rich Designs.

Jennifer had just returned from a delivery and was at the front counter waiting on customers. Detective Charles Lucht, a policeman in the Springs for seventeen years, was standing right in front of her, looking at the fanciful decorations and the parched flowers hanging overhead. He was incognito, wearing a suit and tie. His partner, Michael Lux, also dressed as a civilian, was waiting outside in their unmarked car, a 1986 Mercury Marquis. As he took in the jars of chutney and the colorful greeting cards, Lucht, a solidly built man with a square face and hairstyle, noticed a colleague of his in the corner, Detective Tim Hogan, who had also been working on the case since Wednesday night. Hogan was in plainclothes and speaking with Alaine. When he saw Lucht, Hogan did not sustain eye contact or make any hand gestures, a signal that things in the shop were under control and that he—Lucht—really didn't need to be there.

"Can I help you?" Jennifer asked him, coming out from behind the counter.

"Just looking around," Lucht said.

The phone rang and she retreated behind the counter to answer it, speaking into the receiver so intensely that Lucht picked up some of her words.

He turned and walked outside, jumping into the Marquis and telling Detective Lux to drive them to Fort Carson, five miles to the south and sprawling on the edge of the prairie that extends well into eastern Colorado. The army base, sitting at the foot of Cheyenne Mountain, is often windy and when seen from a distance the roiled dust leaves a sepia tint. This huge military installation, which looks like a city that erupted overnight, somehow feels forlorn, as if it will eventually become a ghost town. For now it holds barracks, drab buildings, and government housing. Jeeps run everywhere and the soldiers' souped-up private cars race their engines alongside them. Young men and women march through crosswalks, looking to the right and the left. People are well armed at Fort Carson but out on these open fields, which stand next to the dark green mountains, everything appears naked and vulnerable.

On their ride to the base the detectives received a call from the homicide bureau informing them that Dr. Howard had determined that the murder weapon was "similar" to a .45 long Colt. Howard had scheduled further tests for this evening. As the men pulled into the parking lot of Fort Carson's Criminal Investigation Division (CID), the police branch of the army, they were astounded to see Jennifer in the lot, speaking with a man in uniform. Her route to the base had not only been different from theirs, as Lucht remarked to his partner, but must have also been considerably faster. The detectives watched Jennifer linger near the curb talking with the officer, who they correctly assumed was her husband. The young couple went into the CID building and Lux and Lucht followed, introducing themselves to the Realis and making small talk. Lucht refused to tell Ben why they had come to the base until after Detective Lux had taken Jennifer into another room.

When they were alone, Lucht said, "What do you know about the murder of Dianne Hood?"

"I heard about it yesterday," Captain Reali said. "That's all."

"Nothing more?"

"No."

Lucht stared at him. "Do you keep any guns here?"

"Sure. I'm a soldier."

"Where are they?"

"In the armory."

"Can we look at them?"

Ben hesitated. "What are you looking for?"

"I can't tell you."

"Why not?"

"Because I'm in the middle of a murder investigation."

The men went to the armory and examined several weapons, Detective Lucht retrieving the long Colt from a locker where it had lain since the previous day, wrapped in a piece of white cloth. Lucht asked Ben to accompany him to his office in downtown Colorado Springs and they left the CID together and rode to 105 East Vermijo Street, the home of the investigations bureau of the C.S.P.D.

Jennifer stayed at Fort Carson, sitting across from Detective Lux and answering questions about her background and occupation. Lux, who wore eyeglasses, a small earring, and hair that fell down over his shirt collar, could have easily passed for a keyboard player in an aging rock band. He was polite and gentle. He spoke in a calm unag-

gressive manner and told Jennifer he was looking into a
shooting that had occurred Wednesday night at Otis Park.
She said she knew nothing more about it than that Dianne
Hood, a casual acquaintance of hers, had been murdered
there. She had heard about it on the radio. Lux nodded and
never raised his voice. After he had queried her for twenty
minutes, two other detectives, Tim Hogan and Brian Ritz,
who had just arrived at the CID office, came into the
room. When Lux indicated that he had finished speaking
with the young woman, Hogan introduced himself to
Jennifer and the other men left.

"Do you know Brian Hood?" said Hogan, who was
round faced and baldheaded. He spoke softly and had
sleepy eyes.

"Yes," she rubbed her cheek, scratched at it.

In the past twenty-four hours her normally smooth skin
had broken out in small reddish sores, little bumps that
gave her the appearance of a rebellious teenager. Her
ponytail added to that image and so did the uncertain way
she sat on the edge of her chair.

"I met him last spring at the U.S. Swim and Fitness
health club," Jennifer said, "and I also met his wife,
Dianne."

"Are you having an affair with him?" said Hogan, as if
he were asking her for the time.

"No."

"Where were you on Wednesday night at eight-thirty?"

"Jogging in Dublin Park."

"What kind of surface were you running on?"

"Concrete."

"Do you like jogging?"

"It's like running on a beach or playing piano. A lot of
people do that to think and I wanted to think."

"Have you shot any guns lately?"

"Ben and I went to Fort Carson in August and took target practice."

"Are you having an affair with Brian Hood?"

"No. He's married and I'm married. He's a big handsome man and under different circumstances things might be different but not now."

"Where were you at eight o'clock on Wednesday night?"

"The Citadel Mall. Shopping. Then I ran and then I picked up the kids from the day-care and then I went home." She touched her cheek again. "Are you thinking I did this?"

"Did you do this?"

"No. I couldn't shoot anybody. I wouldn't shoot anyone."

She stood and walked across the small room. "My stomach hurts," she said. "How do you feel?"

"Fine," he said. "I feel fine. Do you feel trapped in your marriage?"

"It isn't that bad."

"Are you having an affair with Brian Hood?"

"No. I don't like this. You're asking me questions to get me to say I killed an innocent woman. This is absurd."

"Did Ben kill her?"

"No."

"How do you know that?"

"He just wouldn't."

"Where was your husband on Wednesday night at eight-thirty?"

"He was in his office, here at the base. I called him after nine."

"Where was he before nine?"

"Ben had no reason to kill Dianne."

"Who did?"

"I have no idea."

"Maybe, if Dianne was so sick with the lupus, murdering her was an act of mercy."

"She wasn't that sick."

"Some other detectives are talking with Ben right now. They're going to get his gun from the armory and test it to see if it's the murder weapon."

"Ben wouldn't kill anybody. I know he wouldn't."

"Were you wearing a hooded sweatshirt on Wednesday night?"

"I don't like hooded sweatshirts."

"What color is the carpet in your home?"

"Red."

"Do you have a brown dog?"

"Yes. A Labrador. My stomach hurts. Can I get some fresh air and a drink of water?"

"We're finished," Hogan smiled at her. "You're free to go."

She walked out of the room but did not go to her car. Instead, Jennifer lingered at the CID office. Ten minutes later, she wandered back to where Hogan was sitting and writing out his notes from the interview. She paced in front of him, her ponytail swinging behind her.

"Nobody's under arrest," Hogan said, looking up at her. "You're free to leave."

She stopped pacing.

"At eight-thirty on Wednesday night," he said, "I don't think you were running in Dublin Park. I think you were running in Otis Park after shooting Dianne Hood."

"Stop that!" she cried.

Six

Detectives Steve Wood and Kenneth Hilty pulled up in front of the Hood residence and stepped from their unmarked police car. Wood, the lead investigator in the duo, had spent eleven and a half years with the C.S.P.D., the last four with the Major Crimes Unit. Broad chested and wide shouldered, he had blond hair swept back from his forehead in a mild pompadour, a light-colored mustache, and a small rusty voice that always seemed about to crack. His voice did not match his physique, which reminded one of a serious weight lifter. This combination of traits gave Wood a strong-yet-sensitive air and made him a good police interviewer. He could be intimidating one moment and soft the next. He favored tight-fitting suits and elaborately tooled cowboy boots fashioned from the skins of exotic reptiles; the latter added a touch of danger to his appearance even though he hated snakes.

On this Friday afternoon, Sergeant Joseph Kenda, who was running the murder investigation from the downtown bureau, had contacted Wood and asked him to go to an east side watering hole called Frankie's Bar & Grill. The detective had arrived there at 3:40 and listened as Frank Patton, the proprietor, told him that a week ago on September 7, Brian Hood had come into the tavern to inquire about his insurance needs and mentioned that his wife was dying of lupus. Patton, a bearded, bearish, friendly man who looked as if he should be running a bar and grill, had responded with a joke but quickly apologized when he realized that Hood was serious.

"I just wish she'd die and get it over with," Brian had

45

told him. "I've got three kids to raise and I just want to get on with my life."

The coldness of the remarks surprised Patton and stayed with him after Brian was gone. He was further surprised to learn of Dianne's death a few days later, so surprised that he called the police.

Frankie relayed all this to Detective Wood, who thanked him and drove back to the bureau to report to Sergeant Kenda. The sergeant then sent Wood and Hilty to the Hood residence, a modest stucco house, with a vague Swiss influence in its arched roof, and a cramped lawn. Pines hung overhead and a cluster of low shrubs grew near the front porch. The living room's picture window gave a clear view of the sidewalk and street, and on this warm summer evening boys and girls were riding bikes past the Hood address and playing games in adjacent yards, yelling at one another and calling out names. As Wood approached the front door, he wondered how Brian had explained to his daughter and sons what had become of their mother.

He knocked and a man answered the door, saying that Brian, his two oldest children, and his parents were at the Swan-Law Mortuary viewing the body but would return in an hour. Wood thanked him and he and Hilty drove over to the mortuary, but the Hood family was not on the premises. Wood went into the room where Dianne was lying in her open casket, dressed in funeral garb, her hair styled and her face covered with makeup, the stillness of everything filling the air. If asked, the detective would claim not to be religious, but he would also say, "We are here for a purpose." As he looked at Dianne, he felt the unfairness of things and of this death in particular. In his line of work, he had seen a lot of dead people and in many cases he had felt that the deceased persons had done something to bring about their own demise. Maybe they had been killed in a drug deal. Maybe they had associated with the wrong types. Maybe they had tried to harm someone and been slain in return. None of that, as far as Wood could tell, applied to the woman lying before him. She had been a wife and mother attempting to run a household and raise her children to the best of her ability, an obscure woman really, who had always obeyed the law and tried to get along with everyone.

Wood now addressed her in silence, telling Dianne that he didn't know what had happened or who was responsible for her death, but he promised her that regardless of how long it took or how difficult it was, he would do everything in his power to discover the truth and see that her killer was found and brought to justice. Even though she was a stranger to him, he felt, just from looking at her and knowing the little he did, he owed her that much. He said good-bye to her and drove back to the investigations bureau.

The bureau occupies the third floor of what is called the Professional Building, a tall structure with a common brick facade but a lobby full of raspberry carpeting and elevators holding polished mirrors, golden handrails, and crystal chandeliers. At 6:30 P.M., after learning that her husband had been taken here for more questioning, Jennifer drove down, parked her Cherokee behind the Professional Building, and was escorted inside by Detective Hogan, who had just arrived from Fort Carson. She was taken into the holding room of the Crimes-Against-Persons Unit, a small space reminiscent of a poor dentist's lobby, with its worn couch, several old chairs, table, and outdated magazines. Jennifer asked Hogan to sit with her and he did, the two of them chatting pleasantly for more than an hour about skiing, raising children, and their favorite Colorado Springs restaurants.

"Can I see Ben?" she finally said.

Hogan was noncommittal. He excused himself and stood, wending his way back to Sergeant Kenda, who was working on the case in another third-floor office of the homicide division. The division resembles a labyrinth, full of small rooms, oddly angled cubicles, and confusing hallways. The layout is intentionally disorienting: two people being held for questioning about the same crime could be ten feet apart and never know it. Kenda told Hogan that Jennifer could see her husband but only after Ben had looked at the clothing that had been retrieved from Julian Medina's trash cans on Wednesday night.

For the past two days, the garments had been down in Pueblo, where they were being examined by CBI agent Barbara Ray. The discarded jacket did not bear any insignia or military symbols, except for a "US Army" patch over the left chest pocket, but Ray had found two laundry marks—the numbers 35 and 58—in the waistband of the forest green camouflage pants, the kind of marks stamped on items that had been sent to the dry cleaners. As Captain Reali sat in the bureau and conversed with Detective Lucht, the clothing was transported up from Pueblo, arriving at 8:00 P.M. Ben looked over the items and said the jacket appeared to be his; and he had, he acknowledged, taken the camouflage pants to the dry cleaners more than once. They also appeared to belong to him. After he finished examining the clothes, he was escorted into the holding room, where he was surprised to find his wife sitting and looking at some magazines. When the detectives had left the holding room and left the Realis alone, Ben whispered to Jennifer, asking her why she had come to the bureau.

"I wanted to know what they were doing with you," she said. "They think one of us killed Dianne."

He laughed. "That's crazy."

"I know it is."

"They're checking my gun now to see if it matches the murder weapon."

"What if it does?" she said.

He shrugged. "I'm not worried about it. I don't think it will."

"I've been leaving the doors open lately," she said. "Someone could have come into the house, taken the gun out, used it to shoot Dianne, and brought it back to frame us."

Ben shook his head.

Detective Lux walked into the room. "Are you thirsty?" he asked them.

Ben asked for a Pepsi, Jennifer nothing.

As soon as Lux was gone, two more detectives, Hogan and Lucht, walked into the room and sat down with the Realis. Everyone exchanged greetings and then there was silence. They all looked at one another.

"We're getting hungry," Jennifer said. "Can we leave and get something to eat?"

"Yes," Hogan said. "You can go anytime. Nobody's being held here against their will."

Jennifer and Ben glanced at each other but neither of them left their chairs, as if they wanted to see what would happen next. The four people stayed together in the room, talking about a number of things, until Lucht mentioned the hairs and fibers that had been recovered from the ski mask the killer had worn.

"If that mask has saliva residue and we match that residue to someone we have in custody," Lucht said, "the case is broken."

"Are you going to talk to Brian?" Jennifer asked him.

The detective looked at her and did not respond.

Ben also stared at her.

"Are you?" she said.

"I can't answer that," Lucht replied.

It was getting dark when Wood and Hilty drove back to 1015 Custer Street, knocking on the front door of the Hood residence and identifying themselves as police officers. A minute later Brian's father, Andy, came outside and told the detectives that this was not a good time for anyone to intrude on their privacy and grief. Dianne's funeral was in the morning, he explained, just a few hours away, and the family members were trying to prepare themselves for it. They needed to be alone and would appreciate it if the officers could come back later. Listening to this, Wood was surprised, almost taken aback. He had assumed that Dianne's relatives and in-laws would be eager to speak with the police and learn that they were already in the process of obtaining warrants to search the home of a suspect in the murder. All they wanted to do was ask Brian a few questions. Resistance was the last thing Wood had expected from 1015 Custer Street.

"I need to talk to your son now," he said to Andy. "It can't wait until later."

Andy gave him the same response as before. It was not appropriate, he felt, at this time to have Brian leave the house. Dianne was dead. There was no way that going to the police station and talking to them could be of any help to her. He suggested that shortly after the funeral the police could talk to his son at length. His concern was the children. The problem he had was that Dianne had left the house two nights earlier and never returned. The kids knew that. Andy did not want Brian to leave and not be there to support them. He considered it a serious violation of their privacy to have the officers come in when they were grieving and fearful.

Wood waited politely as Andy spoke his piece but he was equally intransigent. It was critical, he said, to speak with Brian this evening. By this time the men had moved off the porch and onto the small front lawn, facing each other in a standoff.

Jeff Taylor, Brian's uncle from California, now came out and joined them. Taylor, an attorney, asked if the detectives were going to interview Brian as a suspect in the case, another remark that took Wood by surprise.

"No," he said.

The lawyer went back inside and spoke with Brian, who sent out word that he was very distraught from trying to cope with his own pain and loss and from attempting to explain to his children that their mother was gone and not coming back. The kids were confused and in shock; he had to be with them now. He also had to deliver the keynote address at Dianne's memorial service at Fellowship Bible Church in the morning and needed time to put together a speech. Why were they interested, he wanted to know, in questioning him now?

Wood conveyed through Taylor that they wanted to ask him about his relationship with a woman named Jennifer Reali.

A few moments later Brian emerged from the house and four men were quickly riding downtown to the investigations bureau, Jeff Taylor and Brian in one car, Wood and Hilty in another. Brian had agreed to make the trip, but only if his uncle could chauffeur him. Once they arrived at the bureau, Wood took Brian into a conference room—just down the hall from where Ben and Jennifer were sitting in the holding room—but Brian refused to talk unless his uncle were allowed to be present. When the detective, who was not aware that Jeff Taylor was an attorney, denied the request, Brian stood to leave.

"You're willing to give up learning who killed your wife," Wood said, "just because he can't be in here?"

Brian nodded.

They argued for almost fifteen minutes before Wood conceded. He let Taylor into the room, offered the men sodas and then read Brian his Miranda rights. When he had completed that, he said, "Who are your close friends?"

"Mark Ramey and David Blue," Brian told him.

"What about female friends?"

"I don't have many female friends."

"Have you had any extramarital affairs?"

"Yes. One nine years ago and one five years ago. Dianne knew about both of them."

"Do you have any female friends who would have known that Dianne was at that lupus meeting at Otis Park on Wednesday night?"

"I have a woman friend at the U.S. Swim and Fitness health club. She's married. Her name is Jennifer Reali and her husband is Ben."

"Are you having an affair with her?"

"No. We're friends. She and I share Christ together."

"When was the last time you talked to Jennifer?"

"Monday or Tuesday of this week. I'm sure it wasn't Wednesday because I didn't work out that day."

"Where were you when you last spoke?"

"At the health club."

"Are you and Ben Reali friends?"

"Yes. I've seen him in church. I talk to Jennifer and try to help her strengthen the relationship between Ben and her. I'm trying to be a support for her."

"What kind of a support?"

"I understand the problems in a marriage when one person is a Christian and the other is not. To someone who isn't a Christian, all is foolishness. I've always told her that it's hard when your husband is not a Christian."

"Describe Jennifer."

"She's just a very sweet, honest person who wants to do what's right."

"Have you ever been romantic with her?"

"No. I think of her as being attractive but we never had a romantic relationship."

"Has she ever made any advances toward you?"

"No. Once we said it would be nice if we'd met under different circumstances but we didn't pursue a relationship."

"What kind of insurance do you carry?"

"A year and a half ago I gave Dianne a permanent life insurance policy. She used to be a rider on my $700,000 policy but then she got a $100,000 policy of her own."

"What did you and Jennifer talk about the last time you were together?"

"She said that she and Ben were splitting up."

"Is there any reason that either Jennifer or Ben would have wanted to harm Dianne?"

"No. Why are you asking me so many questions about her?"

"Earlier today some evidence surfaced that makes her a suspect in this murder investigation."

Brian didn't speak for some time, looking around the room and then settling his gaze on Wood. "That's very strange," he said. "I find that very hard to believe."

Wood thanked him for coming downtown and Brian left the bureau with his uncle.

As nine-thirty approached, Wood found Captain Reali still sitting in the holding room with Jennifer. He told Ben that they were finished with him for the evening but wanted to ask his wife a few more questions, alone. Ben, who had no transportation, left the room and made several calls to see if he could find a ride to the Everett's so he could pick up his children, but none of his friends was answering. He kept calling.

At a quarter of ten, Sergeant Kenda called the home of the El Paso County District Attorney, John Suthers, who was preparing for bed. They spoke for several minutes and after hanging up, Kenda called Wood into his office and passed along his orders. The detective walked down the hall and into the holding room where Detective Hogan was talking with Jennifer.

"You're under arrest for first-degree murder," Wood told the young woman in his gentle rusty voice, which almost carried a hint of apology. He advised her of her rights.

"Are you kidding?" she said, touching the red marks on her cheek.

"No. I'm not."

She made a sound like broken laughter, like someone inhaling and exhaling at the same time.

Wood offered his hand and she stood. He escorted her, without cuffs, along the maze of hallways and cubicles, leading the two of them into another third-floor office, a tiny eight-foot-by-ten-foot room that held a small gray desk, three plastic-seat–covered chairs and nothing else, except the odor of old sweat embedded in the walls and furniture. The rest of the air was stale and there were no windows. A calendar was the only decoration. The baseboards along the faded beige walls were smudged black, as if they had been repeatedly kicked. The face of the desk had been carved with a pen or a dull knife. And the cramped room became even smaller as they entered and looked at one another, three feet apart, the towering heavy-shouldered detective and the trim woman with the frightened eyes and acne on her cheeks. Wood shut the door and they sat down.

"Did the gun tests come back from the lab?" she said hesitantly.

"Yeah. They were positive."

"I didn't kill anyone."

He stared at her, leaning forward and placing his elbows on the desk, struck by how young and innocent and confused she looked. He didn't know exactly what to say.

"What's the penalty in Colorado for first-degree murder?" she asked.

"It depends. There's twenty-four years in prison to life in prison to death by lethal injection."

"Where's Brian?"

"I can't answer that but I did speak with him earlier this evening."

"Did he say that I did it?"

"I can't answer that, Jennifer. I have no information linking him with the murder."

"That's real fine." She looked right at Wood and spoke in a tone that struck him as being perfectly sincere. "What should I do?"

He cocked his head, not used to being asked that question by people in these circumstances. "If others are involved in the murder," he said softly, "they'll hear about your arrest through the media. They'll find out by tomorrow morning. Maybe even tonight. They'll leave town and you'll have to face all the consequences on your own. If you know something, you should tell me now."

"Can I have a nonmenthol cigarette and a glass of water?"

"Sure. Anything else?"

"That's all."

He left and came back a few minutes later, once more advising Jennifer of her rights. She lit a cigarette, puffing it quickly and nervously, holding it upright like an inexperienced smoker, and mentioning that it might be good to have a lawyer present.

"It's Friday night and it's after ten o'clock," Wood said. "Hiring an attorney before Monday morning could be difficult."

He smiled across the desk, assuring her that he would not begin the interview if she really wanted a lawyer in the room, and adding that there was no point in their talking unless she was ready to speak openly and honestly now. Wood wanted only the whole truth.

Yasmin Forouzandeh, an attorney in the El Paso County Public Defender's office, was on duty and watching the ten o'clock news on one of the local stations. Just as a report came on concerning the arrest of a suspect in the Dianne Hood murder, her boss, Guillermo Garibay, called Yasmin to alert her of this development in the case. Hanging up, Yasmin immediately phoned Sergeant Kenda at the homicide division and told him that if Jennifer Reali wanted a lawyer tonight, she could be there at once. When Kenda indicated that the suspect had already waived her right to an attorney, Yasmin asked to speak to her anyway. Kenda said he would call District Attorney Suthers with this request and phone her right back.

Minutes later Suthers himself called Yasmin, repeating that the suspect had waived her rights but if the public defender wanted to talk with her, she could catch up with Jennifer later, after she had been booked and transported to the Criminal Justice Center (CJC) on the southeastern edge of town. Dissatisfied with his answer, Yasmin got off the phone, trying to decide what to do next. From the news program, she had gathered that the young woman was being held at the old detective bureau on Nevada Street, several blocks north of the newer location on East Vermijo. Yasmin drove to Nevada but the suspect was not there.

She drove out to CJC, a trip of several miles over a poorly lit and winding road leading into the countryside, but Jennifer was not there either. The CJC authorities said they did not know where she was. For more than an hour, Yasmin waited in vain for her arrival, before leaving and going home.

Seven

Brian's older brother, John, the architect from California, also tuned in the ten o'clock news. He was in Colorado Springs for the funeral and had been trading reminiscences with his relatives at the house on Custer Street, but when a story about the murder of his sister-in-law came on TV he focused all his attention on the screen. John was slimmer than Brian and more conventionally handsome. He dressed well and conveyed the impression of a man who had not only expected to be successful in life but had turned out that way, the sort of older brother one might be proud of but would not want to compete with. When he and Brian were growing up, it was conceded that John was the smarter of the two and family members affectionately referred to the younger brother as Bonehead.

When the news item ended, John went to the telephone and called the police, relieved that the crime was being solved and anxious to know more about the person in custody. A detective told him that the suspect was named Jennifer Reali and she had told the authorities that she was an acquaintance of Brian and Dianne Hood. John thanked the man and as he was hanging up the receiver, Brian walked past him carrying his younger son, Joshua. The two-year-old was still awake from all the night's activities. When John mentioned the suspect's name to his brother, Brian stopped in front of him.

"Do you know this girl?" John asked him.

"I know her," the insurance salesman said, a stunned expression crossing his large boyish face.

57

The men looked at each other and in that moment John felt certain that he had just been told that his brother "knew" Jennifer Reali in the carnal sense of the word. He was so certain of this that he did not bother confirming his intuition with a direct question.

"Did you have anything to do with Dianne's death?" he said.

"No. Absolutely not."

"But you were involved with this woman and she's been arrested."

"Yes," Brian said.

"I think we should consult an attorney."

The younger brother nodded, the shocked expression still on his face. "Okay."

The family began calling lawyers in their various hometowns, seeking advice. They called people in Houston, San Francisco, and Denver and when none of these produced results they tried some local numbers.

Starting at 10:15 P.M., Detective Wood sat next to Jennifer in the tiny room and began furiously scribbling notes on a legal pad. Despite his years of experience doing this and his best efforts now, he could not possibly keep up with the avalanche of information that came pouring out of the young woman. Whenever she paused for a drink of water or to light another cigarette, he continued writing in order to catch up with her story, but it was futile—no one could have captured all her words or all the nuances of her speech, let alone all her emotion. He needed a tape recorder but he did not have one with him this evening, and once she had begun talking he did not want to stop her so he could go look for one.

"The back door of our house was open last Wednesday night," she said, after explaining how she had met and gotten to know the Prudential salesman. "I'd told Brian he could come in and get the clothes and the gun and kill Dianne."

For the first time in half an hour, Wood stopped writing.

Laying down his pen and leaning back from the desk until his shoulders touched the wall, he crossed one cowboy boot over the other and gave her a long gaze.

She looked away from him. "Someone must have come into the house," she said, "and taken the clothes and found the gun and committed the murder."

"I don't believe that," he said patiently, studying Jennifer, watching her exhale smoke from yet another cigarette. Her eyes were skittery behind the big glasses she wore and she couldn't sit still. She chewed her lips and looked down, her bangs falling over her forehead. She shifted in her chair.

Wood maintained his silence, feeling rather strange. Four or five hours earlier, he had vowed to the dead woman to find her killer, even if that took months of hard detective work on his part and the part of the whole bureau. When he had made that pledge he had felt the kind of abstract anger toward an unknown murderer that one felt when reading about a heinous crime in the newspaper; the killer must have been monstrous to plan and execute such a thing, because no one else could behave that way. Now he was sitting three feet away from the person who might have shot Dianne Hood through the heart and he did not know what he felt toward her. One moment it was sympathy or pity, the next it was anger or disgust. Jennifer did not look to him like a killer or even a petty criminal. She looked confused and lonely.

Wood tried to push his feelings aside and concentrate on the work in front of him. Whenever he interviewed suspects about serious crimes, he tried to put himself in their place and asked himself a series of questions. How would he act in such circumstances? What would he say or not say? Since he doubted that he would have the courage to tell the whole truth, he expected some prevarication, if not outright lies. He had spoken with one man for nine hours straight before getting the information he wanted. He had spoken with another for twelve hours. There was nothing harder, he believed, than confessing to a horrendous act,

especially in front of a police officer, and he admired anyone who could do that. He was prepared to spend all night
talking with Jennifer and even the next day if necessary.
On the other hand, he preferred to resolve things quickly,
so he decided to try a simple ploy. It probably would not
succeed but it might lead him where he wanted to go.

"It wasn't very smart of you to shed the clothes in the
alley," he said.

She looked at him and nodded. "I should have taken
them with me," she said.

He made a note on his pad, trying not to show any surprise at what he had just heard. In truth, he was not that
surprised by her admission. A veteran criminal, the kind of
person he often dealt with, would have become uncooper-
ative hours ago but this was no veteran. Since entering the
bureau, Jennifer had passed up half a dozen opportunities
to leave and go eat dinner or even drive home. More than
anything else, Wood sensed, she wanted someone to talk
to.

"I cleaned the gun on Wednesday night after going back
to the house," she went on. "Was that the wrong thing to
do?"

"If you wanted to remove the evidence," he said softly,
"it was the right thing to do. Did you want to kill
Dianne?"

"I . . . can't tell you that."

"You just told me you did it. Do you want to answer my
question?"

"You know I did it. Why do I have to say it?"

Wood swung around in his chair, suddenly angry at her,
really angry for the first time since she'd entered the room,
thinking about Dianne's children and about how much had
been destroyed and how quickly and for how little.

"Shouldn't I have a lawyer here if I'm gonna talk about
this?" Jennifer said.

"We can stop until you get a lawyer."

She shook her head. "No, that's okay. All I really want
is another cigarette and another glass of water."

He stood and walked toward the door.

She asked him to wait.

"I've gotten by all my life by telling little white lies," she told him. "Right now, I'm being more honest with you than with anyone, ever, and I want to keep doing this. I want to keep talking to you about it."

Wood looked at her and felt another wave of sympathy.

"I didn't think I could kill Dianne," she said. "I'm such a bad shot."

Wood sat down, his anger dissipated.

"Everything that night is foggy," she said, starting to cry and waving her hands in front of her as if trying to shoo away something invisible, an odd, childlike gesture. "It's so hard to remember. I really thought that something would stop me from doing it or that God was watching over me and I'd be safe or that I'd missed with the gun and it hadn't really happened. But I can remember some of it. That proves I'm sane, doesn't it? That proves it."

"Are you sure you don't want an attorney?"

"I'm sure. I wasn't myself that night but someone else. Brian used Christianity to do anything he wanted, to reason, to manipulate. I was given the impression that it was God's plan and, being as vulnerable as I am, if it were to happen, it wouldn't be my fault. I feel like I've been separated from myself. Because of the state of mind I was in, and the money he talked about, I just did it and I still can't believe it."

She cried harder, collapsing in her chair, her face covered by her palms. Wood excused himself and left the room, walking across the hall and informing Sergeant Kenda of what he had just been told. Kenda immediately called several detectives into his office, Lucht and Hogan among them, and they began making plans for the next phase of the investigation.

Wood went back into the interview room, taking along more cigarettes and water.

"You still understand your rights?" he said, sitting down across from Jennifer.

"Yes," she wiped at her eyes. "Is Ben gone?"

"No. I saw him out there."

"Can he come in?"

"We can't do that."

"I want him to hear the story from me and not from the papers or TV. I want him to see me being totally honest with you and with him."

Having a third person present at a murder confession was against regulations, Wood explained, but as he was telling her this he was also considering her remark about the little white lies. He felt that she was experiencing a kind of psychological breakthrough—approaching a level of truth and self-insight she had never known, which might be useful later on—and he wanted to assist her with this process. He excused himself and walked across the hall again, asking Kenda to allow Ben into the room. After some persuasion, the sergeant said yes.

Wood located Captain Reali—who despite many efforts this evening had been unable to find a ride home—sitting by himself in the holding room. The detective approached him and in a soft, even voice said that his wife had been Brian Hood's lover, had murdered Dianne Hood, and she now wanted him to join them for her full confession.

Ben's mouth, which frowns naturally, fell much farther and he jerked back, as if he had been struck. His impressive shoulders, then his whole body, went slack. He made a kind of groan.

"Why should I be in there?" he said.

"It might help her to live with herself a little easier," Wood replied. "The decision is up to you."

Ben made another sound, like a man choking, and shook his head. "This isn't real, is it? You're talking about my wife and the mother of my two daughters."

"I'm sorry but all of the evidence points to her."

"She killed Dianne?"

Wood nodded.

"What should I do?"

"I can't tell you that."

"That's not Jennifer in there. It can't be."

Wood said nothing.

"That's not the woman I married. I know it. That's not my wife."

"You don't have to do this," Wood said. "It's just that she wants you to be with her."

The captain pulled in a long breath, then another, standing up straighter and glancing toward the door. At least for the moment he was a soldier again.

"Let's go," he said.

He trailed Wood into the tiny room and looked down at his wife, who sat against the far wall, weeping in her chair. When she saw him, he too began to cry. Ben leaned over and took her in his arms, embracing her and planting a kiss in her hair.

"My God, Jennifer," he said, tears covering his broad, square face. "Oh, my God."

"Thank you for doing this," she whispered to him.

Ben lowered himself into the chair next to hers and the room was again smaller, not just because of his bulky physical presence but because the atmosphere had also become thicker, even more explosive. Wood shut the door. Smoke filtered through the overhead light and an odor mingled with Jennifer's burning cigarette, the harsh metallic scent of perspiration and fear. The couple sat on one side of the desk, holding hands and looking at the detective. Wood stared back, feeling that someone in the room was going to break but he did not know who. While investigating homicides during the past five years, he had seen a lot of memorable things but he had never seen a husband or wife admit to murder in front of a spouse.

Jennifer slowly resumed her narrative, outlining her activities with Brian in the summer months just past, when Ben had been away much of the time on army business. The captain listened, maintaining control of himself at first, but then he began to tremble and sob, shaking in his chair and grabbing the edge of the desk.

"I'm sorry, Ben," she said. "I'm very sorry. I really liked Dianne."

The young man gazed at her as if he were seeing something that his eyes couldn't register, something that fit nowhere within his previous experience. "You liked her? How could you do this, Jen? Tell me how."

"I don't know. I feel awful for what I've done to you and to our family."

"Do you love Brian?"

"I loved the idea of his being attracted to me. He's tender and loving and a great salesman."

The captain laughed bitterly. "When did you first have sex with him?"

"I can't remember."

"Everybody remembers those things."

Wood had been watching them in silence but now he said to her, "Can you prove that you and Brian were intimate?"

"What do you mean?"

"Did you see any markings on him that you would only see if you were intimate with someone?"

"He has a scar on his chest and some moles on his buttocks."

Ben pushed off from the desk, stood and left the room. In the hallway he walked in circles, then leaned against the wall and cried. The police officers who passed him lowered their eyes.

When he could breathe normally again, he went back into the room and sat down, reaching over to Jennifer and caressing her hand. He said he was all right now. He told her to continue. Detective Wood looked at the man admiringly, surprised that anyone could listen to such a confession, let alone return for more.

Jennifer began talking, but Ben interrupted her.

"Did you do it in May at our house when I was down range on maneuvers?" he asked.

"No. Just some kissing one day and then he left."

"When did you first have sex?" he asked again.

She let go of his hand and faced her husband. "Do you want to leave?"

"No. I'm here. I want to know what happened. Was Brian circumcised?"

She looked at the floor.

"Was he?"

She sobbed in her chair.

"Tell me, Jennifer. Was he circumcised?"

"Yes."

Ben turned to the detective. "There," he said. "That proves she's telling the truth. That's an intimate detail you can check out for yourself."

Wood nodded but said nothing.

Captain Reali looked at his wife. "How many times did you have sex with him?"

"Four. Twice at our house and once in the Cherokee and once in the country when we went out for a picnic."

"When was the first time?"

"It wasn't July, I guess. I think it was June."

"Where was it?"

"In his car."

"It had to be more than four times," Ben said. "I was gone a lot. You made love with him in our house?"

"Yes."

"Where were the girls?"

"Next door. Brian told me that you were an awful husband and a terrible father who didn't love his wife or children. He said you were unfaithful when you were away from me."

"I've never been unfaithful to you, Jennifer. Never. Not once in six years of marriage. Not once in all the times I've been away from home."

"I know that but he was so convincing I believed him."

"All I ever wanted was you. I told you that and told you."

"Brian said I needed a good and godly man who would be around for me, a Christian man. I can't believe I did it, Ben. I feel worth nothing. I feel I've been used. Someone came into my life and sweetened all the evil and I believed him. I believed what he said. I'm going to jail now and I may be put to death. Maybe if I'm a good kid, they'll let me out someday but I'm going away for a long time."

"Maybe we can help you," Ben said. "Maybe you won't have to go away. But you've got to be strong now, Jen, and tell us the whole story."

"I am telling you. I killed her. I shot her. I used your gun and your clothes. Brian said that his wife was so miserable. He said I'd be putting Dianne out of her misery. He said she took addictive drugs and slept all the time. He just . . . didn't love her anymore."

Ben stood and left the room again. Jennifer lit another cigarette and smoked it quietly with her head down. Wood looked at her, thinking of all the lives that were going to be changed by what she was saying—the three parents who were still living, their five children, the two sets of grandparents, the friends and extended families and others whom such an event might eventually reach and alter. Wood's emotions had swung throughout the confession but as he waited for Ben to return, what he felt mostly was a terrible sadness.

The captain stepped back into the room and was trembling. He stood over his wife and shouted in a broken voice, "Why couldn't you stop? Why couldn't you just tell someone what was going on? Why couldn't you tell me?"

"I was too weak, Ben. I couldn't . . . let him down. I've never felt loved. Never. Not by anyone. I've always felt second-best and stepped on by everybody. I'm so sorry for hurting you and our family."

He bent down and embraced her again.

"I love you and I don't want anyone else," he said. "I'll stand by you one hundred percent, Jennifer. You're sick and you need help."

"I know it. I fired the damn shots and killed her. I don't know why. I can't believe what I did to you and the kids and Dianne."

"I've got to go now," Ben said, turning away from her. "I've got to go home."

"Will you come and visit me?"

He stopped and smiled at her, a confused half smile. "Of course, I will."

The captain went into the hall and Wood followed him, finding Sergeant Kenda and explaining to him that Ben should not be left alone tonight, not after hearing the confession. Kenda said that some men from Ben's unit at Fort Carson had been alerted and had driven up to the bureau; the sergeant had advised them to stay with Ben at least until morning.

Returning to the interview room, Wood found Jennifer sitting calmly and no longer crying or smoking, as if she were finally relaxed in his presence. She asked what would happen next and he said she would be taken to the county jail, booked for murder and conspiracy, and then her lawyer would probably schedule a hearing to see if she'd been tricked into talking to the police.

"I don't feel I've been tricked at all," she said. "Thank you for letting Ben come in. I really appreciate it."

Wood studied her, a part of him liking the woman or at least not disliking her at the moment. "You're welcome," he said.

"Just before the murder," she said, "Brian told me that sitting in prison teaching the Gospels would be better than what he'd been living with. I hope he doesn't get away with it. He manipulated and brainwashed me, but I've got to face the consequences."

At 3:00 A.M. on Saturday she was transported to the Criminal Justice Center and placed in a cell. The first time she heard the big iron door slam behind her with its flat resounding clang, she told herself that she would never, no matter how long she lived, get out of prison. Five hours later Yasmin Forouzandeh, the public defender who had tried to contact her on Friday night, was at CJC but by then it was too late to advise Jennifer on what to say or not to say to the authorities, too late to represent her at her first police interrogation, too late to block the confession, too late to offer any kind of legal protection, too late for anything.

Before entering her cell Jennifer had called her parents, Gail and Keith Vaughan, informing them of her arrest and receiving assurances that they were on their way from Seattle to Colorado Springs. It was a very brief conversation. Afterward, her parents both got cold in the house and couldn't warm up, although it was a warm night.

Early that morning the Vaughans received another call, this one from Ben Reali, Sr., who also lived in Washington state. He had just heard the news from his son. Initially, Ben senior had thought that the captain was joking.

"Wow!" he had told his son. "You don't normally drink."

Eight

On Saturday at 12:47 A.M. Detective Lucht delivered an arrest warrant to the home of Judge Douglas Anderson. The judge got out of bed and signed it and then Lucht, along with Detective Hogan and several other officers, drove to 1015 Custer, arriving at five minutes past one. There was still activity inside the Hood residence as well as outside. During the past few hours, strangers had been driving by the house, which had lately become notorious because of media reports about the murder, and some thrill seekers had even stopped to take pictures. Others squealed their brakes and raced their engines. The Hoods were not used to being in the public eye, certainly not this way. Brian's father remembers that when the police arrived very early that morning, the family was sitting together in the living room "extremely afraid and nervous. I looked out the window and saw what looked like four policemen and two plainclothes cops on the sidewalk. It scared me to death. They knocked on the door. I could not believe this was taking place nine or ten hours before Dianne's funeral and that they would be so insensitive. They surrounded the house and came in and put handcuffs on Brian, arrested him, and took him away."

Before the young man left, his parents finally reached an attorney in Colorado Springs, Richard Tegtmeier, informing him of the evening's events. Awakened from a deep sleep, Tegtmeier, who had defended more than one hundred people accused of murder, lost no time in moving from the world of dreams to the realm of lawyering. He immediately got Detective Hogan on the phone and demanded to see the arrest warrant before Brian was driven downtown and booked for first-degree murder. Hogan replied that Tegtmeier would have to talk to Sergeant Kenda about this matter and the conversation ended there. At the moment the attorney could do nothing more for his new client but he was already thinking of a legal strategy, one he would soon announce to the press and not deviate from for the remainder of the case, almost as if he'd had the defense in mind even before he was aware of the crime.

At the Saturday morning memorial service, the Fellowship Bible sanctuary (Brian and his wife had switched to this church in recent years after leaving Village 7 Presbyterian) was filled with people who had come to pay their final respects to Dianne. It was an unsettled gathering for at least two reasons—a young wife and mother was not only dead, taken from them in her early thirties, but she had been murdered. Those attending the service were given a program at the entrance and two more disconcerting things were connected with this slip of paper. The first was odd but trivial: the program mentioned that Brian Hood was to deliver the "Husband's Words" and his name was spelled "Brain." The second was odder still and not at all trivial. Once the service began, it became apparent that the young insurance salesman was not in the sanctuary and his absence caused a great deal of head turning and whispered speculation from the chairs that had replaced the pews in this very contemporary church. Where could he be? people were asking. Why wasn't he present for Dianne's last rites? Was he so distraught that he couldn't even appear in public? A few mourners knew where Brian had spent the past several hours and, as the memorial progressed, this information slowly filtered up and down the rows, causing more rustling and craning and leaving the crowd even more unsettled.

The casket remained closed. The Twenty-third Psalm was recited and everyone sang "Amazing Grace," "Are You Washed in the Blood?", "O Glorious Love," and

"Blessed Assurance." Dianne's "Epitaph," which she had written the previous March when she believed that she might be dying of lupus, was printed on the program and so was her "Insight." It read, "God's plan is perfect for each one of us. Have a celebration day too, for I will be in Heaven." Betty Moore, Dianne's mother, from Texas, stood and asked those who had known her daughter to write down some thoughts about her, words that would be given to her children when they became adults. Scattered throughout the sanctuary was the sound of weeping and one man, to the dismay of other mourners, kept saying, "Praise the Lord! Praise the Lord! Praise the Lord!" Little Joshua Hood, age two, started fussing and had to be carried outside. As he was leaving, he yelled, "Where's my mommy? Where's my mommy?"

After the service, many of the people drove to Evergreen Cemetery, not far from the church, and watched as Dianne was buried in a grave that had not yet been marked. As soon as this ritual ended, Steve Thurman, the pastor of Fellowship Bible, went out to the Criminal Justice Center, where Brian was being held in a different wing from the one holding Jennifer. Pastor Thurman knew Brian reasonably well and had visited his home twice since the murder to offer condolences. The pastor had always thought of the young man as a dedicated and sincere worshiper and he was stunned by his absence this morning. He wanted to ask some questions for himself. At CJC he was escorted to where the accused man was being detained and after they had been left alone, did not stand on ceremony.

"Did you set this up?" the pastor said.

Brian had slept little for the past three nights. His eyes were bloodshot, his face was ragged and unshaved, his fingernails were torn, his hair was dirty, and he looked to be in a deepening state of shock. He had as much previous experience of imprisonment as Jennifer, and his face had gone rigid with surprise. The bright orange prison clothes looked all wrong on someone who had always taken such care with his appearance.

"No," he told the minister. "I did not do that."

"When did you last see Jennifer Reali?"

"Two weeks ago."

"How could Jennifer Reali have possibly known where your wife was on Wednesday night at exactly that time unless you'd given her that information?"

"Well, she called the night before and I told her I had to stay home with the kids on Wednesday evening because Dianne was going to a lupus meeting at Otis Park."

The pastor looked straight into the man's eyes. "Whether you're innocent or guilty, you have an obligation as a Christian to tell the truth. The rules of honesty don't break down, even if you're facing the death penalty. I want to know, Brian. Did you do this?"

He shook his head.

Richard Tegtmeier was a bald, diminutive, well-proportioned man with a very lively face. With his glasses on, his pupils were bright and intense, and with them off they became even brighter and more intimate. They bored right through you. His features were good and his head was perfectly shaped, so it looked natural without hair, like a tonsured monk's. Away from the courtroom he favored cowboy boots, blue jeans, leather jackets, a Harley motorcycle and he was friendly and approachable. But before the bench, he favored well-tailored suits and a guarded manner. He felt strongly about many things and one was his adamant opposition to capital punishment. Colorado Springs thought of him as a quick, tough lawyer who enjoyed, perhaps relished, the art of intimidation.

"People are afraid of him," Detective Wood once said. "He creates a lot of fear. He's a very good attorney and I respect him for that. He'll make the waves that are necessary to help his client and he'll get you, as a prosecutor, to jump through every hoop there is. If you convict someone he is representing, you can damn well believe that they're guilty of the crime they're charged with. That's fine. That's how it should be. That's how our system works."

At a press conference not long after Brian's arrest, his lawyer made a remark that would permanently attach itself to the murder of Dianne Hood and maybe even play a role in its legal outcome.

"This is not," Tegtmeier said, "an exact mirror of the movie, but it does appear to be a case of fatal attraction on Ms. Reali's part."

He was, of course, alluding to the 1987 film *Fatal Attraction*, in which a single woman, played by Glenn Close, has a brief affair with a married man, played by Michael Douglas. The Close character feels rejected by the man and attempts to kill his wife.

By the time the remark had been made, Jennifer's parents had arrived in the Springs and hired another local attorney, Elvin Gentry, to represent their daughter. When Gentry learned of Tegtmeier's comment, he took immediate umbrage at the choice of words—he disliked mixing fictional events with factual ones. Jennifer Reali and Brian Hood, he emphasized to the media, were by no stretch of the imagination Glenn Close and Michael Douglas. This was not a Hollywood picture but a complicated and tragic piece of reality and his fellow lawyers would do well to keep that in mind.

Tegtmeier was anything but apologetic, having just planted in the minds of those who were following the story the image of an unstable, violent woman acting alone and acting out her own murderous intentions. With this one statement, he unleashed the sexual politics underlying the crime and, over the months and years ahead, those politics would not only grow more significant and considerably uglier, they would affect every aspect of the case, turning it into something like a war between women and men.

On Friday night during her confession Jennifer had told Detective Wood that Brian once used a comb at her residence and left behind a single hair in its teeth, which she had removed and placed in a small wooden box as a memento. When the police searched her home, they discovered the box and the hair. Several days later, Charlie Green, a crime scene technician with the C.S.P.D., made Brian strip naked in front of him and then, using a forceps, which gets hair roots out of the human body, Green yanked scalp hair, chest hair, and pubic hair from the man's skin. The hairs were tested to see if they matched the one in the wooden box and they did. Green photographed Brian's buttocks to establish that moles were indeed there and he took pictures of Brian's genitals to show that he had been circumcised. While the young man submitted to all this in a cooperative spirit, he was astounded at what people could do to you once you had been taken into custody.

The evening of Jennifer's arrest her car had been impounded by the police, and the detectives had cut out carpet samples from the back of the Cherokee, in the spots where she had claimed that she and Brian had made love. Lab technicians found semen stains in the samples and tests eventually revealed that the DNA bonding pattern in these stains was also present in Brian's DNA; the frequency of this exact pattern in Caucasian males was one in 26,000,000. That was close enough to be legal proof of their sexual relationship.

Before long Jeanne DeBoe, another of Brian's ex-lovers in Colorado Springs, came forward and told detectives that the insurance salesman had once asked her to run into Dianne with her car. She had emphatically told him no. A friend of Brian's, Michael Maher, told the police that the young man had once requested a similar favor from him. Dallas Salladay, who owned a pawnshop outside the Springs, informed the authorities that Brian had purchased a .45 automatic from him shortly before the killing. And Terry Wenzlaff, an employee of the Colorado Springs Prudential, mentioned a conversation between Brian and himself that took place the previous June, in which Hood had talked about a Christian's being absolved from any sin he had committed, including murder, once he had been saved. Several other local women whom Brian had approached sexually were also interviewed by the police. During a business meeting, one recalled, he had attempted to arouse her by placing his toe against her vagina, and another one stated that he had propositioned her while rubbing the front of his pants.

Despite these findings, less than two weeks after his arrest Brian was released from CJC because of a lack of evidence. He flew to Houston, where his children were now living with his parents, and began an extended stay in his mother and father's high-rise apartment. Jennifer remained in custody—charged with first-degree murder and conspiracy. She was held without bail at the Criminal Justice Center and, because of the circumstances of the case and all the media attention it had drawn, she quickly became one of the most heavily publicized killers in the history of Colorado. Everyone had an opinion on whether she had acted alone or at Brian's command. When his early release from jail was made known through the press, a number of women had strong reactions.

"Even if we don't have all the facts, the public perception is that he's being treated differently because he's a man," said Jan McClure, a political consultant for women's groups in Denver. "Letting him off like that is ridiculous."

"I hate to see this called a 'fatal attraction' killing," said Linda Harroun, director of the Colorado Springs Women's Health Service Clinic. "Most women don't commit murders unless there is some motivational involvement by a man."

"I think women get set up and get blamed for a lot of things," said Mercedes Harden, a feminist counselor in the Springs. "My experience is that women don't plot to kill other women. Mothers don't kill other mothers."

part two

THE STORY
SHE TOLD

Nine

In the 1860s a lovestruck general invented Colorado Springs. William Jackson Palmer, a Civil War hero who had created the Denver & Rio Grande Railroad, decided to build a posh resort that would lure his beloved—a highbred Eastern beauty named Queen Mellen—out West. Palmer chose the moniker Colorado Springs because he thought it sounded like a spa for the rich. The nearest springs were hard by in Manitou Springs but to the general that was a minor detail. He constructed a castle for Queen Mellen but she was not well-disposed toward frontier life and after a year in the mansion, she repaired to the East Coast and eventually settled in England. Palmer stayed on in Colorado Springs and is commemorated in the heart of the city he founded by a large statue of a noble-looking gentleman astride a broad-chested horse.

His resort paradise did not boom until 1891, when a gold rush hit a few miles to the west in the village of Cripple Creek. Tycoons began filtering into the Springs and during the first decade of the twentieth century it became the richest metropolis per capita in the United States. It had then and still retains a certain elegance in the architecture and in the feel of old money floating around. Gradually the town evolved into a tourist mecca and something of a retirement center, and following World War II the armed forces became the local growth industry, reaching its zenith nearly forty years later during the Reagan administration. In the 1980s Colorado Springs boomed again, becoming the fastest-growing American city, but the high times were short-lived. The nineties have brought arms cutbacks and signs of a bust, and the town has made some recent efforts to establish itself as an outpost for high-tech manufacturing.

If its economy is erratic, its political identity is not, as the Springs regularly sends to the state legislature Republicans hell-bent on doing away with various taxes and passing ordinances against homosexuals or other perceived moral threats. In 1991, during America's brief war in the Persian Gulf, the city held many rallies supporting the troops and as soon as the fighting ended, the victory parades began. Xenophobic signs were hung out and the few antiwar students who protested near Colorado College, the excellent liberal arts school just north of downtown, were pelted with eggs. In 1992, a local group named Colorado for Family Values created an amendment to the state constitution that would not allow the legislature to pass any laws giving legal protection to people because of their sexual orientation. The notorious Amendment 2, as this was called, narrowly passed and set off a local firestorm that soon became a national issue. Colorado was quickly dubbed "The Hate State"; the *New York Times* and other papers around the country wrote editorials denouncing the amendment; many groups who had planned to hold conventions in Denver chose to boycott the city and take their business elsewhere; a number of Hollywood stars, some of whom had second homes in Aspen, decried the election; and a few celebrities, including tennis star Martina Navratilova, even decided to leave the state. The force and dimensions of the outcry were something no one could have predicted and the result was that Colorado and Colorado Springs ended up looking, if nothing else, meanspirited.

Since the early 1980s another growth industry in the Springs has been splinter religions. The town has more than thirty evangelical Christian ministries, some of which advertise themselves on large billboards that say things like, "PRESENTING JESUS." New churches have erupted everywhere, from the foothills to the central business district to the suburban strip malls. Each congregation has its own theological spin. In 1985, twelve married couples gathered in the foothills for the initial service of Fellowship Bible Church, meeting just below the spectacular rock formations at the Garden of the Gods, and a month later the group moved to its present address in the heart of town. With its off-white stucco arches and tile roof holding two small towers, FBC resembles a Mexican restaurant. In its brief life, the church has had remarkable success, now offering three Sunday morning services for its thousand-plus members.

Its "Doctrinal Statement" reads in part:

MAN:

"We believe that Adam and Eve were created in the image of God and thus man has great value in God's sight. But man sinned and consequently experienced not only physical death, but also spiritual death (which is separation from God). The consequences of this sin affect the entire human race so that all human beings are now born with a sin nature and reveal this nature by committing acts of sin. While they are able to do some good works in the eyes of other humans yet as to their spiritual standing before God all are lost apart from the sacrificial death of Christ."

THE PAST, PRESENT AND FUTURE WORK OF CHRIST:

"We believe in the personal, bodily return of Jesus Christ to set up on earth a kingdom in which He shall reign in righteousness and peace."

SALVATION:

"We believe that whoever trusts in the Lord Jesus Christ as Saviour receives eternal life. This salvation

is not the result of any human effort or merit. Faith itself achieves nothing; rather, it is the object of faith (Christ and His substitutionary death for sin) which has value. To become a Christian, a person places his trust in Jesus Christ who died in his place, suffering the punishment for his sin."

LIFE AS A CHRISTIAN:

"We believe that all believers are kept eternally secure by the power of God through the indwelling and sealing of the Holy Spirit and the intercession of Christ. In other words, once saved, always saved."

FBC publishes booklets outlining its beliefs and one is entitled "The Inerrancy of the Word of God." The Bible, the pamphlet states, "is WHOLLY TRUE, true in whole and in part, without error in everything affirmed. The Bible may use such things as figures of speech and round numbers, but it is nevertheless truthful and accurate . . . Think about it. If the Bible is 'the word of God . . . breathed out' HOW COULD IT HAVE ANY ERROR WHATSOEVER? It is impossible . . . What should be our attitude towards APPARENT 'contradictions'? First, remember that if the Bible is the Word of God it is impossible for there to exist any contradiction, for God cannot make a mistake. Is it His Word or not? If it is, then no error, mistake, or contradiction is possible. Secondly, study the APPARENT 'contradiction' and ask yourself who you will ultimately declare as confused: yourself or the Word of God? Thirdly, take hold of the attitude of St. Augustine who said: 'If we are perplexed by an apparent contradiction in Scripture, it is not allowable to say the author of this book is mistaken; but either the manuscript is faulty, or the translation is wrong, or you have misunderstood' . . . At Fellowship Bible Church we declare that the Bible is the INERRANT, infallible, authoritative WORD OF GOD . . . and nothing less!"

* * *

Lawyers in the El Paso County D.A.'s office handle murders on a rotating basis. The person scheduled to prosecute the Hood killing was Bob Harward, a veteran deputy D.A., who had driven to Otis Park on the night of the crime and talked with several detectives as they went about their investigative business. Harward is thin, soft-spoken, and gracious, a handsome, prematurely graying man who rarely raises his voice, even when cross-examining people about first-degree murder. He appears to be obligated, because of his job, to do many things he does not enjoy and his most striking trait is his gentle manner. If you were charged with killing someone and had a choice in the matter, you would very likely choose him for your prosecutor.

On Saturday, September 15, Jennifer Reali's first full day of incarceration, John Suthers, the El Paso County D.A., called Bill Aspinwall, the chief deputy assistant in his office, and asked him to help Harward prosecute the case. Not only would there be enough work for two attorneys, Suthers reasoned, but this pair would provide different and complementary approaches to what would be a long, complex, and grueling ordeal. The duo were opposites in almost every way. Aspinwall was shorter and stockier than Harward, with curly reddish hair and a ruddy face. Harward was a Wyoming native and nearly incapable of being offensive. Aspinwall had the scrappiness that many people associate with greater New York City (he was raised in New Jersey) and could be downright gruff in the courtroom. Harward had a gift for friendliness. William Alexander Aspinwall III had a talent for annoying people. If Harward looked vaguely patrician, Aspinwall looked pugnacious, with his upturned nose and his constant expression of a man who smelled something bad. Harward was essentially a vegetarian who liked to jog. Aspinwall ate red meat and looking at him one could never have guessed one of his favorite pastimes—ballroom dancing.

Aspinwall refused to take a gibe, even from a judge,

without giving a harsher one in return. Inside a courtroom he appeared self-confident to the point of cockiness, but outside of it he was surprisingly open and full of self-doubt, finishing many sentences with, "Do you understand what I'm trying to say?" or "Does that make sense?" He had a sharp, practical intelligence and a bottomless curiosity. Away from work he posed so many questions that his friends sometimes felt he was prosecuting them. He not only had a good legal mind, but another characteristic that could be useful in his line of work: he was sneaky. Once, when he wanted an opposing attorney's expert witness, a psychiatrist, to look out of control on the witness stand he made three appointments with the woman and did not show up for any of them. When he questioned her in court, she was livid with him and it showed.

When Suthers called and asked him to work on the Hood murder, Aspinwall was out mowing the lawn. After speaking with his boss, he said he needed time to think about it. From their conversation it was obvious that Suthers wanted to prosecute the case to the fullest extent of the law and that, in all likelihood, meant capital punishment. A few years earlier, when running for the D.A.'s office as a Republican—Suthers had thrashed his opponent—he had promised to pursue the death penalty if at all possible, despite the fact that Colorado hadn't executed anyone since 1967. One criticism aimed at him and at many other D.A.s around the country was that capital punishment was most often sought when a minority male had been convicted of a heinous crime. White people, male or female, generally stood a better chance of not being killed by the state. Rumors around the El Paso County Courthouse held that Suthers had been looking for a case to disprove this charge of prejudice, and some people believed that on the night of September 14, 1990, when Jennifer confessed to Steve Wood, the D.A. had found exactly what he wanted.

Aspinwall, except in very rare circumstances, strongly opposed the death penalty. He was also not entirely comfortable prosecuting cases with another lawyer. His personality was more formidable than many people's and he had very definite ideas about how to prepare for the courtroom. After one phone call from Suthers, he knew that if he were expected to convict Brian Hood of planning the murder of his wife, his main ally in the process would be Jennifer Reali. Aspinwall was unconvinced that Brian was involved in the shooting and, beyond that, he did not like jumping into bed with confessed killers. He did not like that at all.

For several good reasons he did not want the case but for several other good reasons he did. It would be a challenge and he was a competitive man; before every trial he prepared not just his own legal strategy but the defense's and he was always surprised if the opposing lawyers did not use it. His boss had asked him to get involved in this highly publicized murder, which made it harder to say no, and he, like Detective Wood, wanted to do something for the dead woman. The final reason that made him lean toward the case was more elusive. Aspinwall had a sense of duty and, although one had to observe him for a while to perceive it, he was a strange kind of idealist. He worked at least as hard as many defense lawyers and for considerably less money. He passionately believed in the American legal system despite the fact that he knew how difficult it often was to determine the exact truth of a given crime or to grasp who was ultimately responsible for it. And more than anything else, for the past sixteen years he had been an El Paso County prosecutor and throughout that period he had remained highly disturbed and indignant at what human beings do to each other.

"Most people in this office get burned out," John Suthers once said. "Bill never has. After all this time, he still has the fire."

"I don't celebrate when I win a case," Aspinwall says. "I take no personal satisfaction in sending someone to prison for twenty or thirty years. Mostly, I just feel sad for the victims. I'm motivated by the idea of justice which, despite the hundreds of thousands of dollars spent on not serving it, and despite the judges who get appointed to the bench, occasionally does surface. When that happens, I feel good."

He was not popular with his legal adversaries or even with certain employees of the D.A.'s office. He could be crotchety and outspoken and he naturally pushed against the grain. He could be grumpy and his words carried a sting. On one occasion, after a judge had said that he had twisted the facts of a case to make a point, he had jumped up and yelled, "No one calls me dishonest!"

A lot of people had called him uglier things but then, the law was not a beauty pageant.

He spent a couple of days thinking about the murder and as he did his own curiosity increased. He had a sense of what had taken place but wanted to know more of what had really happened among and between the four of them, the Realis and the Hoods. He told Suthers, "Yes."

Ten

Three days after Jennifer was imprisoned, Captain Reali and some of his army buddies moved him and the children from the Briargate house out to Fort Carson. During the next few weeks Ben wrote his wife heartfelt letters, repeating his position of unwavering support and stating his feelings about the recent events:

"You are a warm loving person and . . . a beautiful mother . . . and I know the Jennifer who could not bear to see violence on the TV screen, the Jennifer who was full of compassion and care for others . . . the woman who supported me and stood by me through some of the toughest times . . . I think back to how the loneliness hurt you and made you cry . . . I am so very sorry . . . I feel as if I've failed you. You were vulnerable and I wasn't there for you . . . I know you could never do this under normal circumstances . . . I will never abandon you . . . I need you and our kids need you and you have too much to contribute to society . . . I want you to have a part in our children's life and we can grow old together and we can have a flower shop with a male-female symbol in the corner . . ."

As she sat in the Criminal Justice Center and waited for the legal process to unfold, Jennifer fell into the rhythm of life behind bars—arising at 5:00 A.M. if she wanted breakfast (or later if she did not), being alone for hours in her eight-foot-by-ten-foot cell with only a bunk, a desk, and a commode, trading stories with other inmates, lifting

87

weights, reading, cleaning library books (her prison job), thinking about the future and talking with a few visitors. Guards constantly monitored her to see if she attempted suicide, but she did nothing to harm herself. In jail she was friendly, pleasant, courteous and cooperative, much the way she had been described by her employer at Rich Designs. She cried a lot but that was not unusual for someone in serious trouble for the first time in her life. Jennifer badly missed her daughters, speaking with them on the phone weekly but not allowed to see them in person. Like many people who were incarcerated, she found the other inmates more troublesome than the authorities. One female prisoner, who had been a male before having a sex change operation, called her "a mother-fucking murderer" and imitated the well-publicized stance she had assumed as she stood over Dianne and fired the second bullet. Jennifer learned to walk away from her tormentor without speaking.

Inside the walls of CJC, while talking with her lawyer, Elvin Gentry, or with Dr. Kathy Morral, a psychiatrist hired by her attorney, Jennifer took a long look into her past and the history of her family, hunting for something that might help explain why she had just committed first-degree murder. What had made her dress up in her husband's clothes? What had caused her to lie in wait and fire two shots into a woman she claimed to like, the last one coming from less than two feet away? How could the nice person that many people perceived her to be have done such a thing? She had offered the police one explanation for her actions, having to do with Brian Hood, but she was searching for something more. As part of that process, Jennifer began writing her husband and her attorney:

"October 15, 1990. As I said, when I was young I would try to be bad just to get attention. Brian said that a wife needs discipline, which is a form of love. Our lovemaking was filled with fury. Not abusive but far from gentle. It would hurt."

"October 16, 1990. He [Brian] said that often he would awaken in a dream, jump out of bed thinking there was a snake in his bed. He'd have to search the bed and room before he could get back in it ... Dreams. The ultimate sentence from Hell. I was sentenced to eternity behind bars. He went free. But he had to visit me for a few hours each day. He'd be on the ward, physically hounding me down."

"October 17, 1990. I remember hanging on every minute until he would phone. Just his voice was like a fix. I'd become anxious until I got to hear him. Not necessarily talk, just hear him ... as if I was dependent on that."

"October 19, 1990. The one thing that drives me crazy is why? I don't understand. Was it just a common case of crime of passion? I don't know. What made me click? The never-ending feeling that if God didn't want it to happen, it wouldn't ... Things he'd said echoing through my mind. Not the promise of success and a beautiful future but the threats of a desolate life ahead ... He wanted to know what made me tick. He would search my parched soul and use my weaknesses to get deeper into my mind, my spirit.

"A dream I remember having in April before the affair. It was Brian in a very dark place with candles and people all around. Quiet, stoic. Slowly he'd come to me. I was immobilized in the center of all the people. I was to be initiated into his world of 'religion.' I had the dream more than once."

"October 23, 1990 ... He had just gotten his hair done (permed) and I mentioned how tight it was and that I didn't care for it that way but rather when it was combed. He blew his top. Withdrew like a scolded resentful child. Became distant and curt. Later, he was open to the fact that he was pissed that Dianne was still alive. He blamed me for this. It was okay if he risked his life in a car wreck

but not okay for me to get involved. What kind of love was this? he'd say. He was furious . . .

"The physical and mental numbness of the whole day. Even into the next day. Slow motion. Eyes wide but not seeing. God, I'm scared. Maybe I'm just a true case of fatal attraction. Without losing the man. I'm confused. I feel like there's something I know that I can't give up. I feel so lost. Help me. Sometimes I feel as though I deserve nothing more than to sit in here and rot. Oh, I'll fight it. Rot I won't do. Not until my question is answered and we can all be at peace as to why."

Undated: "Benjamin. I'm not sure of what to say. I hurt terribly. Right now as I lay down in my small dark room alone I . . . I don't know how to express how I feel. When I put my hand across my body, I shiver at how I let it hurt you and others. If I could discard my hands, get rid of my private places, for there is nothing good about them. I deserve nothing . . . I search myself to see. Perhaps I never loved you. As I search and search I remember the feeling of love, my heart racing, my mind and body soaring with joy at just the thought or sight of you. Was all that a lie? I don't think so . . . but maybe. I never felt you really loved me. Your love was conditional. I was tired. I felt unnecessary, unimportant. I'm trying to change. I'm trying to grow. I'm trying to be honest with myself and with you. I feel so mis-used and I'm sure I've done my share of using. Please try to understand. I'm trying. Jennifer."

Undated to Ben: "When I look at our past, I'm angry. You were a selfish man. You assumed I was so strong. You loved me as long as I lived up to your standards. It was always a battle for me to be good enough to keep your love, return your love. I did things I didn't like to please you. I honestly tried to enjoy the things you enjoyed. Yet you criticized me for . . . not taking time to clean the house, fix a good meal, get the right groceries, buy enough razors . . . not buying ice cream! I was always so scared *that I'd not do whatever I was doing right. You criticized me for not drawing or painting. You always thought I was having an affair, you were always picking my friends. I wasn't 'allowed' to make decisions for myself. I got tired of trying. When I became depressed or wanted to seek counselling for me or us, your career wouldn't allow it. It would go on your record and damage your career. Not caring about what damage no counselling would do to me. Always trying to please you, always falling short . . . I never wanted to hurt anyone yet I did and I must live with that and pay for it. How much I must pay I don't yet know. I know I will never be able to forget the past but I can try to work with it, learn from it, forgive those around me and myself . . . Try."*

Elvin Gentry's spacious office was just south of the El Paso County Courthouse. His visitors' chairs were covered with soft blue leather and the window near his desk gave a broad view of Pikes Peak. A sign on the wall stated that unless he was getting paid for his time, he would much rather not be working. Large and blondish and friendly-looking, Gentry evoked a good character actor, someone who could always find work in Hollywood. His voice was gruff but not menacing, his laughter husky and pleasant. He had a masculine presence and at any moment you had the feeling that he might tell you a funny off-color joke. He smoked filterless Pall Malls but promised to quit once Jennifer's case had been resolved. He had promised that before.

When he talked about the young woman not long after the crime, his eyes moved toward the window and gazed into the middle distance, in the direction of the great mountain, as if he were looking for something critically important but invisible. While doing this he leaned so far back in his huge leather chair that one worried about his crashing to the floor.

"Sometimes people only make one mistake in life," he said, "but it's a royal fuck-up."

He lit a cigarette and took a long drag, blowing smoke across his desk. "The only way this case makes any sense is for Jennifer Reali to have a mental defect. If something offends common sense, then you have to check it out psychologically. Given her background, which is pristine in terms of law-abidingness, her actions do offend common sense. She's like an overachiever in many ways, the kind of person who would never kill anyone. Ever. That's not just my opinion but the opinion of all the people who know anything about her. They are absolutely shocked."

Before going to law school in 1967, when he was thirty-one, Gentry taught Spanish and Latin-American literature at Colorado College in the Springs and before that he pursued a Ph.D. on the novels of the Mexican Revolution at Case Western Reserve in Cleveland. When he decided to practice law, he completed the course work at the University of Colorado in two and a half years. In 1970 he was hired as a prosecutor by the El Paso County D.A.'s office and four years later he become a defense attorney, which he had been ever since, representing several people accused of homicide. His entire legal career, covering more than two decades, had been spent within a few blocks of the El Paso County Courthouse, which is a way of saying that he knew the people and the procedures on both sides of the law in Colorado Springs very well. Soon after Jennifer was arrested, a reporter asked Gentry if he had been offered a deal for his client in exchange for her testimony against Brian Hood.

"All I've been offered," he grumbled, "is to throw in the towel. I didn't go to law school to learn to do that."

Then he started negotiating with the D.A.

Eleven

Before long Gentry had made a deal with the prosecution: in exchange for his client's testimony against Brian in the upcoming grand jury hearing—and for that same testimony if he later came to trial for murder—D.A. Suthers had agreed not to seek the death penalty for her. Her life had just been saved. Suthers had also agreed not to use anything she said at these proceedings against her in the future, and if she were fully cooperative with his staff, he would consider writing a letter to the governor asking for a commutation of her sentence. In the second week of December, Jennifer went before the grand jury and talked for several days. Between fits of abject weeping, she started from the beginning and told them how, in the fall of 1989, she had developed stomach pains and made an appointment with a doctor at Fort Carson. There was nothing much wrong with her, the man said, but she was suffering from tension and needed a hobby, an outlet for her stress. The Realis joined the U.S. Swim and Fitness health club on the north side of town, not far from their home in Briargate.

Jennifer was quite good at physical activities—running or kicking a soccer ball or wielding an oar and once, after receiving encouragement from her high school coach, she had even considered going to Harvard and trying out for the rowing crew. At U.S. Swim and Fitness, she began jogging, stretching, lifting weights and using the Stairmaster, a treadmill-like device that simulates walking uphill. Her daughters usually accompanied her to the spa and she left them in the nursery before going to work out.

Afterward, she liked to sit in the Jacuzzi and relax, closing her eyes and letting the warm water swirl against her shoulders and back. One day in March of 1990 a tall, handsome, powerfully built man joined her in the hot tub. He introduced himself, said he was an insurance salesman, and asked what she did for a living.

"I'm a housewife," she replied.

"You say that," Brian told her, "like you're embarrassed about it."

"Not many people now are just housewives."

"I like women who are housewives. That's what my wife is."

She went to the club almost daily and, mysteriously, Brian usually arrived there shortly after she did. The two of them regularly met in the Jacuzzi and began trading stories about their backgrounds and their spouses, Jennifer saying that she and Ben were looking for a home to buy and Brian telling her about his religious convictions and how much he liked children. He had once been a drinker, he said, who was constantly tempted by lust, but Christianity had changed his life and made him a good family man. He invited Jennifer and Ben to accompany him and Dianne to Fellowship Bible Church some Sunday morning. Jennifer was noncommittal. She enjoyed these conversations but found the man to be very forward, perhaps even flirtatious, despite all his talk about his newfound faith and recent transformation. He sat very close to her in the water, he lightly brushed against her arms or legs, and he leaned toward her and asked pointed questions. She was perplexed by his being at the club whenever she was, so in April she began working out later in the day and stopped using the Jacuzzi, but regardless of when she went to the spa, he showed up a few minutes later.

Thinking that a job would help remove her from the situation, she looked in the newspaper for part-time employment and found an opening at Rich Designs. On May 1 she started at the floral shop, working Mondays, Wednesdays, and Fridays and going to the club on Tuesdays,

Thursdays, and weekends. Jennifer disliked aerobics but signed up for a class because Brian had expressed disdain for that form of exercise. He was soon in the group's front row, standing right next to her, jumping, clapping, and waving his arms. When she dropped out of the class, he did too.

At the club's front desk she left him a note, stating that she was confused and needed clarification. Given his Christian ethics and his claims as a family man, something seemed wrong; she wanted to know his intentions. He invited her to lunch, she accepted, and during the meal he said he had no interest in divorcing his wife. He was, however, seeking a "physical relationship" outside his marriage. Because of Dianne's lupus, there was no sex at home and not much love. Dianne was dying of a terrible illness, was miserably addicted to drugs, was irritable with him and the children, and said things that were hateful. She never had any energy and the fun in their marriage had long since ended. She would not do anything exciting and could not even sit in the sun without getting a rash.

Jennifer dismissed his proposition, saying she had never been unfaithful to Ben and was opposed to infidelity. She made a counteroffer—that the Hoods and Realis go out socially—but Brian's answer was no, that wasn't what he had had in mind. Jennifer was very pretty, he said in the Jacuzzi, and her husband was a fool to be gone so much of the time on military business. If she were his wife, he added, he would take care of her financially, protect her, and be at home each night with her and the children, instead of traveling the country playing soldier and chasing women. Listening to Brian, she realized how lonely she was, with few friends and no family in Colorado Springs. Why had that never been obvious until now? Brian was so large, sitting beside her, that she felt safe in his presence.

On a Tuesday morning in the second week of May, he made an appointment to come to her home to discuss what he called "long-range insurance strategies." Ben was on maneuvers in the Mojave Desert and the Reali girls had

been sent over to a neighbor's house to play. As Brian and
Jennifer sat on the couch drinking coffee and eating
sweets, he explained that every family needed a well–
thought-out economic plan, especially when a couple had
small children and wanted them to attend college in the
distant future. He himself had a $100,000 policy on his
wife in case she died and a much bigger policy on himself.
The Realis already had a savings program for Tineke,
Jennifer told him, and were thinking of starting one for
Natasha. When she went into the kitchen for a refill on her
coffee, he followed, standing next to her. He bent down
and kissed her.

"This isn't right," she said, pulling away.

"No, you're right," he agreed, taking a step backward.
"I guess it isn't."

She walked to the stairway leading down to the basement and hesitated at the top step.

"There's no reason for us not to have an affair," he said,
coming up to her and putting a hand on her shoulder. "I
know you want to. All you have to do is take your head,
unscrew it, and set it over there. Then you can just enjoy
life, take it as it comes."

He kissed her again.

She went downstairs and he followed. She showed him
the finished basement and a computer in Ben's office and
then sat with him on a sofa, turning the pages of a photo
album of her children. When he kissed her again, she
stood and said it was time for him to leave. Brian did not
argue but asked if she would iron his shirt, just touch it up
where it had been wrinkled by their embraces—he could
not meet his next appointment with it looking this way.
She said she would.

He unbuttoned his shirt and she carried it into the small
downstairs laundry room. He followed, looming over her,
and watching her find the iron and plug it in. Coming up
behind her, he turned her around by the shoulders and
kissed her again, more passionately than before, kissing
her over and over in a full embrace. At first she resisted

but then she closed her eyes and returned the kisses as fervently as he gave them. He lifted her onto the washing machine and held her in front of him, quickly removing her clothes. They made love but only briefly, neither of them consummating their desires. He pulled away from her, straightening his clothes and hair and asking again if she would iron his shirt. She did this, and he said goodbye and left.

When she thought about it later, a part of her was very disturbed by what had happened yet she had enjoyed the encounter and was attracted to this handsome man with the confident manner, easy patter, good tan, and blondish curly hair. Ever since they had met, one thing had been consistent and unusual in her experience with him: the attention he gave her was total. He listened to her, he sought her opinions on things he was thinking about, he constantly asked her questions. He focused on her—Jennifer—not as a wife or a mother or a floral arranger but simply as an adult woman, with her own thoughts and hopes and desires.

When she saw Brian again a few days later, they talked about what had taken place in her basement. Because they had committed adultery together, he said, they were now one in the eyes of God; they had sinned and he had been taught that to God all sins were equal. She asked him what that meant. If you looked at someone with lust, he explained, that was a sin and exactly the same thing as making love with that person. If you had hateful thoughts about a person, he went on, that was the same thing as killing him.

At the end of May the Realis celebrated Tineke's third birthday party (her actual birthday was earlier in the month but Ben had been out of town working). Friends and neighbors were invited, along with the Hood family and Jennifer's mother, Gail, who was visiting from Seattle. When meeting Dianne, Jennifer was surprised at how normal she appeared, having heard for two months that she was dying and drug-addicted and had a shrewish personality. She did not strike Jennifer as being a shrew at all, but a warm and lively presence with a soft Southern accent. The only thing that indicated the lupus was her need to sit down often and catch her breath. Everyone enjoyed the party except Ben, who was more than detached, sitting off by himself behind a wall of silent disapproval and anger.

When Captain Reali was away again on maneuvers, Brian began calling Jennifer at the flower shop or at home two or three times a day, telling her that if she wanted a better understanding of herself and other people, she should study the Scriptures. He would tell her what to read, then explain what the verses meant and how they applied to their own lives now. To Jennifer, who had basically had no religious training of any kind, Brian seemed to know just where everything was in the Bible and he quoted from it at will—while riding in the car or on the phone or in the Jacuzzi or after intimacy. He had the words for nearly every occasion. He began Jennifer's instruction by asking her to memorize certain passages.

One came from Matthew: "You have heard that it was said do not commit adultery but I tell you that anyone who looks at a woman lustfully has already committed adultery with her in his heart. If your right eye causes you sin, gouge it out and throw it away. It is better for you to lose one part of your body than your whole body to be thrown into Hell. And if your right hand causes you sin, cut it off and throw it away."

A second one also came from Matthew: "It has been said, anyone who divorces his wife must give her a certificate of divorce. But I tell you that anyone who divorces his wife, except for marital unfaithfulness, causes her to become an adulteress, and anyone who marries the divorced woman commits adultery."

Another was from I Corinthians: "Now I want you to realize that the head of every man is Christ and the head of every woman is Man, and the head of Christ is God . . . A man . . . is the image and glory of God; but the woman is the glory of Man. For Man did not come from woman but woman from Man; neither was Man created for woman, but woman for Man."

Another came from Romans: "There is no difference for all have sinned and fall short of the glory of God ... If you confess with your mouth 'Jesus is Lord,' and you believe in your heart that God raised him from the dead, you will be saved."

And another passage read: "Jesus Christ laid down his life for us and we should lay down our lives for our brothers."

Jennifer began perusing her husband's Bible, a gift to Ben from one of his friends who had fought in Vietnam. Having never read the book before, she was fascinated with its stories and parables, reading them voraciously and asking her husband what they represented. Ben had grown up Catholic but was no longer enamored of organized religion; it was a personal issue with him now, he said, and he did not have much time to discuss theology. He watched his wife devouring the Bible and could not understand why she was doing this, but when he thought about it her spiritual hunger did not seem like a bad thing.

Near the end of May Jennifer and Brian met for breakfast at a downtown restaurant and then went for a drive, parking near the city limits and making love in his Honda Accord. Afterward, he said that once a person had been saved and accepted Jesus Christ as his Savior, he could be forgiven for any sin—for lying, for adultery, for murder—except divorce, unless it was established that his spouse had been unfaithful. Brian knew that Dianne had never cheated on him, so divorce was not only forbidden him but a violation of his deepest convictions and a sure way to lose his Christian friends at the church and the Prudential office. Even his boss, William Bramley, the man who had given him a job, would disown him if he left Dianne. He told Jennifer that he was falling in love with her but he could never divorce his wife.

Brian had majored in psychology at Angelo State and he told his lover that he knew, from his studies and from closely observing Ben, that the captain had never really cared for Jennifer. Ben's passion was for the military and moving up its ranks; everything else was secondary and that would never change. Jennifer had told Brian that whenever the soldier left home for an extended stay down range, he would say to her, "You're gonna be good, aren't you? You're gonna be a good girl?" And each time she would answer, "Yes." Upon his return he would ask if she had been faithful and again she would always say yes. It was a kind of ritual. From his psychology studies, Brian explained, he had learned that when one person repeatedly asked another person if he or she was doing something wrong, that meant the first person was really the guilty party; it was Ben himself who was being unfaithful. Because of this, there was no reason for Jennifer not to have an affair and no reason for her not to get a divorce. She had not been saved, at least not yet. If she were to leave her husband now, it would not damn her at all in the eyes of God.

In mid-June the two of them drove to the Black Forest, a wooded area north of Colorado Springs, where they had a picnic and made love. Every time they met, Brian used a phrase he would often repeat in the weeks ahead: "Right life, wrong woman." His life was fine, he said, but he had wed an impossible partner. Meeting Jennifer at the health club was not mere chance, he added, but something much more than that. Divine purpose had brought them together as part of God's plan to help both of them escape painful situations at home. They were supposed to be married to each other, not to Dianne and Ben, and they were supposed to be living somewhere far away from Colorado Springs, probably in the Northwest, where Jennifer's family lived and where he had always wanted to settle. Their future was ordained, if only they could act on it.

On the night of July 12, the Realis' sixth wedding anniversary, Ben was on maneuvers in southern Colorado and

Brian came to his home. Tineke and Natasha were at the baby-sitter's. Jennifer cooked dinner, they drank wine and made love, and later that evening Brian called all of this "a test drive" for the life that was opening up to them. As he was describing that life, the phone rang and Jennifer, to his dismay, decided to answer it. Ben was phoning from down range and his wife talked with him for several minutes, Brian listening to her side of the conversation, growing angry at her for speaking gently and being kind to her husband. Brian was sitting in a rocking chair in his underwear and had been thumbing through Ben's Bible and looking at certain verses, the same Bible that Jennifer had been reading of late while underlining several passages in red. Brian rocked harder, waiting for her to get off the phone. When she hung up, he scolded her for using a loving tone of voice with the very person she was supposed to divorce.

He quoted some Scriptures on human nature—old Testament lamentations about man's inherent wickedness, jeremiads on how everyone is capable of adultery and murder—while rocking and holding up the Bible before him. Brian explained that only one perfect person had ever lived, Jesus Christ, and all others are filled with sin. If Jennifer didn't believe that, she was seriously deluded.

Once a week, in order to revive their marriage, Brian and Dianne went on "dates" to movies or restaurants. He told Jennifer they had been doing this for some time and it had recently occurred to him that if he were to turn left into traffic at a busy intersection on one of these evenings, and if an oncoming car were to smash the passenger side of his vehicle, Dianne would be gone and that would be an act of mercy for everyone. She would be done with human suffering and in a better place with Jesus. And the two lovers could get on with their lives together.

"Can you handle raising five children?" he asked.

"Yes," Jennifer said.

He had also thought of other ways of ending his wife's

suffering. One was by giving her a drug overdose. She took so many pills that it would be easy to alter the amount or the content. If a branch fell from a tree in his backyard, he could beat her to death with it and make it look as if the limb had struck Dianne and killed her. Or he could take her to a movie, leave her standing in front of the theater, park the car, ride past on a motorcycle, and fire a pistol at her—drive-by shootings were becoming commonplace. Maybe he would take her into the woods and simulate an abduction, a rape and murder. He had already gone so far as to steal male pubic hairs from the health club in order to strew them on her dead body.

Twelve

One Wednesday evening in July Brian made a left-hand turn with Dianne sitting beside him, narrowly missing an onrushing vehicle.

"Do you want us to be with Jesus tonight?" she said.

"No," he said, suddenly realizing that he too could be injured or killed. He never attempted another car wreck.

On July 27, while Ben was out of town and his children were at the baby-sitter's, Brian again came to the house in Briargate, where he drank wine with Jennifer and they made love. Afterward, he found Ben's long Colt .45 downstairs and picked up the gun, turning it over and aiming it at the wall, examining it carefully.

"You're willing to let me or my wife die in a driving accident," he said, "but you're not willing to participate in this."

"You're right," Jennifer told him. "I'm not."

Because she felt in need of some spiritual guidance beyond what Brian was giving her, she began visiting Fellowship Bible Church by herself or with her daughters, going to a different service from the one the Hoods attended. She liked being there. It was a chance to get out of the house and meet new people and it filled an inner vacuum she had felt for too long a time. When she told Brian what she had been doing, she expected him to be happy, but he was furious with her.

"Why didn't you tell me you were there?" he said.

"I don't know."

"Why are you being secretive?"

"I'm not."

"What are you hiding?"

"Nothing."

"Why haven't you divorced Ben yet?"

"We've talked about it."

"But you haven't done it."

"You haven't filed for a divorce, either. You're still with Dianne."

"I can't get divorced. I told you that. You can leave Ben because you're not saved. You don't really want us to be together, do you?"

"That's not true."

"Then get rid of him. Get him out of the house."

Jennifer called Wendy Phillips, a friend of hers who also attended Fellowship Bible Church, and said that she knew a couple in a distant state who were devout Christians but having serious marital problems. The husband was so distraught that he was thinking of killing his wife. It was Jennifer's understanding that in God's eyes all sins were equal, so murder was no worse than divorce. Did Wendy agree with that?

"In Christian marriages," the young woman replied, "divorce is not an option. Husbands and wives are supposed to work things out or wait for God to change their spouse."

Sin is sin, Wendy said, and the nature of the sin really does not matter.

Not long after Jennifer had this conversation, Brian mentioned someone in Texas who might kill Dianne for a substantial amount of cash—money that would become available from her $100,000 double indemnity life insurance policy after her death. Maybe he would talk to him about that.

Very early one morning Brian drove to Rich Designs after Jennifer had arrived at the shop but before she had opened the doors, and the two of them drove in her Cherokee up a slender mountain road known as Cheyenne Canyon, which led into the foothills west of town. The canyon held dense foliage and the pavement wound in and around huge boulders. Between the tree limbs they could glimpse mountains looming ahead, the vast red face of the Rockies. Sheer overhanging rocks gave a sense of danger to the road, a sense of being able to slip into the woods and hide from everything. Jennifer parked the Jeep on a secluded pulloff and they made love in the back of the Cherokee. Afterward, Brian told her about a convenience store called the In & Out just east of downtown at the intersection of Platte and Institute, where he and Dianne frequently stopped in the evenings for milk or gum. He had been scouting this neighborhood lately, driving up the lilac-bordered alleys and down the narrow streets, circling and recircling the blocks, until he had found an abandoned A-frame garage behind a home on Prospect. It was just a few hundred yards from the In & Out. Maybe his Texas friend could go to this garage, change into some camouflage clothing that had been stashed there, then walk to the mart. There he would find Dianne and Brian inside, commit a robbery, and in the process shoot and kill Dianne. Finally he could run back to the garage to shed the clothes before vanishing into the night.

It would look better, Brian reasoned, if more than one person were shot—if the store manager, an Asian woman, were also killed—because that would make the robbery appear more genuine.

"Could you do this?" Brian asked her in the first week of August.

"Do what?" Jennifer said.

"Carry out this plan."

"You mean . . . no, absolutely not."

"Are you sure?"

She looked at him, as if she were not quite sure if he were serious. "Are you crazy?"

He asked her what time of the month her period occurred and gave Jennifer some psychology tests he had retained from college. She answered over one hundred questions and Brian analyzed her responses, telling her that she was an active and energetic woman with strong masculine traits, a powerful woman, quite capable of committing murder. In fact, she was perfect for the act, because no one would suspect that a female would put on a man's army fatigues or think that a woman could use a heavy weapon like Ben's long Colt .45. The plan was foolproof and even if they were caught, he had decided that he would rather spend the rest of his life in prison than one more day with his dreary wife.

In the second week of August, Brian rented a Lincoln Town Car and drove Dianne to Sun Valley, Idaho, for a business vacation he had earned from his work at Prudential. Other insurance agents and executives attended the conference, including his parents and his boss, William Bramley. Before leaving Colorado Springs, Brian had told Jennifer that in Sun Valley he was going to start making public displays of affection toward his wife—a necessary step if she were going to be killed in the near future—and indeed when people at the conference saw the couple hugging and kissing in the motel lobby, they were pleased that the Hoods' much–talked–about marital problems were apparently behind them.

While the Hoods were in Idaho, Ben nearly moved out of the Briargate house, leaving one Sunday morning in a huff but returning later in the day. His anger had been unleashed after Jennifer told him that her friend from the health club, Brian Hood, was a model father who cooked meals, cleaned up the kitchen, changed diapers, regularly bathed his kids, and was always home at night with his family. Captain Reali had listened to all this and slowly simmered, before jumping into his army vehicle and driving away. During his brief absence, Jennifer drove to Fellowship Bible Church and attended a service. She found that environment soothing.

In spite of the church's bedrock Fundamentalist doctrine, it does not have a fire-and-brimstone atmosphere or impassioned sermons that fly against the walls. The sanctuary holds no pictures of the blood of Christ and the hymns sound much more like pop tunes or Muzak than music of the soul. The church conveys neither thunderous self-righteousness nor old-fashioned Christian primness, but rather something not quite expected. It is modern, bland, and sweet. More than anything else, FBC seems like a nice place run by well-intentioned people who are serving a congregation committed to reasonableness and decency. The sanctuary stirs no awe or wonder. It offers pleasant numbness instead.

Jennifer sat on a folding chair, surrounded by contemporary wall hangings. A quasi-rock band played at the front of the sanctuary, while a screen was mechanically lowered from the ceiling and the words to the hymns were flashed on it so the gathering could sing along. Musical staffs and notes were unnecessary; all the melodies sounded the same. At first Jennifer hummed but gradually she began to sing out loud. She had a good voice and enjoyed using it and by the end of the service she was comfortable joining in with the others.

That evening, after Ben had returned home, she decided that the time had come to sit down with her husband, open a bottle of wine, confess to her affair with Brian, and discuss the strange religious ideas the young man had introduced her to. She had even decided to tell Ben about Brian's constantly evolving plans for killing Dianne. Weeks ago, she had broached the topic indirectly, by mentioning to Ben that her friend from the health club was so unhappily married he had been praying for his wife's death.

"That's really warped," the captain had replied. "I think you should put some distance between yourself and him."

Ben had a native distrust of insurance salesmen and told Jennifer that if he unexpectedly died, he hoped she would not marry a man like Brian Hood.

On that earlier occasion when she had tried to open this subject, she had felt that Ben had not really wanted to talk about it. As she thought about it again on this Sunday evening, she told herself that he probably would not want to discuss it now, not when their own marriage was already in such turmoil. In fact, it seemed to her that no one she knew wanted to dwell on unpleasant things. Not Ben, anyway, and not Wendy Phillips, her friend from Fellowship Bible Church, who had not really wanted to focus on the idea of comparing the two sins of divorce and murder. And not her own mother, certainly. Earlier in the summer, when Jennifer had told Gail Vaughan that a married man had been paying considerable attention to her, Gail had said that was a definite "no-no" and the conversation had died there. And not Renate Reali either, who was Jennifer's mother-in-law. One evening in the fall of 1989, when Ben and his father were away and the children were sleeping, the two women began drinking wine at the Briargate address and Jennifer opened up, talking in some depth about her family with Renate for the first time. She had always felt sorry for her mother, Jennifer said, and always disliked her father because he was controlling. Renate briefly listened to this confession but then stood and said it was time to wash the dishes. Seven or eight months later, on a summer afternoon, Jennifer saw Dianne Hood walking across the parking lot of a shopping center. She wanted to approach the woman and have a conversation with her, tell her everything that was going on between her and Brian, but she quickly dismissed the notion as absurd.

She did not tell Ben anything that Sunday evening, mostly because she was afraid to but also because Brian had sworn her to secrecy. Despite her promise to keep silent, Jennifer thought about calling Pastor Thurman at Fellowship Bible Church while Brian was in Sun Valley. Ministers had moral authority; they dealt with difficult and complex issues all the time; Pastor Thurman would know what to say if she just told him the truth. He would help her because that was his job. Yet she hesitated in picking up the phone. He was a very busy man, after all, with many people to attend to and more important tasks than counseling a new attendee at his church. She was not even a member at FBC. Finally, after debating the question inside herself for a day or two, she resolved to call him and decided to look up his number. Just then the phone rang and she answered it.

Brian said hello from Sun Valley and then, "I just got the feeling that I was losing you. I want to make sure you still love me and you're still with me."

"Yes," Jennifer said. "I do love you."

They spoke of other things and she never did call Pastor Thurman.

Soon after returning from Idaho, Brian drove over to Rich Designs one day at noon, picked Jennifer up for lunch, and asked if she was ready to execute the convenience store plan.

"No," she said. "I can't do it."

He slapped the dashboard so hard it rattled the car windows and the interior, echoing throughout the Honda Accord.

"Our relationship," he said, "is over."

She had never seen this large man become violent and his anger was so palpable and so frightening that later on she could not recall what had happened immediately after he had struck the dash. She did remember that when things had calmed down inside the car, he smiled and told her he loved her. He had not meant that remark about their relationship being over and once again he started talking about their happy future together.

In the days ahead, the couple began visiting the convenience store over the noon hour or later in the day—they went twelve times by Jennifer's count—circling the neighborhood and driving through the alleys, looking at the abandoned A-frame garage he had discovered and making small purchases at the In & Out. Brian showed her some diagrams he had sketched of the area and told her who worked in the mart and that it had neither a security camera nor a button under the front counter that triggered an alarm. He asked if Ben had some army clothes lying around the house that would not be missed. Since Jennifer herself would not shoot Dianne, he would have to find someone else who would and he needed the camouflage clothing on hand now, squirreled away in the musty garage, so the killer could go there and fulfill the plan. Could she get one of her husband's fatigue jackets and a pair of his military pants, drive them to the alley, and drop them in the shed?

She did not say yes at first, but a good salesman asks a lot of questions just to get a positive answer to something—yes to the good weather, yes to the joys of watching children grow up, yes to the benefits of life insurance, yes to the importance of religion in family life. After a while she took Ben's clothes to the shed and left them there.

It was critical, Brian began saying, to shoot Dianne twice. One shot might leave her alive but maimed and the only thing worse than living with a lupus victim was living with one who was permanently disfigured. Two shots would work. Two shots from very close range. And it would be best to jam the gun barrel into her stomach and shoot up toward the heart.

At a pawnshop outside Colorado Springs, he bought a .45 automatic for $300, but then he told Jennifer that the gun could easily be traced to him and could never be used for the shooting. What about one of Ben's firearms? What about the long Colt .45? Could she provide it for the killer to use? Could she use it herself?

On August 28 Jennifer purchased ammunition for the long Colt at a sporting goods store and wrote her husband a note that both surprised and delighted him. "Let's have a hot date," it read, "on the firing range." In years past Jennifer had occasionally gone to military ranges with Ben and at times appeared to take an interest in his weapons. She had once purchased for him two pistols with consecutive serial numbers, a coup in the world of gun collecting. Now she wanted them to shoot together at Fort Carson and when Ben saw her note, he was elated. He loved sharing his knowledge of guns with others and taking target practice with her might even help their marriage.

They went to the base and shot at an "E Type silhouette," a humanlike cutout figure that the army employs on its ranges. Jennifer used only one gun—the long Colt—and shot up most of a box of ammunition, rarely hitting the figure from twenty-five yards, although Ben had just given her a refresher course in how to load, cock, and fire the heavy, awkward revolver. He liked her enthusiasm but wished she were more skillful; in Europe she had once shot a hole in the floor. They left the range with six live .45-caliber rounds, which Ben took home and placed in a silver container, shaped like an apple, in their upstairs bedroom. The bullets were there for Jennifer's protection, he explained, to be used in case anyone broke into the house or threatened the children. She might need more protection soon because he could be half a world away, fighting a war in the Persian Gulf.

While target-shooting she was relieved to see how badly she performed, telling herself that she could never harm anyone with Ben's gun or any other.

Thirteen

Once Dianne was dead, Brian explained, they would move to Portland and start their life together with the $200,000 collected from her life insurance policy. They could teach a Sunday School class and get some Christian marital counseling if they needed it for what had happened in the Springs, but if God truly wanted Dianne to live, He would intervene and keep her alive. For planning the crime, Brian told Jennifer more than once, he was the greater sinner of the two.

"Anything I do," he said, "you do. And anything you do, I do. And if you do this to Dianne, you may be there physically but it's not you doing it, it's me. And if I could do it and get away with it, I would have done it years ago."

On August 29, the last Wednesday of the month, the Hoods' date night ended at the In & Out convenience mart at 9:00 P.M. sharp. Ten minutes earlier, Jennifer had arrived at the intersection of Platte and Institute, parking just north of the store so she could see it without being easily seen herself. She watched Brian and Dianne get out of the Honda and walk into the shop. Dianne purchased milk while Brian scanned some magazines, taking his time, examining several carefully but not buying any. Five long minutes passed before the couple came out, stepped into the car, and drove toward their residence. Jennifer followed at a distance, certain now that Brian was serious about killing his wife. He let Dianne off at their house and took their baby-sitter home, Jennifer still tailing the Honda in the darkness. When he was finally alone, she pulled up alongside him and they parked.

"Where were you?" he said, as they stood together beside the cars. "I waited for you to come to the In & Out tonight."

"I was there but I couldn't do it."

"Where were you?"

"Watching from the corner. I saw you and Dianne go inside the store."

"Why couldn't you do it?"

"I can't."

"Why not?"

"I just can't, Brian."

"You don't want to, do you?"

She shook her head.

His tone of voice had been gruff but now he embraced her, giving her a warm kiss and saying good night. They drove off in different directions.

Five days later, on September 3, the Realis and the Hoods separately attended a church picnic at Monument Park, where a Labor Day sermon was delivered by Pastor Thurman. After the minister had spoken, Ben and Jennifer, who were spread out on a blanket eating their meal, began to quarrel over his treatment of the girls. He didn't understand them, she said. He didn't know how to interact or play with his children and was too impatient, too brusque, or too tired when he was home in the evenings. He was gone so much that Tineke and Natasha barely knew their father. The spat intensified and Ben stood, going for a walk in the park by himself. When he returned he saw his wife waving to Brian, who was sitting with Dianne and his children across the way. The salesman waved back.

"What's going on?" the captain asked Jennifer.

"Nothing," she said.

"Why were you doing that?"

"Doing what?"

"Smiling at him."

"It's nothing."

Brian approached the couple and asked Ben if he wanted to play volleyball.

"I don't trust you with my wife," the captain said.

Brian grinned at him, his large boyish grin. "Your wife? I just wanted to play volleyball," he said, walking away.

A few moments later he was back asking Ben if he wanted to play basketball. The captain motioned for the two of them to step away from the others and they did, squaring off face-to-face, one man tall, broad-shouldered and wearing a sun-bleached permanent, the other stocky and solid beneath his crew cut. Jennifer watched the men and strained to catch their words. Ben said that he was having some difficulty in his marriage right now and just wanted to be left alone. Brian smiled at him again and replied that he understood, promising not to disrupt their picnic anymore.

At the Fort Carson commissary, Jennifer bought a gray sweatshirt and claimed that Brian purchased a black ski mask at another clothing store. He gave her the mask and a pair of worn gloves, completing the camouflage outfit. She took the mask home and sewed the eyeholes and mouth hole smaller, using dark thread. If the mask covered her entire face, Brian had said, and if the murder occurred after dusk, it would look as though a black man had done it. And the Colorado Springs police were predisposed to thinking this is what black men do so they would naturally look in that direction for a suspect.

On Wednesday, September 5, the Hoods had another date night and stopped at the In & Out on their way home, but this time Jennifer refused to go near the convenience store. On the phone the next morning Brian yelled at her for breaking their agreement, telling her that Ben was going to leave her soon and she would be left without a husband or a lover and no one would want a divorced woman with small children. That afternoon he called back to say he loved her and that evening he phoned the house three

times but hung up each time before Ben could answer it.
The dial tone on the other end of the line drove the captain
wild.

On Saturday, September 8, Jennifer, after much inner
debate and turmoil, finally asked her husband to move out
and by sundown he was gone. In her diary that day, she
wrote,

"Years pass. The more things change, the more they
stay the same. I'm so very unhappy in my life right
now. I doubt Ben's really the man for me but perhaps 'he' doesn't even exist. Too many ugly words,
dissatisfied weeks, months, years. He's only now
taken a responsible interest in our success in finance,
etc. Hard to believe how easy it's been to run so
much . . .

"What do I want? Yes, you, Jennifer Vaughan. I
want a man who can love me for me. Let me be me.
Give me security, strength, love, tenderness, children, etc. What price must I pay for that which I
long for?

"On the verge of tears always. Moods swing like
a pendulum. Who am I? What is my purpose? Why
must I question?

"Ben loves me as only he can. I often feel as
though I deserve each and every pitfall, every down
day. I'm so tired. I'm such a strong/weak person.
I'm so afraid of hurting others at the expense of my
happiness.

"Perhaps I'm odd, wanting a sabbatical from my
life. I have my children, my family, my hobbies once
I get into them. What can I say?

"Anxiety. Frustration. I need to be strong. To be
calm. To examine everything and really not worry
who I hurt as long as I look out for me. That is very
difficult for me to do. I always worry what everyone
else must be thinking. I'm a good person. I'm intel-

ligent yet I'm confused so greatly in my own little mind. Fighting battles within myself.

"Sometimes, I wonder if it is all worth it. Life, though meaningless in a sense, is so monumental. I question my personal validity on this planet. Perhaps I shouldn't question, rather I should just remain numb and not wonder.

"I neither feel young nor old . . . There is no sense of urgency. I just feel so very torn within myself. For what reason I don't know.

"I feel lost. I feel abandoned. I feel alone. I feel tethered. Lord, help me. I'm in great need now of your wisdom and strength . . ."

The next morning, a Sunday, she arose early and drove the girls to Fellowship Bible Church. The Hoods sat a few rows away from her, but she did not speak to them. Jennifer went home, called Brian, and talked about the Christian message that Pastor Thurman had just delivered, which had convinced her, once and for all, that she could never go through with the plan. Killing Dianne was simply crazy. If Brian hated his wife so much, she told him, why didn't he just get a divorce? Again, the man explained in a calm and reasonable voice that she was not saved yet and did not know how to interpret sermons correctly. Jennifer distorted the verses and did not see that God always won out over Satan. If she studied the Scriptures more deeply and listened more carefully to what was being said in church, she would see that it was her duty to kill Dianne.

"Go to hell," she replied.

That evening at six o'clock the Hood family had made plans to walk around the pond at the Broadmoor Hotel, one of the most famous and attractive landmarks in the city, and then eat ice cream. On their way home Brian was going to stop at the In & Out at exactly 8:00 P.M..

"Will you be there tonight?" he asked Jennifer, while

they were still on the phone discussing her religious education.

"You want me to shoot Dianne in front of your children?" she said.

"Yes. It's God's will for her to die."

"You are absolutely out of your mind."

"I believe that if God doesn't want something to happen, it won't happen."

"Maybe He doesn't want us to do this."

"Sometimes, you have to force the hand of God. I can't wait any longer. Dianne is so strong. She'll live to be ninety, just like her mother."

"I can't do this, Brian. I'm not that kind of person."

"If you want to see what kind of a person you really are, go read your Bible. It will tell you what you're capable of. It will tell you that you're just like everyone else. Everybody is filled with sin. There's no reason you can't do it. If you go look in the mirror, you won't see Jesus."

She hung up, feeling exhausted and lonely. She missed Ben, missed her family, and missed having a confidante, a close girlfriend. She called her older sister, Erin Dudley, who lived in Seattle, and they had a brief conversation, but Jennifer revealed nothing about her recent experiences. She called her mother-in-law, Renate Reali, who also lived in Washington state, and complained about being alone so much. Renate told her, "You knew you married a soldier and you have to learn to deal with that. I've been married for thirty-two years and I still feel those things."

"That's not enough for me," Jennifer said, right before hanging up. "I want it all and I want it now."

She called her younger brother, Rick, but they had not been particularly close since a dispute over music in the early 1980s. Rick was a guitarist and Jennifer was accomplished on the saxophone: in high school she was the only white person in an otherwise black combo and she had once won an award at the Reno Jazz Festival. She and Rick had played together in a band but disagreed over her level of commitment—he thought she devoted too much time to the opposite sex and not enough to practicing her instrument. They argued about it and fell out.

After speaking with his sister on the phone, Rick called his parents and said that Jenny was acting strange and bitchy, not at all like the person he had expected to talk with today. What was wrong with her? Why was she so angry and upset? Was she having marital problems again? Keith and Gail Vaughan had no answers for their son. They had also seen and felt the mystifying changes in their daughter lately but had told themselves that perhaps it was just a phase. Rick's call disturbed them and when they got off the line with him they phoned Jennifer, who chatted with them for a while and said that everything was fine.

That afternoon she went to the health club, taking the girls along and leaving them in the nursery. While exercising she received a call and when she picked up the message from the front desk she was told that her husband had phoned. The number on the slip of paper, though, was Brian's (by now she had long since realized how the salesman had always known when she was at U.S. Swim and Fitness; he had simply called the nursery first, asked if the Reali children were there, and driven straight to the club). When Jennifer returned his call that afternoon, Brian apologized for the things he had said that morning about how it was her duty to kill Dianne. He was sorry for making those remarks and for his harshness.

Driving home, Jennifer realized that there was one person above all with whom she wanted to speak, one person who might be able to offer her some genuine help. Derek DeJong had been her boyfriend nearly a decade earlier, when the two of them worked at the Pike Place Market in Seattle, and he had always remained in her heart and mind. He was not her first lover but the young man had affected her in ways she still did not fully understand. Brian, she had come to see over the past several months, reminded her in some ways of Derek. Both were tall and powerful-looking, both could be intimate one moment and distant the next, both knew exactly where she was vulnerable, both made her feel loved but also made her feel very weak. Maybe Derek could explain Brian to her and tell her what to do about his insistent overwhelming presence, maybe he could assist her in getting away from the man. She dialed his old phone number in Seattle but it had been disconnected and when she called directory assistance there was no listing under his name. She searched her mind, trying to think of anyone from her past who might know how to reach him but came up blank.

That evening, after Brian returned home from his family outing at the Broadmoor, he called Jennifer and demanded to know why she had once again failed to show up at the convenience store at the appointed time. Why had she not been there, dressed up like a soldier and ready to kill Dianne? Why had she let him down again? Why could she not keep her word? Why did she not want them to be together?

Exhausted and confused, she hung up and dropped into bed, but sleep was elusive.

Fourteen

Early the next morning Brian called from a north side restaurant and asked Jennifer to meet him there. When she arrived he was sitting with two business associates and talking about insurance, so they rendezvoused a short while later in the parking lot of a nearby Bennigan's. Brian was not angry at her now, he said, just disappointed. He could provide her with a better life as her husband and the father of her children, and she needed a Christian man, a good and godly man. They could never be married, though, until the hand of God was forced and she was not willing to do that, at least not yet. When she said she could never follow through with the convenience store plan, he surprised Jennifer by agreeing with her.

"Maybe it's all a crazy idea," he said. "Maybe it's better if I do it myself."

She felt very relieved.

Three hours later he called to say that Dianne was attending a lupus support meeting at the Otis Park Community Center this Wednesday evening, just two days from now. Emilia Vargas, who worked in his office and also suffered from the illness, had given Brian the park's address and told him when the meeting started and when it would finish—8:30 P.M. That would be perfect, Brian said, because it would be dark enough for her to hide outside the community center until Dianne emerged. Jennifer listened to him, her relief suddenly gone.

In mid-afternoon he called again from his car phone, as he was riding around Otis Park and looking at the grounds.

There was some foliage near the community center, he told her, and a parking lot, a tennis court, a track, and an alley that ran north of the building, which she could use after shooting Dianne. Before and during the murder, he insisted, she should puff up her shoulders and walk like a man. And she should wear a jogging suit beneath the army fatigues so once the camouflage had been shed, she would look like any other female runner getting her exercise on a summer evening.

The following morning Jennifer drove to Otis Park with her children and put them on the swing set, the young mother pushing the girls gently on the swings, catching them in the sunlight, and pushing them out again. When they had finished playing, Jennifer walked over the grounds and looked around to see if the layout matched Brian's description, which it did. After she had returned home, he called and told her the best place to park the Jeep ("as far away from the center as possible"), told her when to get to the meeting ("right at dark") and said once again how many shots had to be fired ("Two. It has to be two"). That afternoon she met Brian at the spa, where they sat in the Jacuzzi and spoke in whispers above the warm swirling water, the man saying that he would be home the next night between eight and eight-thirty calling his relatives long-distance, which would establish in the phone records that he could not have been at Otis Park at that time on Wednesday night. He gave Jennifer some maps he had sketched on pink slips of paper, drawings of the park and the neighborhood.

That evening he called again at eight-thirty, telling her to look out the window and see how dark it was now, dark enough in mid-September to hide the movements of a person who was lurking in the dusk. She had to phone him right after the murder—"I'll let it ring twice," he said, "and you hang up"—their signal that Dianne had been shot so he would be prepared to act stunned and grieving when the police arrived.

"I love you very much," he told Jennifer and hung up.

Before going to bed on Tuesday night, she wrote in her diary,

> "Finding it very difficult to stick to my guns. My needing time away from Ben. He's frustrated. I'm frustrated. I feel so calm and anxious. So perplexed yet sure. So bitter yet content. I need a beach to walk on. Maybe that would help me."

At seven o'clock on Wednesday morning Brian and Jennifer met at Rich Designs and took the Jeep Cherokee up Cheyenne Canyon for their final meeting, at least for a while. Once Dianne was dead, he explained, they could not be seen together or talk on the phone and if they met at the gym, they were to ignore each other. Jennifer had made plans to fly to Seattle in mid-October for the birth of her sister's first child and Brian wanted to attend a Christian Businessmen's Conference in Portland around the same time. The Northwest, he said in the Cherokee, was the ideal place for them to come together—well after Dianne had been buried and the murder investigation had begun to cool.

In the canyon, Jennifer parked on a turnoff and showed Brian the army jacket and camouflage pants which she had recently retrieved from the A-frame garage behind the In & Out. He told her how to wear them and reminded her to walk like a man. They discussed their future together, where they wanted to live, and how they intended to educate their children (he preferred a Christian school). They both desired to settle near the Pacific Coast and he confessed a long-suppressed dream of buying a sports car and opening a photography studio. They held hands, embracing and kissing in the front seat, growing more passionate until they were soon fumbling with each other's clothing. Jennifer noticed something behind them and pulled away. She turned and saw a police car—then gave a cry and began straightening her hair.

Officer Daniel Gonzalez, the Cheyenne Canyon patrolman on weekday mornings, stepped out of his vehicle and walked up to the driver's side of the Jeep. He took out a pen and pad.

"Good morning," he said.

"Good morning, officer," she replied, trying to steady her voice.

"What's your name?"

"Jennifer Reali."

He looked across the seat. "Yours?"

"Brian Hood."

"Is anything wrong here?" Gonzalez said.

Brian smiled at the policeman. "Do I look like a rapist?"

"What does a rapist look like?" Gonzalez shot back.

Brian shrugged.

"If you could tell me what one looks like, it would make my job a lot easier."

Brian just looked at him.

Gonzalez wrote down both of their names and gave them a long gaze. "Are you sure everything's all right?"

"Yes," Brian said.

Jennifer nodded at the officer.

"Okay," Gonzalez said, walking slowly toward his car and starting the engine.

As soon as he was gone, the couple left Cheyenne Canyon and on the way back to Rich Designs, Brian was moody and irritable. He was angry because he had to wait until this evening, more than twelve hours from now, before the sun went down and Jennifer could do what she was supposed to do so they could be free.

"If you don't do it this time," he said just before they parted, "you'll be raising your children alone. I've waited as long as I can. Ben will leave you and so will I."

Later that morning he called the flower shop to reassure her that she could fulfill the plan and that afternoon she saw him briefly while making a delivery. During this last visit, he said he loved her and quoted another Biblical passage on the nature of sin, telling Jennifer that his wife was sicker than ever and they had to put an end to her misery. After work Jennifer drove home to Briargate, drank two beers, and changed into her running clothes. At seven she called Brian, who was at home watching his children and installing a telephone answering machine that Dianne had bought the previous weekend at a garage sale. His older son, Jarrod, was helping him with the installation. His wife, Brian said, had already cooked dinner for the family and left for the meeting. She was wearing a denim skirt, a white top covered with purple flowers, and tennis shoes painted to match the top, and she was carrying a large straw bag. It would be easy to recognize this outfit, Brian told her, even though Jennifer would not be able to wear her glasses under the ski mask.

"There's gotta be two shots," he said again, "and call me right afterward and let the phone ring twice."

"Does Colorado have the death penalty?" she said before hanging up.

"Don't worry about that. The police here aren't very good."

She glanced through a window and saw the sky growing dark.

She drove to East Junior High School, parked the Jeep, put on the army fatigues, and walked to the community center, a dozen blocks away. Hiding behind the center, she smoked a Marlboro Light and then another. The night was warm and she was overdressed but felt cold, her skin damp. Underneath the fatigues she wore blue running tights, a green sweat-top, and a pink shirt, and on her feet were white Nike running shoes. Over this layer of clothing was the grey sweatshirt she had purchased from the commissary. Her hair was braided and the black ski mask sat atop her head, a pair of green wool glove liners on her hands. The long Colt was under the jacket, loaded with the six rounds left over from the day, two weeks earlier, when she and her husband had gone shooting at the firing range.

In near-darkness she walked around to the front of the

community center, sat on one of the concrete planters, and smoked another cigarette. Listening to the lupus meeting within, Jennifer peered through a window and looked for Dianne but was unable to find her. A woman came out and leaned against a wooden post, just a few feet away. Jennifer, her mask still up, stood and walked right past her, moving to the east side of the building and kneeling in the shadows next to a pine tree. A minute later she had returned to the dark spot behind the center and as she sat there shaking and smoking again, she thought of leaving, of shedding Ben's clothes and running away from Otis Park and getting in the Jeep and picking up her children from Kay Everett's and going home and calling Brian and telling him this could never happen and . . .

She walked halfway around the center, hiding in the shadows again. Other women were in front of the building now, chatting and smoking, and as she came closer and stared at one of them the woman stared back. Jennifer stood near the pine tree, hunching her shoulders, trying to look bigger and squarer, trying to look like a man. Dianne came out and talked to the smokers, laughing and standing in the patio lamplight, Jennifer recognizing her voice—that rich Southern drawl she remembered from Tineke's birthday party. The mask was still up and she strained her eyes to see Dianne's clothes and handbag, to make sure it really was Brian's wife. Dianne had frosted hair now; Jennifer could barely make out the tint in that light. She turned away and went behind the center once again, crouching down and thinking, trying to come up with a reason to run. She fumbled with the gun and pulled down the mask.

As she came around the building, Dianne was still talking to one of the women. Jennifer had an odd fleeting desire to walk over and join them, to take off the mask and introduce herself to Dianne and ask how she was, but the impulse passed. She lingered next to the pine, puffing up her shoulders inside the army jacket and remaining perfectly silent. Dianne and her companion started for the parking lot and when they reached it Jennifer began to run after them, holding the Colt .45 in her left hand and grasping for Dianne's bag.

"I don't remember cocking the gun," she told the grand jury, "but I remember shooting and I remember her falling and I remember shooting again. I remember hearing the shots. I remember things going through my head—'It has to be two shots'—so I shot her again, whether she was dead or not. I don't remember anything except trying to run away and falling and running and running and I didn't know what happened. All I knew was that I was supposed to run. So I ran. I took off the army clothes in the alley and I was a woman again. I was me, Jennifer.

"I remember thinking I'd missed. I didn't—I didn't miss. I kept hearing his voice: 'Two shots. She's gotta be dead, gotta be dead.' He got his wish. He kept pushing me and pushing me. There was no way out. I didn't have a choice. I was so scared. God, if I could have just grabbed her and said, 'Dianne, your husband wants to kill you.' If I could have just talked to her.

"But I was scared and I was numb. I couldn't feel anything. I couldn't feel hot or cold. I couldn't feel. All I wanted to do was die. I kept thinking, 'Oh, God, I hope she's alive.' I went home, put the kids to bed, and hugged them. I felt so awful. I didn't want to touch myself or be near myself but I had to go clean the gun, so I did. I put it back where it had been—under the mattress that Ben and I slept on. The gun repulsed me. I was shaking. Brian and I had discussed where I would put the gun after I cleaned it. Everything was discussed. Down to the wire. Everything.

"We discussed how he was gonna react when he got to the hospital. He'd act shocked and everyone would look at him and say, 'Poor, poor pitiful Brian. He's lost his wife and has three kids to raise.' He'd even made plans to play golf with a buddy on the Friday after the murder so it wouldn't look like he'd left time open for the funeral arrangements. He usually golfed on Wednesday. He had everything down.

"I wanted to call Brian the next morning and tell him I couldn't handle it and I would do my darnedest to get rid of myself so everybody wouldn't have to worry about me anymore. I'm sorry Dianne's gone. I didn't want to hurt her. I didn't want to kill her. I never wanted to hurt anybody. I thought something would stop it. But . . . nobody would ever understand. I felt like I was just floating on air. When Ben called on Friday and said he had to talk to the police at Fort Carson, I was relieved because I could finally tell somebody. I was scared of telling, but I couldn't live without telling, and it just isn't right. I'd been floating for days but I finally landed.

"I felt so trapped inside myself and trapped inside that little room where I talked to Detective Wood. I didn't really know what had happened but there I was, sitting with a policeman who was not only charging me with first-degree murder, but hey, I did it. And it doesn't make any sense. I've wondered if somebody else was there. I'm just not that kind of person but I'm sitting with a cop and all the evidence points to me. Wood said, 'If I were your accomplice, I'd be in Tijuana tomorrow.' What am I supposed to do? I knew I'd have to tell the truth some time or I couldn't live with myself, so I did.

"I've had a lot of nightmares in jail. I wake up and see Brian's face. He's angry with me. He's saying, 'She's gotta be dead, she's gotta be dead.' I hear the shots and I have a pain in my chest, like I've been shot there. Then I think Dianne is in my room. It's very hard to sleep.

"I don't know to this day why it happened and I don't know if I'll ever know. I don't know if I want to know. He was just pushing me and it felt like if I didn't do it, the whole world would fall underneath me and if I did do it, the world would fall, so what did it matter?"

She paused and wiped away some tears, looking out at the jury members. "I'm sorry," she said.

Fifteen

After hearing Jennifer's testimony, the grand jury indicted Brian on three counts of solicitation, one count of conspiracy, and one count of first-degree murder. On December 21, 1990, he returned from Houston, where he had been living with his parents and preparing for the Christmas season with his children, and voluntarily surrendered to the Colorado Springs police. Before filing the charges, the El Paso County D.A. John Suthers had decided that Brian's plans and his influence on Jennifer had laid the foundation for the crime, and because of this he was seeking not just a murder one conviction but also the death penalty for the young man.

Brian was sent back to the Criminal Justice Center, the same facility where Jennifer was still being held. Although their cells were on different floors, one morning they came face to face in a hallway and he gave her a big smile and said hello. She froze, unable to speak, then scurried away and burst into tears. What did his grin mean? she wondered. That he loved her? That he was enraged with her and trying to disguise his feelings? That he intended to do something bad to her? Through the ever-present and highly imaginative prison grapevine she had heard that he intended to have her killed.

It was not only Jennifer's testimony that had brought about Brian's indictment or the severity of the charges filed against him. Two of his other acquaintances, Jeanne DeBoe and Michael Maher, also told the grand jury about the man's efforts to get them to harm his wife, and their words led to two separate counts of solicitation to commit murder. Officer Gonzalez testified to seeing the lovers in Cheyenne Canyon on the morning of the shooting; he said they had seemed skittish and alarmed. Jeanie Brooks, the legal investigator for Jennifer's lawyer, Elvin Gentry, had been working closely with the D.A.'s office, providing information that also substantiated their client's story. Jeanie told the police where to look in the phone records to corroborate the long-distance or cellular phone calls Jennifer said Brian had made. Jeanie told them about a small bank withdrawal Brian had made eight days before the crime, money that Jennifer claimed he had used to purchase the black ski mask. Bank records seemed to bear this out. Jeanie told them about the gun Brian had bought in late August, a gun that police found in his car trunk six days after the killing.

Most everything Jennifer said checked out, until the police began visiting ski shops in Colorado Springs, looking for exactly the same kind of mask that Jennifer had worn at Otis Park. Only one local store, the Ski Haus, not far from Jennifer's home or Brian's work address, had these masks in stock. When Officer Jeffrey Huddleston asked Sandra Biereichel, a saleswoman at Ski Haus, if a man had lately purchased a black one, she said no, but she did remember selling one to a young woman—on August 31, her receipts indicated—and the sale was memorable because people almost never bought ski masks this early in the season.

"I tried to talk her into a neoprene mask, one that didn't cover all of her features," the saleswoman said, "but the buyer insisted on the full-length model, which has holes for the eyes and mouth and gathers tightly around the neck. I said, 'What are you going to do—rob a bank?' She said she was going on a camping trip to Steamboat Springs with her husband and children and needed something to keep her face warm. She said her nose was always a problem in chilly weather."

When Officer Huddleston asked Sandra to pick Brian

out of a photo lineup, she could not, but when shown pictures of six women, the saleswoman identified two of them as closely resembling the buyer of the mask. One was Jennifer. When Rich Schell was questioned by the police, he recalled that his favorite employee had not worked at the flower shop on August 31 but phoned in and said that her children were sick.

A month after the grand jury hearing, on January 10, 1991, a bond hearing was held for Brian in the courtroom of Judge Mary Jane Looney, and Jennifer was called to testify. Sandra Biereichel came to the hearing and was able to study the young woman at some length. Nearly four months had passed since Sandra had seen the photo lineup containing half a dozen female faces; part of her difficulty in making a positive identification back then was that when she had first seen Jennifer on television right after her arrest, there were little markings all over her face, like a bad rash. The woman who had bought the mask had had no skin problems. At the bond hearing Jennifer's complexion was clear and as Sandra sat in the courtroom and watched her, she reached a definite conclusion: this lady had purchased the black ski mask.

Brian's bond was denied and he went back to his cell to await trail.

In January of 1991, Jennifer was examined by another psychiatrist, Dr. Arthur Roberts, a mental health specialist in Colorado Springs who was known for delivering expert testimony at criminal trials. A distinguished-looking man with a strong jawline, prominent eyebrows, and a smooth consonant voice, Roberts saw Jennifer five times for a total of about eight hours and he also interviewed her parents and read her diaries. Jennifer told him many of the things about her past that she had lately been remembering in her cell and mentioned one night when she was a teenager. She had gone to sleep in her bedroom but had come to standing in the kitchen holding a knife, pointing it at her

Jennifer Reali and defense investigator Jeanie Brooks at Jennifer's sanity hearing in April 1991.

Photo by the Colorado Springs Gazette.

Dianne Hood.

Illustration by Mark Daily.

Brian Hood listens to opening statements at his first degree murder trial in Fort Morgan in November 1991.

Photo by the Colorado Springs Gazette.

Captain Ben Reali testifying at Jennifer's sanity hearing in April 1991.

Photo by the Colorado Springs Gazette.

The Reali home in the Colorado Springs suburb of Briargate.
Photo by Joyce Jacques.

Brian and Dianne Hood's home near downtown Colorado Springs.
Photo by Joyce Jacques.

The Otis Park Community Center in Colorado Springs where Dianne was murdered.

Photo by Joyce Jacques.

Elvin Gentry, Jennifer's defense attorney, in his Colorado Springs office.

Photo by Joyce Jacques.

Prosecutors Bill Aspinwall and Bob Harward *(l-r)* in the law library of the El Paso County District Attorney's office.

Photo by Joyce Jacques.

Richard Tegtmeier, Brian Hood's defense attorney, in his office in Colorado Springs.

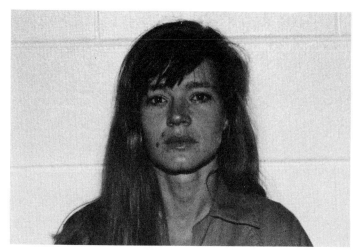

Jennifer Reali's police photograph taken on the night of her arrest. *Photo courtesy of the Colorado Springs Police Department.*

Brian Hood's police photograph taken soon after his arrest. *Photo courtesy of the Colorado Springs Police Department.*

chest, terrified of committing suicide. When she had calmed down, she went back to bed, telling no one.

Dr. Roberts eventually decided that Jennifer was not "mentally impaired," as her first psychiatrist, Dr. Kathy Morral, had diagnosed her, but something well beyond that. She was, in his opinion, legally insane. Under Colorado law, legal insanity is defined as the inability to distinguish right from wrong at the time a crime is committed. Roberts conveyed his views to Elvin Gentry, who passed them on to Jennifer. To her the news was just one more jolt. If she was as distraught and confounded as everyone else by her recent behavior, she did not see herself as mad—not at all. When Gentry suggested that she enter a plea of "not guilty by reason of insanity," she argued with him, reiterating that she was not crazy and did not want to be perceived that way.

She argued heatedly about this—with both her lawyer and her father, Keith Vaughan—but as Keith explained to her, Gentry and Dr. Roberts were experts in their fields and the Vaughans were paying them substantial amounts of money to help her.

On Valentine's Day, 1991, Jennifer did as they advised and her sanity hearing was scheduled in Colorado Springs for the upcoming April 15. Her father would one day testify that she criticized him for an entire day for letting her plead insane.

part three

ROCKING AND CRYING

Sixteen

By mid-April the seasons have begun to change at lower elevations, but at 6,035 feet winter lingers in Colorado Springs. Pikes Peak looms white and glowering, young trees bend naked against the wind, and the town feels cold, disappointingly and utterly cold. The early spring weather is not unlike the El Paso County Courthouse, the site of the sanity hearing, a chilly gray slab of cement designed to look something like concrete venetian blinds, opened up and stood on their side. Across the street sits the former county courthouse, occupying a square city block, an impressive old structure surrounded by beds of marigolds and geraniums, and with a gazebo off to one side. Its grave facade, spraying fountains, cupids over the front door, red latticework on the windows, and weathered clock tower that rises into the sky all reflect a lost grandeur in public architecture. The interior is even more stately—huge marble columns, a bird cage elevator, frescoed ceilings, beveled glass in the arched doorframes, and sparkling chandeliers. The central courtroom is vast and high-ceilinged, the echoes of impassioned legal arguments still faint above the gallery. This building, now included in the National Register of Historic Places, is the kind of place in which one feels one should behave and reveals how much respect the law once commanded.

The new courthouse evokes boredom, like a factory for the numb. In good weather people who work there carry brown bags over to the benches that encircle the flower beds in front of the old building and eat their lunches in the shadow of a more elegant time.

* * *

Bad weather could not keep people away from the courtroom. From opening day the fourth-floor hallway was jammed with spectators waiting to enter the chambers of Judge Mary Jane Looney, a youthful soft-spoken woman with a benevolent smile. Her manner on the bench differed from that of many older judges and many male judges: she was gentler, appeared more open-minded, and let attorneys pose many leading questions. When asked to make a ruling, she did nothing by rote but hesitated and thought a while before speaking. When the lawyers sparred in front of her, she did not scold them as many judges would have done but smiled down at them from the bench, like an indulgent mother looking at her unruly sons.

Women jammed the courtroom. The judge was a woman, the bailiff was a woman, the stenographer was a woman, and several of the armed guards, who were always there to watch Jennifer and escort her back to her cell, were women. Eight of the fourteen jurors were women, the media contained numerous women, and the defendant herself, of course, was a woman. But the real female contingent was in the gallery. It held aging women, middle-aged women, young women, and teenage girls, women of varying shapes and colors and in different styles of dress, women who looked curious and women who stared angrily, unforgivingly, at Jennifer. It held married women, single women, pregnant women, and women who worked in the courthouse and took their coffee breaks at the hearing. It held female attorneys, female legal investigators and law students, female schoolteachers who had brought their high school classes to the proceedings, with the idea of showing the kids that crime does not pay and can be extremely embarrassing.

The assembled women were clearly fascinated with Jennifer, and often whispered among themselves. They scrutinized her, nodded back and forth, critiqued her clothing, hair, makeup, jewelry, and shoes. The defendant had dressed down for the hearing—way down, according to some observers. She usually wore a cream-colored sweater with small pink flowers embroidered on it, a garment that quietly proclaimed her innocence. She wore pearls around her neck and white high heels or black patent leather sling-back pumps. In place of the embroidered sweater, she donned a crisp white blouse with a Peter Pan collar. She wore glasses and a mid-calf green plaid pleated skirt—like the bottom half of a Catholic schoolgirl's uniform. Women in the gallery who sympathized with her predicament found her clothes to be sensible, if not always tasteful. Others said that her courtroom image was a calculated fraud, designed to conjure up the image of a helpless virgin, a ploy which only made her look guiltier.

She cried throughout the hearing and especially when photographs of the dead woman were shown to the jury or when the murder weapon was made an exhibit or when her family and friends testified. When she was not crying, she rocked back and forth in her chair, arrhythmically, hypnotic to watch, her eyes fixed downward on the defense table. Hands in her lap, her shoulders slumping forward, she appeared to be talking to herself or singing. The scene evoked *The Scarlet Letter,* the classic American novel in which the early New England settlers looked upon the adulteress, Hester Prynne, with anger and scorn. Jennifer was not on trial for mere adultery, however, but for murder. And the victim was a young wife and mother, like many of those in the gallery, who had made sacrifices for her husband and children, who had tried to hold a marriage and family together, who had learned to adjust to disappointments and ailments, who had lived with suffering and had attempted to overcome all that and find a decent life.

From the expressions of many of the women in attendance, it was as if by shooting Dianne Hood Jennifer had violated not just the law or social norms but something deeper, something in womanhood itself.

* * *

"We intend to present to you," prosecutor Bill Aspinwall told the jury, while concluding his opening remarks, "the evidence that Jennifer Reali is sane and knew that what she was about to do was entirely wrong. She did it not because she didn't know the difference between right and wrong but because she thought she could get away with it. She could get away with it in our eyes, by fooling the police, and in God's eyes, through forgiveness. She committed adultery with Brian Hood, which is a sin, and she committed murder, which is a sin, because she felt that she would be forgiven by God."

Jennifer's lawyer stood and walked over to the jury box, facing its members and giving them a modest smile. Elvin Gentry has a friendly courtroom manner and is good at letting jurors know that they have a long, difficult, unpleasant job in front of them and that all of them would rather be doing something else. If his client was unpopular for having committed adultery and murder, he was well aware that she might appear even more unsympathetic for pleading insanity. Lawyers use this defense in less than one percent of all criminal trials and rarely succeed with it. In 1981, after John Hinckley, Jr., shot President Reagan and was subsequently found insane and exonerated, forty states, including Colorado, passed laws making it tougher to win with this strategy.

Gentry began by giving a biographical sketch of Jennifer, saying that "she always wanted to be a boy because she thought boys had power and could do what they wanted to do . . . Our expert witnesses will say that she is suffering from major depression and a dependent personality disorder. Both of these are acknowledged by the American Psychiatric Association as mental diseases. You will hear that this last disorder became dominant when it was to Brian Hood's advantage to have his wife murdered. I'm not standing here telling you that Brian caused her mental illness, only that he exploited it. He used mind control and brainwashing and, as strange as it sounds, she came to believe that it was right for Dianne Hood to die, right for both Dianne and Brian. We will show that Jennifer held the gun but Brian pulled the trigger, and this was all a product of his evil mind. Dr. Arthur Roberts will say that Jennifer resisted this insanity defense and wanted nothing to do with it but it was mandated by this doctor and by Dr. Kathy Morral.

"If you want to make human sense out of this case, discard logic. Throw it out. There is no sense to it. She was insane at the time of the killing. Otherwise, the alternative is too strange to contemplate."

Seventeen

The hearing lasted three weeks, nearly sixty people testified, and many tedious days were spent presenting the evidence the police had gathered and the various statements Jennifer had made to the detectives. All of this greatly annoyed Elvin Gentry, who protested loudly and often that he had already conceded his client's part in the crime and that the only relevant issue was the psychological one: based on her past and on Brian Hood's behavior toward her, did Jennifer know the difference between right and wrong when she pulled the trigger? Prosecutors Bob Harward and Bill Aspinwall took exactly the opposite tack—her state of mind was best revealed by her actions before, during, and after the shooting.

The prosecution's most intriguing witnesses were, strangely enough, the friends and coworkers with whom Brian had shared his religious beliefs. They were young men with strikingly conservative ideas, who were generally successful in business and who were moving up in the community. They spoke with candor about Brian's past and repeated many of the things that Jennifer had said Brian had told her about his faith. David Blue, the owner of an orthopedic company, had attended a two-year Bible study group with the Hoods and purchased insurance from the man.

"Off-the-cuff," he testified, "Brian once mentioned in my office, 'Sometimes Dianne wishes she were dead and so do I.' This was around six months before her death. He asked me what I thought about divorce and if I'd look down on him if he got a divorce. I said, 'Absolutely,' because the Biblical interpretation is that divorce is not an option. We only talked about this once. He was frustrated. I said, 'I'd still love you if you got a divorce' but it wasn't an option."

Had Brian, Gentry wondered, ever told him that he was sexually dissatisfied with his wife?

"Yes, sometimes," Blue said. "I'd come home and share with Darla [Blue's wife] what Brian had shared with me. And Darla would encourage Dianne about this and pray with her."

"Did she tell Dianne how to be more creative and give herself to Brian?" Gentry asked.

"Yes," said the soft-spoken Blue, "she did."

Mark Gabelman, a life insurance broker at Prudential, told the court that Brian was "really opposed to divorce. He didn't want to lose face with God and with his church buddies. And he didn't want his children to grow up in a broken home."

Mark Ramey, who supervised Prudential agents, had attended both Village 7 Church and Fellowship Bible with the Hoods.

"If Brian had gotten a divorce," he testified, "I would feel that he'd made the wrong decision and be disappointed in him. I had a high opinion of Mr. Hood. He mentioned having affairs with women outside of his marriage prior to making his profession of faith, but after that, no."

The most provocative of these witnesses was Brian's old boss, William Bramley, a shorthaired, bespectacled man with a soft, flat voice. In the winter of 1991, after a long run as the Prudential general manager, he had retired from the Colorado Springs office and begun a second career as a Christian missionary in prisons. On the witness stand, he was as unflappable as granite.

"Brian held me in high esteem," he testified. "He knew that I don't tolerate negative attitudes and would call him upon it. He did not talk about divorce with me or tell me that he was seeing another woman. My view of divorce is that, with the vows he'd taken, it would not be acceptable, unless there was infidelity. But other than that, it was not an option."

He went on to explain certain parts of his spiritual belief system, which he'd taught to Brian back in the mid-1980s, prior to hiring him, when they were both pursuing the Timothy Study in his office at 6:30 A.M. This part of his testimony exactly corroborated what Jennifer had told the grand jury.

"All sins—including adultery or murder—are equal," Bramley told the courtroom. "I shared that with Brian and showed him the parts of the Bible that support that view ... Brian was counseled that to think about or to look lustfully at another woman was equal to committing an adulterous affair."

"And he had Biblical Scriptures to back this up?" Aspinwall asked the man.

"Yes. And others told him the same thing."

"Can you be forgiven for all sins, even murder?"

"Yes. He had a basis for that."

"He had Scriptures to back this up?"

"Yes."

"And he believed this?"

"Yes, he did."

When Captain Reali entered the courtroom as a prosecution witness, the gallery whirled around and stared at him. Ben was still married to the defendant and under Colorado law one spouse cannot be forced to take the stand against the other but he had waived that right and decided to testify. Actually he had gone much farther than that and now felt it was his duty to prove that his wife was sane at the time of the killing and should stand trial for first-degree murder. Seven months earlier, he had promised to support Jennifer one hundred percent but since then he had learned more of the details of the crime, had had time to absorb what Jennifer had done in the summer of 1990, had thought about the future of his daughters, and had started seeing other women. This past December he had filed for divorce and begun pursuing sole custody of Tineke and Natasha. In addition to these things, he was also aware that his wife had been very forthcoming with her attorney and her psychiatrists about the most intimate details of her married life. The more she talked about it, the worse Ben was portrayed—as a lover with abusive and violent tendencies. When Ben himself was questioned about this by the police not long after the murder, he had said that sex had never been a problem between them and that Jennifer was eager to make love at any time or any place, and under any conditions.

The captain did not wear his uniform in court, but opted for blue jeans and a blue denim shirt instead. The clothes were markedly casual, as if he had interrupted fixing his Jeep to come to the hearing. On the stand he rarely looked at Jennifer and he appeared—in the downsloping wings of his mouth, in his sad eyes—deeply baffled and hurt, the very image of a man who had never thought that his wife could do something highly unpredictable, let alone have an affair or kill someone. He conveyed numbness and rage— his lips occasionally trembled—yet he retained some of the trappings of his old military confidence in his step, in the aggressive way he leaned forward in the witness chair, and in the youthful brashness of a soldier whose army, in the past six weeks, had declared victory in a war in the Persian Gulf. His voice was surprisingly soft and his smile tried to assure everyone that things were under control. With his barrel chest and his boxer's jaw, he looked handsome but frayed, as if he had aged considerably in the past year. Throughout his testimony tears seemed imminent but they never came and he only looked happy when talking about his guns.

As he spoke, Jennifer rocked hard in her chair, staring down and weeping.

"Over the time you've known your wife," Bob Harward asked him, "was her mind ever not working or making sense?"

"Sometimes, in the past, I saw her being easily and greatly influenced by her parents and that concerned me. Her parents didn't approve of our marriage. They didn't like the fact that I was in the army, but I thought she could deal with this and say, 'This is my husband, the father of my children—lay off.' But that didn't happen."

"Did you ever see her have delusions?"

"No. Jennifer did good work at the architectural school at the University of Washington. She's very pragmatic and very logical. She has a good memory and she's smart. I believe there is some type of mental disorder where she is easily influenced by outside things. The easiest thing to do to upset her is to argue with her or—"

"Okay," Harward said, cutting him off with a wave of the hand. The thin quiet-spoken prosecutor had winced at the phrase "mental disorder." Harward craned his neck to the right and took a deep inhalation of air, flaring his nostrils, as was his custom when hearing something detrimental to his case.

"Did she ever," he said, "do anything to indicate that she was out of touch with reality?"

"Well, she told me about Brian being an ideal father because he didn't travel and was home all the time. I didn't think this was very realistic. I thought her perception of him was very unclear and I took offense at this. I began to wonder what I was doing wrong and concluded that she wasn't looking into it deeply enough."

As Gentry began his cross-examination of Ben, the tension between the two men was obvious and over time it would only grow sharper. Right after the shooting, the captain had helped Jennifer's parents find this attorney for their daughter. Ben had then believed that he and Gentry were going to be allies, but now they were severe adversaries, facing each other in a courtroom struggle that would determine if Jennifer would be sent to the state mental hospital for an indefinite period of time or, quite possibly, sent off to prison for life. If the killing of Dianne

Hood would prove nothing else, it would clearly demonstrate, as the weeks and months of legalities unfolded, that murder can indeed make very strange bedfellows.

"Did you," Gentry asked the soldier, "notice anything different about Jennifer on the night of her arrest?"

"Her voice changed," Ben said. "It dropped down very low."

"Had you ever heard that voice before?"

"No."

"You went outside and told the police that that wasn't your wife in there?"

"Yes."

"And you've testified that the shooting was so out of character that something in her must have snapped?"

"Yes. After her arrest she was really stunned and shaken. She said, 'I thought Brian really loved me. I thought he loved me for me.' And he was a snake, an evil man. She thought he was something to strive for, someone to please, someone who was in her self-interest. So from my perspective, as I've had a chance to think about it, something in her snapped."

Gentry thanked him and sat down.

Harward stood for redirect.

"Do you believe, Captain," he said, "that at the time of the murder, your wife knew the difference between right and wrong?"

"Yes. Otherwise, she wouldn't have been secretive and I would have caught on to what was going on. She made a very poor choice in her life and in the life of her children and in the life of Dianne Hood, a bad choice all the way around. The woman I knew before Brian Hood would never have deceived me. A marriage only works when two people put energy into it. Somewhere along the way, she left it and never told me."

Lengthy courtroom proceedings resemble family gatherings. The same people tend to show up at them over and over again and offer a lot of strong opinions. One young man in the gallery came every day wearing a Boston Celtics jacket and stared constantly at Jennifer, winking at her and smiling, her only groupie. Others came to glare at her and say nasty things. The spectators provided a running commentary:

"I've been watching her since this started and it's all an act. That rocking is a mannerism. People who are crazy rock in rhythm. She just rocks when she thinks she should. And she is very conscious of how her hair looks. People who are insane don't worry about their hair."

"Women get blamed for these love affairs, while men get away with murder."

"There's a dead body in the cemetery and over there is the mousy-looking woman in glasses who killed her—and she keeps crying and crying. Something is missing here."

"She's obviously crazy. This whole thing has done nothing but make lawyers money."

"If she's crazy, we're all crazy. No one knows anybody. Husbands don't even know their wives."

"She is crazy. She wasn't crazy when she did it but she is now. Killing Dianne drove her crazy."

"You can't kill someone unless you want to. You can't force a person to do this."

"Isn't it odd that she dressed up in a man's clothes—her husband's clothes—for the shooting?"

"This is my first trial. I came here because I've done things in relationships I couldn't believe I did. I thought this might give me some insight into that, but watching it has just scared me. I think she's insane."

"Monsters have so many different faces."

"Jennifer will be sad when the trial's over. All her life she's wanted attention and now she has it."

"Women tell women their secrets. They tell their

mothers or their female friends or their sisters. She didn't tell anyone anything."

"Only someone who doesn't know what death is could have done something so awful. That's why she feels so shattered now. She didn't just kill someone, she destroyed her innocence."

Eighteen

On the morning he was to begin presenting his defense, Elvin Gentry entered the courthouse nervously chewing gum and pushing a dolly heavy with legal documents. Walking beside him was Jeanie Brooks, his legal investigator, a nattily dressed woman who favored blue high heels and a golden ankle bracelet. Walking beside her was Archie Belford, who was employed by Gentry as a "body language expert," but in earlier years he had been an instructor pilot for the United States Air Force, a car salesman, a leader of national seminars in hypnosis for police officers, a commercial real estate appraiser and, according to his résumé, a "National Level Multi-Level Seminar Communication Instructor." Archie was a big man with a big happy smile, huge feet, large hands, and a large head. When he laughed his entire body rumbled and he looked like an overzealous teenager.

Archie had developed a complicated system of perception and analysis that broke human beings down into four basic categories: 1) Slow, Non-Emotional 2) Fast, Non-Emotional 3) Fast, Emotional 4) Slow, Emotional. Numerous personality traits were listed under each heading and he had created intricate drawings with arrows to back up his ideas. Based upon this "Natural Learning" theory, Belford believed that he could instantly peg the intelligence and emotional responses, conscious or unconscious, of anyone who walked into a courtroom. At Jennifer's hearing, for example, he would glance at each incoming witness and whisper across the defense table: "One,"

"Two," "Three," or "Four." Gentry knew what each number meant and took it from there.

Belford had another formulation—"Positive Multilevel Communication Actions By Archie"—which he recommended for success in business or other endeavors. He enjoyed using his concepts and when encountering someone new, he sized him up in something under a minute, then nodded and said, "Yep, you're a two all right. You're action-oriented, non-emotional. You like to do it now, don't you? Don't like anyone or anything standing in your way. You'll take a risk. You're definitely a two." There were things about Archie that might have led one to think of him as a flimflam man, but his enthusiasm for his own theories was so great that one gave him the benefit of the doubt. Watching him in court, with his long feet dancing under the defense table and a grin playing around his mouth, even an amateur observer of the human body could tell that he was glad to be employed.

"That body language expert," said one aging woman in the gallery, "is just there to tell Jennifer when to cry."

Keith and Gail Vaughan lived in the same attractive comfortable Seattle home they had occupied since 1964. Located in Washington Park, the contemporary two-story house, which sat atop a hill, had been designed by Jennifer's father and was estimated to be worth more than $300,000. In the months following the murder, the Vaughans had sat in their residence, awaiting the daily collect call from their imprisoned daughter, and begun the difficult process of thinking backward, of dredging up the past and looking for a hidden trauma or a buried memory, anything—anything at all—that might explain Jennifer's violence and help to establish that in September of 1990 she had been legally insane.

The testimony they delivered at the hearing was remarkable because of what they did not say (and because of what one had come to expect in these kinds of circumstances). They did not talk about child abuse, the neglect of their kids in any manner, things they might have done differently, serious family strife, or where they had gone wrong with Jennifer. They in no way perceived themselves as her enemies or seemed to be hiding anything or appeared to have any understanding whatsoever of why their daughter had shot someone to death. A cynic might have asked: How could they have seen themselves as her enemies when they were paying for the hearing, which was costing them $100,000? To date their daughter's legal work had forced them to take out a second mortgage on their home, to sell a car, and to set up the Jennifer Reali Defense Fund in Seattle, in the hope that friends would help them out financially; very few had. But there was nothing cynical about the Vaughans. They openly told the court how they had attempted, throughout their children's lives, to provide them with emotional stability, financial security, many educational opportunities, and love.

When under duress, Keith had a tic around his mouth, much in evidence in the courtroom, but even when nervous he spoke in a firm, resonant voice. On the witness stand the short, white-haired architect, who favored dark suspenders and flannel shirts, handled himself gracefully, impervious to the angry stares directed at his daughter. More than anything, he showed a tremendous intellectual curiosity, as if he simply wanted to know the truth of what had happened. How could his daughter, one of the nicer and more thoughtful young women whom a number of people said they had ever known, have done this? Where was the hidden logic behind the crime? What was the stimulus for something that, on the surface, defied all reason?

Gail's testimony did not run nearly as smoothly as her husband's. She was angry and hurt because the prosecuting attorneys had the right to ask disturbing questions about her family's emotional dynamics; more than once she snapped at Harward. This small woman with bobbed greying hair and clothes that revealed an absence of vanity, presented a warm smile when she was comfortable and

a stern expression when she was not. In the courtroom she
was all glares and frowns. She conveyed a great sense of
strength and determination, and a fierce underlying protec-
tiveness toward her children. Watching her try to maintain
control on the stand and repeatedly give in to tears (many
women in the gallery cried along with her) caused one's
stomach muscles to tighten and evoked the mysteries and
profound fears that come with being a parent. During
Gail's testimony, Jennifer looked not at her mother but
down at the floor. She looked shamed.

The Vaughans' first potentially significant recollection
of their middle child came from 1968, when Jennifer was
six and had gone on a field trip with a girlfriend to the Seattle Center, the site of the 1962 World's Fair. Throughout
the hearing much was made of this incident—it was even
described as a case of sexual molestation—but its thinness
revealed just how desperately her parents were searching
through the past for an explanation.

"Jenny came home from this trip," her father testified,
"and told us that a man had shown interest in her. She was
approached by him and something happened but she did
not very successfully convey what it was."

The little girl was blond and slender but when she
reached puberty her hair darkened and her body changed
dramatically. She began to hide inside baggy clothes and
by age twelve she was so self-conscious about her appearance that she asked her mother if there was an operation for reducing the size of her breasts (her bust,
strangely enough, was larger when she was a young teenager than when she became an adult). Because the murder
had occurred two days before Jennifer's period started,
her long-standing menstrual difficulties were also discussed at length in the courtroom. "Her right ovary has
given her a lot of pain all her life," her mother said. "Her
moods went up and down whenever she ovulated, in the
middle of the cycle, so for her it was like having two pe-
riods each month. She wasn't as bubbly and bright then,
but that is how women are."

Keith vaguely recalled a long-ago occasion on Vancouver Island, when Jenny was playing on a low flat beach and the tide began washing in. She became frightened and her father saw this but made no move to help her. "I was the kind of parent," he testified, "who wanted his kids to work their way out of their problems. Jenny panicked and was terrified. She felt abandoned on the beach, but I wanted her to swim out of the situation. She felt she couldn't. A man was nearby watching this and he pushed a log over to her. She grabbed it and was all right.

"Nothing was ever quite enough for Jenny and she was a black hole as far as attention was concerned. She always wanted more. Around the house she was a model child, washing the dishes after meals and making us cookies and bringing her mother flowers. If a problem came up with our kids, our kind of discipline was straight talk and discussion. I never spanked Jenny. I didn't believe in that. We would all sit at a table in the living room and her mother and I would talk about how miserable their characters had become. They would be unhappy about it until the next morning."

In 1975, Jennifer was thirteen when her father's successful architectural partnership exploded over a serious disagreement with his colleagues. He was suddenly expelled, out of work and depressed. "For three to six months," he said, "I was down and it affected the kids. Our older daughter, Erin, got caught shoplifting during this time and our son, Rick, made angry phone calls to the other men in the firm. Jenny didn't react at all. She didn't do anything. She was just always there for us. During this time she stayed home with us and smothered us with care and love."

"She was a very happy child most of the time," Gail testified, "very comfortable in her world. When she wanted something, anything, she would go out and achieve it. She was a perfectionist and an honors student and attended a weekend leadership training program in high school. She was a self-motivator."

"Everything Jenny did," Keith said, "she wanted to be the best at. She was 'stroke' oar on the Garfield High School crew and captain of that crew. She went to the Junior Olympics in rowing. She was a good soccer player. She was a solo alto saxophone player in the high school jazz band. She was very self-confident in those years but that changed as she got older."

At sixteen she began dating a boy named Willis Black and was soon pregnant. The young couple decided on an abortion, through Planned Parenthood, and after the operation had been successfully performed, she told her parents what she had done.

"We weren't too happy about this relationship," Keith said, "but we thought she and Willis handled the situation in a mature manner. Jenny took the abortion very seriously and tried very hard to act responsibly, but she wasn't herself again for two or three months."

"Willis Black," Gail told the court, "was a very disrespectful young man. I threw him out of the house once because he didn't respect our curfew. I thought he was too controlling of my daughter."

Jennifer did not leave home to attend college but enrolled at the University of Washington in Seattle, a choice influenced by another young man. As a teenager, while working at a flower emporium at Pike Place Market, the colorful and vibrant collection of open-air shops that borders Puget Sound, she met Derek DeJong, a tall intense-looking young man who worked in a nearby store that sold fish. DeJong was not exactly handsome; he had large strong features which did not quite fit together, somewhat reminiscent of the French actor, Gerard Depardieu. In Derek's face were both tenderness and ferocity—his eyes shone with intensity and sometimes reminded you of the eyes of a boxer who had been hit a lot but refused to go down. Jennifer fell utterly in love with him, the kind of attraction that usually happens only once in life and usually when one is very young, the kind of passion which leaves the lovers (or just one of them) convinced that nothing like this has ever happened before to anyone.

Photographs of Jennifer from this time reveal a contented-looking young woman, her features rounded, her appearance healthy and full. She was getting a lot of attention. One day, after she and Derek had been living together for several months, he came home and announced that he was moving out. Within hours he was gone. He had refused to talk about his decision or explain his feelings to her, although years later he would say that he left because he has difficulty being close to people. He did not depart without a fight: Jennifer screamed and threw a beer can at him, missing.

Following the breakup she began dressing almost exclusively in black and could not stop crying. There was evidence of bulimia, her weight swinging up and down on a weekly basis. A picture of her from this period shows her with splotchy cheeks, swollen red eyes, and a puffy face—she looks wounded, awful, as if she had been beaten. She looks like someone else. For six months after Derek left, she did not menstruate, but all of these physical reactions gradually went away and her body returned to normal. It was the frozen image of her distorted puffy face—an image that her attorney put on display in the courtroom—which hinted at the damage that is emotional and invisible and does not fade with the years, but grows deeper and more insidious until one is forced to come to some resolution with it, or else.

Nineteen

Well before Derek moved out, Jennifer had planned a trip to France, where she intended to study art and live for several months with a family in Avignon. In January of 1983 she flew from Vancouver to London— her parents paid for the excursion—and spent several days there, too frightened to walk the unknown streets. In her diary she wrote:

> "Everything's been running fairly smoothly. I'm just apprehensive about stepping outside the hotel lobby ... Sitting in a plush velveteen chair, waiting for something to happen. No appetite. Very tired also. I walk around afraid to confront anyone. Afraid to go into places I want to go. Afraid that a single woman should not go into those places."

She wrote about Derek and about a young man she had recently met named Benjamin Reali, who was attending the University of Washington and serving one weekend a month in the United States Army. The military had agreed to pay for his schooling if he would commit himself to the armed forces after graduation. "I miss Ben so much now," she confided to her notebook when she arrived in France. "I want to cry. I want a hug. I wonder what he's doing."

The diary, which was also displayed in the courtroom, reveals a lively, intelligent young woman, with a good eye for observation, away from home for the first time and just beginning to experience the world beyond Seattle. Her entries indicate that she will one day become an artist or an architect or a writer or a cosmopolitan traveler with a great appetite for discovery.

Jennifer's months in France are the only time in her life when she is genuinely alone and essentially uninvolved with a man. One can almost feel her stretching her limbs and her sensibility, as she begins to examine her own rich and complex interior. The process is bumpy and self-absorbed but full of excitement, hope, and poetry. She was twenty years old.

January 12, 1983: "I am learning things about myself, a lot. Solitude is a great necessity for me here and I enjoy being on my own ... I haven't taken a shower in a week. Time to get ready for dinner. I want to call home so bad. I feel different than I've ever felt. Maybe it's just one of those homesick pangs for 'mommie's orange juice.' "

January 23, 1983: "We rode our bikes out to Fontaine de Vacluse ... Following a country road through vineyards, flowers and everything else that can grow here, up into the small village that begins with a paddle wheel alongside the five or six stone houses topped with ochre roofs. Here we passed under an old Roman bridge which stood about five stones high. Now in a canyon whose walls are white and the rock formation was shifted ... A little further on we came into the main square in Fontaine de Vacluse and having arrived just after 1:00 all the shops were closed for lunch. No bread, cheese or wine for us. So we meandered up to the fountain which was nestled in the base of the canyon ..."

January 25, 1983: "I have nowhere I have to be. Such a nice thought. I want to break those strings from everything. I want to be individually secure and perfectly content with solitude. I wonder if I'll ever find my own. The only way to find it is to cut out the outside familiar stimulus and wander inside by myself."

February 1983: "We started for home from Lille at 8:00 on Sunday evening thinking the train would take us straight through to Avignon but ... [it was] a milk run which took six fucking hours. This is where I fought with the smelly Frenchman. It's amazing what one can get out in another language when one is angry ..."

February 1983: "Everything seems so temporary. Nothing fully crystallizes before it melts on to someone or somewhere else. What a crazy rollercoaster ride ... A toe dipped here, a finger dipped there. Just long enough to see if the water's warm or cold, clean or dirty—what's next? ... Maybe I just need a good cry. It's been a while now ...

"Once again I have the desire to move on and escape ... I could stay here in Europe for years exploring. On down thru Africa, Egypt and just move east. Slowly establishing a reality at each stop. Superficial or concrete depending on the length of stay. But ... back to this reality. I bought some paints today and a wicked black mask to be painted for the Mardi Gras. Anything goes. Another toe dipped into another wild pool of water!"

February 12, 1983: "ON THE BUS ... Smoked the weed yesterday and it was shit but ... we had a good time rotting. Snow in Nice. Go to the Cote D'Azur to get cold. Running low on ink. Things are getting better. My depressed state arises from—I have analyzed it—my desire for home. I'm yes, I'm HOMESICK! Desiring things of small individual significance that just fill the spaces in a routine more established than I had thought ... This autoroute is crazy. Damned socialists. Have to stop at every so many kilometers to check in or pay something."

February 1983: "At times I miss Ben and I wish not
to think of it. I want to separate myself from the
pressure and the security. I can't be sure or even
think that I will be with him when I return. The one
I seem to think of often is Derek. Worse yet, I sup-
pose, no hope there. Sometimes I wonder if the letter
I sent was too much. If he sent it to me I would
smile and feel love ... but one never knows. Sometimes, it's best to be detached ..."

February 22, 1983: "I am really missing Benjamin
right now. Three letters, a dozen roses just after Italy. Too much for me to handle. Am I in love or
longing?"

February 26, 1983: "Stark raving naked just ready to
hop into a bath after weighing myself. The phone
rings. It is for me but it takes me a moment to figure
out that it's Derek ... just called to say I love you
and I miss you. Flabbergasted is the term, shocked,
elated. I never expected that kind of reaction to the
letter I sent him. I've got to keep everything in a
good honest perspective from a good strong distance.
Why? I don't want to go home and deal with the two
of them."

March 9, 1983: "Derek called last night. I kept my
distance even though I was excited. He said he'd call
again next week before I leave for the beach ...
man, am I FAT!!? No, I'm not surprised really. But
I should do something about it before it's real hard
to lose.

"Derek ... I cannot let myself love you the way
I once did. My limb, that I so freely ventured out on,
is shorter now. Tho you will always be a warm
thought to me. Yes, I'm scared of you and yes, ever
since you left me I've wished you would desire to
see me when I returned. Silently! ... My memories
of you have been dominant and with your presence,

though distant, they have reawakened and I'm not ready for them now. Now I need to be me and me alone. Caught in a world of uncertainty and constant change. Nothing is ... or I should say everything is temporary. I'm moving on, trying to find me and the me I wish to be. In a sense I'm afraid to go home ... apprehensive to see what is there and how I react to it. I would like to go home and spend some time by myself to sort things out ...

"New forms of beauty catch my wandering eye constantly. From the Alps to the ocean. Spring forest flowers to gothic castles. What a feast for the soul. Lost in nature's playground. A constant spring of discoveries. Yep ... I miss you."

March 10, 1983: "I came here for the experience yet maybe I'm not pushing hard enough ... I'm sorry I don't have the time to seek out a job or maybe it's the guts. No, if I had time and it weren't too difficult, I'd try to find a job sailing."

Undated: "Grey skies on Italian Mediterranean coast. Tranquil anticipation of week to come ... Another dream of death in a courtroom, with steps leading up to a field ... A dream occurred a month ago. A man kissed me and melted away to the ground ..."

Undated: "I don't want to create in my mind a Derek that won't be there ... There are no obstacles save the ones I create for myself. If I argue for my limitations, sure enough they'll be mine. So much freedom can be stifling. I'm not sure where to start and I feel as tho I missed first base somewhere along the line and I want to go back and catch it. Time loses its relevance in changes. There need not be a relationship here. I never wish to cling but instead to flow with the current wherever it blows me."

April 21, 1983: "There is no problem so big that it can't be run away from."

April 27, 1983: "Now sitting in the corner of the blue couch, a glass of wine at my side and the beautiful late afternoon Seattle sun shining over my shoulder onto the rug, roses and light hardwood floor. Yep, I'm home and it's hard to believe. I don't feel as if I ever left. I'm not sure which one is a dream, knowing what all those people are probably doing right now halfway across the world and wishing I were there. I want to cry or I feel the burn of tears rising to flow yet it is only instantaneous and I can get away from it back to this real city."

May 5, 1983: "I feel lost in my own familiar world. My mind battling out the questions of education, employment, social life and love. Each one carrying quite a heavy hand and they joust with each other. Some need research, some need distance, all need time. Ben, the loving sweetheart, playing cool and the aggressive Derek trying to get his foot into a door that is afraid to open."

June 21, 1983: "The cream-colored moon sits almost full in the misty indigo sky at the end of the longest day of the year. A pleasant numb repose waves thru my body as I gaze at the perfect brightness of Venus, shines out to tempt the moon . . . those hollow feelings of sweet loneliness bleed into my aching soul. It has been years since the wars which tore us apart and I cry to the moon for answers to questions that I may never know."

Twenty

Returning from France, Jennifer soon became pregnant by Ben and had another abortion. She kept this operation from her family and most of her friends, none of whom was particularly taken with the young soldier. While attending the University of Washington, Jennifer lived with her sister, Erin Dudley, and Ben briefly moved in with them. They clashed—Erin wanted Ben to pay rent and get his guns out of their home; Ben worried that reports of Erin's occasional indulgence in drugs would filter back to the army and damage his long-range plans for a military career.

"Ben reacts quickly and angrily to things and is uncomfortable to be around," Erin told the hearing. "I always felt that he was an ass and that he humiliated my sister. He would point at women on the street and say that's what a woman should look like. Jen told me that Ben told her what friends to have and what clothes to wear or not wear."

"After Jenny and Ben got together, I saw her much less," testified Elena Lamont, who had known Jennifer in college and gone on to manage the public relations for the Seattle author Robert Fulghum. "Ben came between our friendship. He felt I was a bad influence on her life and he isolated her from her long-established friends. Jenny always seemed self-assured before meeting Ben but after that, she gave up music, writing, and athletics. Her spirit was squashed."

Jennifer Zavatsky, a Seattle lawyer, was Jennifer's best friend in adolescence and had spent many days and nights in the Vaughan home. As she explained in the courtroom, she'd reacted to the news of the Hood killing with something well beyond amazement. "Jenny was the last person in the world to be accused of jaywalking, let alone murder," Zavatsky said. "When we were growing up, her family was more normal than normal. They were the family the rest of us wanted to be in."

Zavatsky and Ben also clashed.

"He worked very hard to get Jenny," she said, "and when he got her, he won and the rest of us lost. I recall him saying that once they were married, we'd never see her again. When we were teenagers, I always thought of her as independent and the leader of our group. A trendsetter. She was very outgoing and made friends easily. Marrying Ben was not an independent thing."

In mid-1984 Ben was scheduled to graduate and then report to a military base for the start of active duty. He gave Jennifer what she would later describe as an ultimatum: marry him before he left for the service or their relationship was over. If the young man entered the army with a wife, he would receive higher pay, better housing, and more status. Virtually everyone who knew Jennifer told her the same thing—wait and see what the future brings.

"Ben would rarely let her be alone with me," Zavatsky testified, "and, sometimes, the girls just wanna be with the girls. He didn't let her out of his sight and he got really concerned about this when he was demanding that she marry him. He was afraid we would talk her out of it."

"Jenny was very confused," Gail Vaughan said. "She told Ben she wanted to wait but he said, 'No, it's now or never.' I hadn't raised a child to respond to these kinds of ultimatums but she was an adult now and made her own decisions."

"Ben always seemed a little macho to me," Keith said, "but I thought that might pass. Beneath that macho and military attitude was a decent guy. I wanted to like him."

"The wedding was on and then off and then on," Erin Dudley said. "The wedding was weird, very sad. I was the maid of honor. Jenny cried right after the vows and during the reception and then she went to my parents' house and cried on my mom's dress. I didn't think brides were supposed to cry that hard."

"She cried on the way up the aisle," Keith said.

"She drank a lot at the wedding," Gail said, "but I really thought it was all right."

"She got loaded," Keith said. "Ben wanted to honeymoon on the Oregon coast and the night of the wedding they didn't leave our house until midnight. The next morning she awoke in Oregon, sat up, and started to cry. When they came back to Seattle, Ben said, 'Is there any return on this model?' We didn't think much about it."

"After the wedding," Erin said, "they left Seattle and moved to Fort Benning, Georgia. Jenny started wearing big hats, more makeup, and fancier clothes and jewelry. Ben likes beautiful women and wanted her to look good. She was cocky now and talked a lot about herself. When Ben wasn't around, she was more of the Jenny we'd always known. She just enjoyed a cup of coffee and didn't dwell on herself so much."

"Once they were married," her father said, "Jenny dyed her hair strawberry blond, the same color as her mother-in-law's hair. She said that Ben liked her hair this color. We weren't very kind about it and said that it looked silly. Ben called her 'Jennifer' now and that was always her 'trouble' name in our home. We only used it when she was in trouble. When we visited them, Ben asked us to call her 'Jennifer' and we couldn't. He said, 'We call her Jennifer now' and that seemed to us like a fairly strong suggestion."

For decades Keith Vaughan had been concerned about the mental health of his children, and with good reason. In the early 1940s, when he was seven, his mother fell into a serious depression and the boy was sent away for a while to stay with relatives. On another occasion, after his mother tried to kill herself, she was hospitalized because of fears that she might hurt her own family members. After receiving electroshock therapy, she was functional until 1959, when the shock treatment was successfully employed again. Had it not worked, she would have spent the rest of her life on a psychiatric ward. When her sister, Bertha, was twenty-eight (the same age as Jennifer in September of 1990), she burned down her house on the Canadian coast. Bertha was committed and never released. As a boy Keith was told that his Aunt Bertha had arthritis so bad that she couldn't leave her institution.

When he grew up and had children of his own, Keith was not as silent as his parents had been about the potential hazards of mental illness. He testified, "My wife and I tried to stress to our son and daughters that these depressive patterns were there and this genetic link was there and to just be careful. But we didn't talk about it that much." In the summer of 1988 at a family reunion in Alberta, Canada, Keith and one of his cousins decided to document the familial pattern of female depression. Their interest had been piqued when one of their relatives stated that over the past several decades there had simply been too many emotional problems for them to continue to ignore. After conducting some research, Keith discovered that, within the past four generations, eleven out of twenty-five women in his family had had "significant depressive episodes."

In 1975, when his architectural partnership suddenly disintegrated, Keith himself became depressed and made his first visit to a psychiatrist. The loss of his long-standing business and some important friendships, the doctor told him, would depress anybody. What he was experiencing was normal.

"After hearing that," Keith said, "I didn't feel so bad."

He came away from the psychiatrist convinced that mental health experts could be very helpful.

After moving to Fort Benning, Georgia, Ben and Jennifer began the series of transfers that would quickly take them to West Germany, to Italy, where Tineke was born, to Fort Huachucha, Arizona, where Natasha was born, and finally, in the summer of 1989, to Colorado Springs. That autumn the Vaughans came to the Springs for Thanksgiving. For years they had known that their daughter had marital difficulties but they had managed to keep an optimistic outlook and to avoid becoming involved in the conflict. It was not in their nature to be intrusive, at least in the past, but the young couple now had two small girls and the tension in the Reali household had grown more severe. What was the proper role for grandparents who did not like the environment in which their granddaughters were being raised? What was the right thing to do?

One evening during their visit Ben came home and was visibly angry. He had never enjoyed Jennifer's parents—they did not approve of his gun collection, they held political opinions that were much more liberal than his own, and there were other differences.

"I was raised with a very strong sense of right and wrong and I tried to raise my children that way," Keith told the court. "Jenny's values were always something that I admired but I thought that she and Ben were developing artificial values. They were very concerned with their appearance—with their clothing and working out and improving their bodies. This isn't the way our family conducted its affairs. We dressed nicely but we didn't sacrifice for that."

"We helped them with money," Gail said. "They'd had money problems earlier and these continued in Colorado Springs. We loaned them over $15,000. Jenny never borrowed money before she married Ben. She was a saver. She could make a nickel turn into a dime. When she was young, we'd borrow cash from her. She and Ben bought a Mercedes Benz and a computer and a lot of other things like that. Whenever we'd go anywhere with them, Ben would find a gun store and buy guns."

On the night Ben arrived home upset, he found his

daughters making noise and throwing food. Keith watched him take Tineke upstairs and spank her, something the older man did not believe in.

"There was such an atmosphere of disapproval in their household," Keith said. "I was very upset by this spanking and I told Ben that I wanted to have my say. I said to him, 'Things are awful here and both of you should seek counseling.' To my surprise, he thanked me for my input and said that he thought counseling was a good idea. I'm a fairly sensitive and emotional person and all of this bothered me a lot. I told my wife, when we were returning to Seattle, that I didn't want to go back there anymore. Two months later, in January of 1990, Jenny called and I asked her if she'd gone to a counselor yet. She said, 'Don't worry about it, Dad. You get used to it.'"

After the Thanksgiving visit, Ben told his wife that her parents were no longer welcome in their home. The Realis never did go into counseling but the young couple, on the advice of a Fort Carson doctor, joined a health club. Jennifer began exercising on a regular basis, three, four, even five times a week, releasing some of her anxiety by working out hard and then releasing some more by sitting in the Jacuzzi. Soon Brian Hood would join her there.

Twenty-one

Elvin Gentry's first expert witness, Dr. Arthur Roberts, spent a whole day recounting the history of "the white sheep" of the Vaughan family. He portrayed Jennifer's life as one depression after another and one emotional crisis leading to the next, all of them culminating in a time when she would descend into madness and homicide. Roberts's testimony was a compendium of modern female ills: mood swings, repressed anger, hormonal imbalances, premenstrual troubles, the search for an identity, codependent behavior with the opposite sex, the inability to find a good man, severe stress, sexual abuse (during her childhood visit to the park), two abortions, bulimia (she had once vomited so hard that her eyes hemorrhaged) and finally, and perhaps mostly, the indignities she suffered at the hands of her husband.

"Ben would rape her anally," Dr. Roberts testified, "a practice which she hated but she submitted to it in order to please him. He put cliplike devices on her nipples and this was painful but she felt she had to do it. She felt a great deal of distaste for sex but did it for her husband. She internalized all of this. Internalizing is feeling a sense of dis-ease within yourself, feeling defective within rather than being comfortable enough to express what you want and need. She only knew how to present herself as the perfect child who was never any trouble or as the adult who had become very skillful at having a smile on her face because that was how she got rewarded."

Dr. Roberts spoke in detail about the number "two," a code word that he claimed Brian had repeated over and

167

over to Jennifer in order to produce a hypnotic effect and a form of brainwashing.

"Two was always a symbol for them," he said. "Brian would often call her at home, let the phone ring twice and hang up. At Otis Park there were to be two shots, he told her, and two deaths. Two deaths, not one. And two rings on the phone at his house after the killing occurred. On Friday, two days after the shooting, Jennifer was driving and stopped at a traffic light. She felt that Brian was with her in the car and she suddenly remembered that two people hadn't died that night. She felt that she was supposed to be the second death. That would have completed the mission. She felt this in a flash—that she had to commit suicide. I've been concerned about her killing herself ever since I met her."

His diagnosis of Jennifer was threefold: she suffered from a "major depression recurrent," which is recognized as a disease by the American Psychiatric Association; she had "premenstrual syndrome" and had killed Dianne Hood near the end of her monthly cycle; and she had a "dependent personality disorder," also a mental disease according to the APA. Because of her family's history of female depression, Roberts said, she was "genetically loaded" in the direction of madness—her chances of having a serious crisis because of these depressive leanings had been very good and at age twenty-eight she had met the perfect man to unleash these dormant tendencies.

Dr. Roberts compared Brian to several world-famous destructive leaders—Jim Jones and Adolf Hitler, for example—declaring that the insurance salesman himself had been like a cult figure. "But in this case," he said, "it was a one-on-one cult and that is even more intense. A charismatic person can replace a group's or an individual's needs with his own. That's the mark of a sociopath. With coercive persuasion, ordinary decent people can violate their morals. If their needs are being relieved by their leader, they can do unspeakable things.

"Jennifer is the model of someone who can be exploited

by a sociopath. Brian scanned his environment and sought
her out. He understood her needs at a basic level and used
techniques well known by cults. He repeated the same
things to her again and again. He withheld or gave sex
based upon what she did for him. He created a kind of per-
verted religion. He repeatedly put her in a trancelike state
and spoke to her in a soft voice—'two shots, two deaths,
two phone rings.' She was always a gentle romantic person and he got her to do exactly the opposite of what she
usually did. Because of all of these things, I believe she
meets the criteria for insanity and was unable to distinguish right from wrong at the time of the act."

With Roberts on the stand, Gentry played a tape record-
ing of Jennifer performing a spiritual she'd written in her
cell. She sang it in harmony with Robin Krisak, another
inmate at CJC:

"Jesus, sweet Jesus, by the grace of God I am
Rinsed by the blood of the lamb . . .

I'm free in Jesus, sweet Jesus, with the spirit
of you I'm free.
I'm free in Jesus, sweet Jesus, no matter where I
may be . . .

Oh faithful Jesus, sweet Jesus, you know my pain
and grief.
Oh faithful Jesus, sweet Jesus, I'm rich through
my faith in you . . ."

The gospel filled the courtroom and the gallery sat rapt.
The song was both touching and haunting, and Jennifer's
voice, strong and rich, passed through a listener, leaving
behind a chill. Had the prisoner found in Christ someone
to believe in at last—someone who would never leave
her—or had she turned to yet another male authority figure
to rescue her from the burden of her past? Was this salvation or one more attempt at escape? Hearing the song

made her life in prison become instantly real—the tiny space she now called home, the hard walls, the countless hours that had to be filled, the other inmates, the pervasive aloneness. The hymn ended but its overtones hung in the air, evocative and poignant, as if you could not just feel but actually see the pain behind the music.

The courtroom was silent and one now understood the essence of her defense—she felt so bad about the murder that the legal system should acknowledge this and treat her with gentleness; she had suffered enough. After listening to her sing, a veteran reporter sitting in the gallery shook his head and said, "She's gonna get off."

When questioning witnesses, Bob Harward tended to dance with the rostrum, holding on to it and moving back and forth in small steps, and this mannerism became more elaborate when he posed ticklish queries. For half an hour he mildly cross-examined Dr. Roberts before saying, "Derek DeJong has told our investigators that Jennifer liked anal intercourse and he did not, but he did this for her."

Roberts, a craggily handsome man with tousled graying hair, cleared his throat. It was a highly indignant sound. He tilted his chin upward and outward, like someone posing for an immortal photograph. "I don't believe that," he said. "I don't believe that women enjoy anal intercourse."

The spectators rustled on their benches and Judge Looney turned pink.

"From my work with many female patients," the doctor added, "I've observed that they don't like it but do it to please their husbands or boyfriends. It hurts."

"Do you think," Harward said, now weaving in front of the rostrum, "that Jennifer Reali has given you inaccurate information or that some of what she has told you about her past may be wrong?"

"Perhaps, but a person's perceptions are their reality. The facts may be wrong but this is their feelings. If you think somebody hates you and you believe it, that's your reality."

"Then there's no point in asking you the question, is there?"

Dr. Roberts stared at him, mute.

"If Mr. Hood was so important in her life and so controlling of her, why was he never mentioned in her diary?"

"I don't know."

"Did you perceive any psychosis in Ms. Reali?"

"No."

"Does she show signs of delusional thinking?"

"Yes. She believed that if she was arrested, Brian Hood would somehow appear and lift her from the police station and absolve her of all this."

"So your testimony is that she was programmed to do all of these things and had no thinking or will of her own?"

"No critical thinking."

Harward looked over at the jury. "If a policeman had come up to the center at 8:30 P.M. on September 12, 1990, and gotten out of his car and seen Jennifer and said, 'How are you?', do you think she would have gone ahead and committed the crime?"

"No. That would have been an intrusion."

"Why wouldn't she have done it, if she'd suspended all sense of right and wrong?"

"Well, she wasn't an automaton."

"Then she had the capacity to tell right from wrong?"

"I don't think the intrusion of a police officer would have stopped her from doing this. If a psychotherapist had intervened in this sorry tale, that would have stopped it but no one ever did."

Derek DeJong's entrance into the courtroom, like Ben Reali's before him, revived the whispering. The tall, ruddy-faced man, who looked straight ahead and seemed oblivious to his surroundings, marched to the stand and gave his ex-lover an affirmative nod. She could not meet his eyes. Jennifer, he said, "had a real good sense of right and wrong, but she always looked to her peer group to justify this."

Bill Aspinwall cross-examined Derek and in the course of this he brought up a report that Detective Brian Ritz, working in conjunction with the D.A.'s office, had put together after traveling to Seattle months earlier and conducting numerous interviews, including one with DeJong.

"You've read the report?" Aspinwall said.

"Yes."

"Is it accurate?"

Derek shifted in his chair and his face grew redder. "It reads as if this activity of anal sex between Jennifer and me was an ongoing thing. I only remember two occasions. As young lovers, we tried it and didn't like it and didn't do it again. Jenny's previous lover liked it and in her eagerness to please me, she thought I would like it too." He smiled at the prosecutor. "The numbers that Ritz wrote down about us having sex three or four times a day are inaccurate. He must have thought I was very strong in those days."

"Did you feel there was anything violent or perverse about your relationship with Jennifer?"

"Never."

"What is your opinion of her parents?"

"They're great people. Her mother and father were a very important part of her peer group."

"Was her relationship with her family healthy?"

"Absolutely."

"Was her father dominant?"

"I wouldn't use that word. He has a strong personality, but when they made decisions, they all talked things over a lot."

After being excused from the witness stand, Derek rode the elevator down to the cafeteria in the courthouse basement and slowly drank a can of soda. He looked disturbed in ways he could not articulate.

"I've worked at the Pike Place Market in Seattle for fifteen years," he said, "and I've met hundreds, maybe thousands of people. Of everyone I've ever known, Jenny is the last person I would have guessed to be involved in something like this. It's a total mystery to me." He took a sip from the can. "I never liked Ben Reali. Never. But in this case I really think that his punishment is worse than his crime."

Two women at the next table were discussing the case and one said, "Jennifer's wonderful loving family is the problem. They care about her, they've listened to her, nurtured her, and paid a lot of attention to her. She's looked for that in the outside world and can't find it in a man. That makes her anger and frustration all the more intense. Her parents taught her that life is like that and it's not. Most men won't listen to your problems and nurture you. They just won't."

During her testimony, Jennifer's older sister could not stop crying. Erin's face was contorted, her short dark hair flew as she sobbed wildly and she looked utterly lost in this setting. If the hearing had a feeling of unreality anyway, her presence only deepened it. When asked to describe Jennifer, she said, "I think of her in terms of fresh flowers. She likes coffee and dessert. She's very loyal, very giving and caring, a good friend. Like a good Labrador dog."

While telling the court how the murder had ended the plans Jennifer had made to visit her in October of 1990, when Erin's first child was born, her voice finally broke altogether and she went into a painful keen: "Jenny was—gonna come—home," she said, wiping at her cheeks. "It was—gonna be so nice. She'd help me with my baby. She was—gonna bring her girls and—we all hoped she would stay in Seattle. I thought she was—comin' around and—comin' home to us. Jenny Vaughan could not have done this. She just—couldn't." Erin gasped for breath. "She told me she wants to have more children. To have a little girl—and name her Dianne. That gave me the shivers."

When the lawyers had finished with her, Erin ran out

into the hallway and broke down again, weeping with such force that she could be heard during the subsequent testimony. When, a short time later, the judge ordered a recess, the prosecutors immediately went into the hall, where she was still huddled over and sobbing. Aspinwall and Harward knelt beside her, speaking to her softly and stroking her arm, thanking her for appearing in court, although they were her legal adversaries.

While the attorneys consoled Erin, Jennifer's parents stayed in the courtroom, talking to each other and looking over at their daughter. During the breaks, the defendant, without any prodding from the armed guards, usually walked briskly toward the holding cell adjoining this room but today she lingered, several feet away from her mother and father, smiling hesitantly at them, leaning in their direction, and fighting back tears. Gail Vaughan began to cry, trying to muffle the sound with her palm.

"Jennifer," a burly guard said, motioning with his hand toward the cell. "Come on. Let's go."

She pivoted away and moved through the open door. Her parents turned away too, awkwardly hugging each other, looking terribly alone.

Twenty-two

Three people came to the hearing with a special purpose. Pat Cooperrider arrived each morning with a broken wrist, damaged in a recent car wreck, and a well-thumbed Bible. As testimony was being delivered, the stocky middle-aged woman sent Jennifer unwavering support or wrote her letters. When the defendant cried, Pat asked God to give her more strength. One of the few people with a general clearance to enter the Criminal Justice Center, Pat was neither a psychiatrist nor a social worker but a self-employed chaplain, an ordained minister who counseled incarcerated women and offered spiritual guidance. Soon after Jennifer was arrested, Pat had driven out to CJC and watched the new inmate in the day room for a week before introducing herself.

"She stayed her distance for a while," says the minister, who has an impish grin, as if she knows something you don't, "but then I began to get to know her. I see people all the time who have been hurt by abuse of the Bible. They've been forced to go to church or to be religious or whatever. I wanted to give her a different slant to the Scriptures than what she'd had from Brian Hood. I don't know where he got his religious ideas but . . ."

Pat and Jennifer began going through the Bible, verse by verse and word by word. This activity, and their friendship, were a great comfort to the inmate and helped fill her days. She started writing spirituals, completing fifteen of them by the time the hearing opened and copyrighting them through her lawyer. She sang alone in her cell or with Robin Krisak, her closest acquaintance inside the jail.

Krisak was three years older than Jennifer and had been indicted for seventeen break-ins and involved in perhaps as many as seventy of them. "When I first met Jennifer," Robin says, "I couldn't understand what a nice girl like her was doing in a place like this. I thought she'd been framed. But as I got to know her, she became more and more dependent on me as a friend and I could see how she could become more and more dependent on someone else and if that person wasn't careful, they could get her to do almost anything. A man came into her life who was the epitome of a beautiful physical specimen, very intelligent, a good Christian man, an excellent father, and he told her that she was the perfect woman. There were no conditions on this. He didn't say, 'You're perfect except for your hair or your clothes or your weight.' He said, 'You're perfect right now.' Jennifer has told me that she loved him but more often she's said that he loved her. That was the thing."

For a while Chaplain Cooperrider spent time with the Reali children, escorting Tineke and Natasha to Sunday School at her own Agape Community Church in Colorado Springs, but Ben refused to go with them and he soon wanted the activity stopped.

"Jennifer's daughters were looking for someone to love," Pat says. "They would go up to women on the street to see if that person was their mother or someone they could love. The saddest part of Jennifer's story is that she's been separated from her girls."

For the past half decade, Pat had counseled imprisoned females—thieves, con artists and murderers—but this particular case was the most unusual one she had yet seen. A high percentage of the women she encountered had been sexually molested or physically abused as children, often by someone within their own family, and these early traumas had played a significant role in the crimes they had committed. The chaplain could more or less follow the pattern of violence in their lives and the process by which they had become violent. None of that seemed to apply in this instance. Gail and Keith Vaughan were ultrasupportive of Jennifer, which made her actions even more puzzling.

"In all the conversations I've had with her parents," Pat says, "I have never, ever, heard them put down their daughter. Once, they called me at 11:00 P.M. and I slipped and said that Jennifer was selfish and demanding and spoiled. They kind of held on to that for a while. No one likes to have their child called spoiled."

Pat eventually baptized Jennifer at CJC.

"I've dealt with a lot of women in prison who have a flaky relationship with Jesus Christ," she says, "but what Jennifer has is true. If she remains loyal to God on a daily basis, I don't believe she'll ever have to go through anything like this again. Her faith makes a difference in her life but at times it doesn't make things any less frustrating. Jail is hard, hard on your body, hard on your mind. You sit there all day and watch depressed people come and go. They're angry and violent. Only Jennifer's faith is going to maintain her. Others can pray for you but when it's midnight and you're awake in your cell and a cancer is eating away at your body, it's between you and God.

"She's not like a lot of women I've met in prison. She doesn't crave physical contact and that tells me something. It tells me that she wasn't looking for sex with Brian Hood but for a father for her children. Brian had a way with children. If they were near him, they were all over him. Some men can't have kids crawling on them, but he could. All I've heard from her is that she wanted a father to be there for her girls. There's a cliché that says, 'What you'll compromise to get, you'll lose.' To get what she wanted she subjected herself to all of his demands and then she lost what she thought she was getting. Jennifer met a false prophet and had a terrible lesson.

"Evil starts with deception, and goes on from there. The darkest evil force in her life was lies or deception, total lies or deception. People are sincere but sincerely wrong, because they've been told lies. She told herself a lot of lies and was told lies by others. If your defense is down, evil will come in."

Tony DiVirgilio worked in a large, comfortable Denver office furnished with a fireplace, latticed windows, French doors, a painting of three buffalo, and a sign on the wall that read, "No Wimps." The windows were wired for security. The office needed to be large because DiVirgilio paced when he talked and he was a tall man with a long, aggressive stride. A Brooklyn native, he had attended Wichita State University and after graduating had gone back to New York City, thinking his degree would assure him a job with the N.Y.P.D. A lot of other people there also had degrees and similar ambitions. In 1970 Tony packed his Buick Wildcat and aimed west, stopping in Denver, where he knew the chief of police.

He became a suburban policeman but few people would have taken him for a cop. His shoulders were sloped, his hair rose in small curls above his ears, and he wore glasses, all of which gave him a thoughtful, intellectual air. He learned to speak legalese with the best of them, and talked very fast, with strains of Brooklyn on his tongue. In 1983 he decided that he wanted to work for himself and make more money.

"I could see that the older cops were just hanging on," he says, "counting the days till retirement. The stress in police work doesn't come from the street—you get adrenaline out there and that's rewarding. The tough part is the internal politics. After nearly fifteen years of it, you doubt your ability to do anything else. I had to make a move or lose all my confidence, but it was a hard move. I had young kids, a house, everything. I'm pleased with what's happened but I can't say that I haven't curled up into the fetal position a few times or won't again."

He took an early retirement as a captain and crossed over to the other side of law enforcement, becoming a private investigator and going to work for some of the best defense attorneys in Colorado, using his police experience and his considerable mental powers to keep people accused of crimes out of prison. The job was very challenging—how do you beat a system that you know from the inside out?—and the pay was more lucrative. On numerous cases he had been employed by Brian's lawyer, Richard Tegtmeier, and within weeks of Jennifer's arrest, Tony had gone down to Colorado Springs and begun gathering facts. No one gathered more.

Early on he knew that Sandra Biereichel, the saleswoman at the Ski Haus in Colorado Springs, was convinced that it was Jennifer, not Brian, who had purchased the black ski mask. He knew that the gloves that Jennifer claimed Brian had given her for the shooting were military gloves, the kind that a soldier like Ben Reali was likely to have in the house. He knew that Jennifer had told Detective Wood that she had lived her whole life telling "little white lies" and Tony wondered if her lying had ever stopped. He knew a lot of other things and fed all of them to Tegtmeier, who was already preparing for the day when he would cross-examine the young woman at Brian's trial (the lawyer had a reputation for being utterly merciless in the courtroom). Tony had created a computer program to hold the tens of thousands of facts in the case, a program that would allow him to sit beside Tegtmeier in court and retrieve any piece of evidence within twenty seconds. One purpose of this instant retrieval system was to see if a witness had changed testimony from one occasion to the next. It was not a good idea to lie when DiVirgilio was around.

During the sanity hearing, he drove down to Colorado Springs to sit in on the proceedings, learn what kind of case the prosecution had against Jennifer, and pick up any useful information for Brian's upcoming trial. He wanted to observe her behavior in the courtroom, to see her tendencies or weaknesses under pressure, to know if she would crack. Then he returned to Denver and began laying out a legal strategy for Tegtmeier and his client. When thinking out loud, he paced, and when doing both of these things he puffed Salems, so in the spring of 1991 there was a lot of activity in his office and a lot of smoke.

"This Elvin Gentry thinks he's clever," he said one day near the end of the hearing. "He's already got a sweetheart deal with the D.A., getting Jennifer out of the death penalty, and he thinks he can almost get her to walk. If her testimony can convict Brian of first-degree murder, Gentry will go back to the D.A. and ask for another plea bargain. But he's ignoring that she bought the mask and lied about it. If your case is built on her and you find out that she's lying, how can you ignore that?"

He moved lightly across the green carpet in his office, turned, and walked the other way. He lit a Salem and bent down for a sip from his coffee cup. "Jennifer has admitted that before the shooting she took the ski mask home and sewed around the mouth hole and eyeholes to make them smaller, so none of her skin would show through. Is that premeditated or what? She's testified before a grand jury that on the night of the murder she's in a trance and can't even remember being in her Cherokee as she drives over to the community center to kill Dianne. She says she's so mesmerized by Brian that she's like an automaton. Says she's just following orders."

He snuffed out the cigarette, opened a window to let the smoke escape, waited half a minute, and shut the window tight.

"A reasonable person would see through all of this. When you go back and examine what she did and follow it step-by-step, it's one hundred percent her doing. It's her motivation to buy the mask and to put together the other clothes. It's her idea to get the sweatshirt from the commissary. It's her volition to get the gun from her husband and to hide it under the mattress after the murder. Jennifer is tomboyish and strong-willed. She's aggressive. She always wanted to be a boy. Gentry said that in his opening remarks. She has a go-getter personality, not at all the weak mild lamb who's drawn into this by Brian. Back when the murder happened, some local feminists were saying that a man had to be responsible for it. I thought feminists believed that women were perfectly capable of making their own decisions and taking their own actions, but they have to blame this on a man. There's this perceived feeling that men have this dominance over women, but you have to look more deeply into it than that. Who's really the dominant one in this murder? It's Jennifer. She plans it and does it and then turns everything around and turns it on the men in her life. When Brian didn't show up at the police station and rescue her on the night of her arrest, like the knight in shining armor on the white horse, she turned on him and hurt him as badly as she could. She blamed him for everything."

He paced, lit another Salem, and reopened the window.

"Common sense tells you that there's more to it than her being under the spell of this handsome man who's quoting her Scripture. Who knows what she thought before all of this happened? Did she have thoughts of suicide? Did she want to kill her husband? There's a fine line between suicide and homicide. Some people can't force themselves into killing themselves so they find another means of self-destruction. Maybe she had all of these feelings inside of her before she ever met Brian and then he walked into the picture and set them off.

"You have to understand. Brian is a guy who talks to everyone about whatever comes into his mind. His every thought is a spoken word. He talks about Dianne's disease and how this has ruined his home life, his sex life, his kids' lives. Dianne's sick, she's gaining weight, she's no fun. She can't take care of their children and in private she's grouchy, not at all the saintly suffering mother everybody sees at church. He thinks of divorcing her but the people in his church would shut him out if he did this. His whole world revolves around the church.

"Brian said all these things about Dianne to other people. He tells them that he gets so depressed he even thinks about killing his wife. He struggles with himself about having affairs with other women. Is he guilty of evil thoughts? Yes. Is he guilty of turning left into traffic with Dianne in the car? Yes, and that doesn't sound good in light of the terrible and tragic thing that Jennifer did, but none of the other people he talked to jumped at killing Dianne, nobody except her. Maybe the whole thing was in her mind more than his. Maybe she was more upset than he was that he wouldn't divorce his wife. Maybe she sensed that he didn't really love her.

"If Jennifer hadn't been caught, she and Brian would not have gone off to the Northwest and lived happily ever after. Look at his past, his pattern. She was a good lay to him, that's all. He had a need for women outside of his marriage. He's narcissistic. He wants to see himself through the eyes of women and be desired by them. He sees himself as a big good-looking man who can bullshit them. He had this affair with her, this short-term infatuation. He didn't leave Dianne for the other girls he had affairs with and I don't think he would have ever met Jennifer later in Oregon, as she said he would."

He took another sip of coffee.

"It's very interesting that she never tells Brian she can go through with this. There is never an agreement per se, not even that last morning in her car in Cheyenne Canyon. She's the one who creates the murder. If she hadn't been caught, Ben or someone else would have eventually turned her in. She was doomed from the start."

Walking over to a large table holding evidentiary files on the case, he sat down, picked up a computer printout cross-referencing the data he had gathered, studied it for several moments, and jumped up and began pacing again.

"Normally I deal in forensics and fact-finding missions—calibers of firearms, gunshot residue, the angles of shooting, blood splatters, and those types of things. In this case, all of that is conceded. Jennifer pulled the trigger. The key here is her state of mind, her intent, and that's a much more intellectual thing. How do you get that theme down and then corroborate it?"

He lit another Salem, talking faster.

"Jennifer and her lawyer say that she was manipulated by Brian—that he is an evil guy who wanted his terminally ill wife murdered, for God's sake—but it's not that way at all. The El Paso County D.A., John Suthers, will go along with whatever she says because Suthers wants to burn Brian. Suthers made this God-awful decision to go for the death penalty on him instead of her—her!—this cold-blooded killer, this heinous shooter. They're all wrong but how are we going to prove that?"

Pat Mika, who also visited the hearing a few times, was what people call an over-achiever. He was born in Arkansas in 1956; graduated Phi Beta Kappa in English literature from the University of Arkansas; attended UA's law school, where he headed the Prison Project, designed to help poor inmates with their postappeals work; represented the United States judo team at the Pan American Games, the Goodwill Games, and the U.S. International Games; was at various times ranked first, second, or third in judo in the country; moved to Colorado Springs in 1982 to be near the Olympic Training Complex but "burned out" on the sport before making the Olympic team, and then decided to devote full time to his legal career. He became a successful attorney.

"It was an easy transition for me from judo to being a defense lawyer," he said one morning in his office. "It's just you and your client against the world and the powers that be—the government, the law, and all of that. So I could be competitive here too."

Mika had exceptionally good features and muscles everywhere. Even fully clothed, he looked immovable. He wore sharp suits, costly ties, and his office walls were covered with his degrees, his judo awards, and newspaper clippings of his most publicized cases, along with some prints by Millet and Courbet. His voice was quiet but carried the fervor of the true believer. In years past he had had a wife.

"Good lawyers can't leave their work at the office when

they go home," he said. "Good lawyers involved in criminal trials don't sleep at night. My marriage deteriorated and was lost because I worked so much. I had a hundred cases at one time. To the people you're representing, their case is the most important thing in the world and if you don't feel what they're going through, then you can't really be effective for them. One time I got involved in a case where my client was a twenty-three-year-old man who was accused of sexually assaulting a four-year-old girl. He was also accused of giving her gonorrhea. Other people didn't want the case but I took it. That was the beginning of my problem at home. I got probation for the guy."

He defended another man whose five Rottweilers had attacked a blind woman. Mika got probation for that client too. Another one of his clients slipped some pesticide in his wife's I.V.

"For some reason," the lawyer said, "I seem to attract a lot of weirdos."

He had once been a partner in Richard Tegtmeier's office but had eventually moved out on his own. When the District Attorney decided to seek the death penalty against Brian, Tegtmeier petitioned Judge Looney to provide him with another lawyer for whom the court would pay, a standard procedure in capital punishment cases. He had submitted Pat's name as his first choice and the judge selected Mika. He was attending Jennifer's hearing to prepare not only for Brian's trial but for the death penalty phase of it, which would come afterward if the man were convicted of first-degree murder. Neither Mika, Tegtmeier, nor Tony DiVirgilio had ever handled a death penalty defense from beginning to end and that added a note of solemnity to a group that was already very serious.

"This case," Mika said, "is the biggest challenge any lawyer can ever have. It's one thing to save a man's freedom, but it's another thing to save his life. From the start the prosecution of Brian Hood has been politically motivated. Suthers ran for office on the idea that he would seek the death penalty in homicides and he's been true to form. He's needed a case where he can answer the criticism that D.A.s only seek capital punishment against black and Hispanic defendants. This time he went after a white male.

"Suthers gave Jennifer her life so that she would help him take away Brian's. It's that simple. She was the killer and he wasn't even present at the crime. To seek the death penalty for him is contrary to everything in the law. You don't see this kind of poor judgment exercised elsewhere but he's making his political stand in Colorado Springs on Brian Hood."

Pat frowned, growing even more solemn. "To do your job right, you really have to absorb this case, the emotions and fears and angers and pain of every person in it. If you don't do this, you can't communicate effectively to a jury. I want Brian's jurors to understand that he's scared to death because he might be convicted and executed for something he didn't do, and all because he made a mistake and got involved with this woman. He may have done something improper and disgusting but not legally wrong."

Twenty-three

No one expected Jennifer to testify in her own behalf at the hearing and she did not. Gentry's last defense witness was another psychiatrist, Dr. Kathy Morral, an attractive, well-dressed, black woman with huge glasses and padded shoulders. Dr. Morral spoke in a slow, soft, rich voice, bending certain words and giving the impression of someone who had just been awakened from a good sleep. In her private practice and as the staff psychiatrist at the Denver County Jail, Dr. Morral had, as she put it, "a special interest in women who kill." This was her 356th courtroom appearance. During her visits with Jennifer at CJC shortly after the murder, the doctor had concluded that the defendant had a dependent personality disorder; was "delusional in terms of her religious ideas"; was depressive but did not have a major depressive disorder; and could not tell the difference between right and wrong at the time of the shooting.

"A dependent personality disorder," Dr. Morral testified, "is a maladaptive way of functioning. The dependency with Jennifer is that she would substitute the values and feelings of others for her own."

"What is a religious delusion?" Gentry asked her.

"It is a fixed false belief system of any religious background. Religious delusions are frequently a part of serious psychiatric disorders. When people are very sick, their confusion about religion often comes to the fore, especially in our culture."

"Have you questioned many people who've tried to fake insanity?"

"Yes. They tend to lay it on with a shovel."

"What about Jennifer—did she try to fake it?"

"No. I never saw any indication that she had much emotional investment in the legal outcome of this case. She was unrealistic about what might happen to her—thinking she might just spend a little time at the state mental hospital in Pueblo—but that was all. There was a vacuum in her, an emptiness, a feeling that I thought should be a part of her that wasn't there and that was a cause of concern for me. So, she could either be a cold unfeeling person or this was evidence of a serious disorder. I didn't think she was a sociopathic murderous personality but that her difficulties were serious and she'd lost some of her ability for emotional expression."

"Does this case make sense to you, if she is not insane?"

"No, it does not."

Throughout most of the hearing, Bill Aspinwall had not displayed his tenacious courtroom manner. There was little point in grilling the Vaughans, Derek DeJong, or Erin Dudley, in part because they seemed to know so little about what might have caused the murder, but expert testimony was another matter. It often holds more sway with jurors than the testimony of nonexperts (when on the stand, police, private investigators, attorneys, and psychiatrists stare confidently at the jury; other witnesses look uncomfortably at the person who is questioning them). Aspinwall would not be so gentle with this woman. Her credibility and the entire notion that psychiatrists can penetrate and explain the mystery of violence was going to be harshly tested. For several hours he peppered Dr. Morral with inquiries, one right after the other—most of them concerning the facts of the case. Gradually she began to tire. The more exhausted she became, the harder he pressed, not attacking her psychological theories but what she actually knew about the events leading up to and surrounding the murder.

"For the majority of her life," Aspinwall said, "Jennifer Reali could tell the difference between right and wrong?"

"Yes."

"But for a few minutes in the summer of 1990, she could not?"

"Yes."

"At that time she had accepted that killing Dianne Hood was the religious and right thing to do?"

"By the twelfth of September, she'd accepted the fact that what she was doing could relieve Mrs. Hood from her suffering."

Aspinwall fired off six more questions about certain details on the night of the shooting, then six more in his brisk staccato fashion, then six more. Dr. Morral seemed only vaguely familiar with many of the things he was asking about.

Gentry stood and told the judge that the prosecutor was badgering his witness. Jennifer looked down and rocked hard in her chair, mumbling to herself. Gentry's investigator, Jeanie Brooks, reached over and stroked the defendant's arm, while the body language expert, Archie Belford, looked gravely at Dr. Morral, as if she were faltering under pressure. Keith and Gail Vaughan, who had been allowed into the courtroom to watch the proceedings after they had testified, stared at the psychiatrist with a beseeching expression. Chaplain Cooperrider clutched her Bible and shut her eyes, deep in prayer.

Judge Looney, after a pause, ruled that the prosecutor was not badgering the witness and could continue.

Then Aspinwall really badgered her—one factual question after another—and the psychiatrist was quickly lost.

"Did Jennifer Reali tell you why she pulled the black ski mask down over her face?"

"No."

"Did she tell you why she did not want to be detected for doing this good and godly thing to Dianne Hood?"

"Because Brian told her that that was not part of the plan."

"Did you ask her why she sat at home with a needle and thread and sewed up the eyeholes of the mask so they would be smaller?"

"She didn't tell me she did that."

"She didn't?"

"No."

"You weren't aware of that?"

"No." Dr. Morral slumped in her chair.

"Why did Jennifer want this good and godly act to look like a robbery?"

"Because that's what Brian wanted."

Aspinwall took a pen from the pocket of his suit jacket, tossed it in the air and caught it. Putting it away, he said, "One of the first things Jennifer said when she was confronted by the police was, 'Dianne was not that miserable.' And yet you've said that killing her was an act of mercy on her part. Doesn't that trouble you?"

"This was not a lady trying to avoid responsibility. She was very troubled by what she'd done."

"On the night of her arrest, she told the police, 'I killed her because he told me to and for the money.' Does that trouble you?"

The doctor shrugged wearily.

"Was finding her insane a close call?"

"There are cases where you have a clear idea of what is insane, cases where you struggle with this, and cases where you never decide. I've reached my conclusions here after a struggle." She looked out at the defendant and when she spoke again, it was as if she too, like Elvin Gentry, were in the difficult position of trying to make sense of something that was beyond her grasp and perhaps beyond the grasp of current psychiatric understanding.

"Jennifer," she said, "killed Dianne as a sign of her love and commitment to God."

The startling sentence hung in the air, filling the silence before drifting away, but in its wake many unanswered questions floated through Judge Looney's crowded courtroom. A middle-aged man who was sitting in the gallery leaned over and whispered to his female companion, "Dr. Morral doesn't have a strong enough theory for Jennifer's problem. Nobody does."

"I feel that I know everything about her and I know nothing," replied his friend.

Since Captain Reali's last appearance at the hearing, several things had arisen in testimony, and especially in the testimony of Dr. Arthur Roberts, that the prosecution wanted him to rebut. Once the soldier had entered Judge Looney's courtroom and been sworn to tell the whole truth and nothing but the truth, Aspinwall did not stand on ceremony with him.

"Did you ever sexually assault your wife?" the lawyer asked.

"No," Ben said.

"Did you ever have anal sex with her?"

"No."

"I'm sorry I have to ask you that. Did you ever give her an ultimatum to marry you?"

"No. We discussed marriage and she was enthusiastic. Then she went and discussed it with her parents and came back very discouraged. We went over to her parents' house and drank some wine and they said to me, 'Go overseas for three years, play army, come back, and marry her.' I told them I might stay longer than three years and I wasn't just playing army. I said if she wanted to wait that was fine, but I wouldn't make any promises to marry her because that didn't seem realistic."

Jennifer stared up at her husband, incredulity fixed in her eyes. Ben avoided her gaze. When Archie Belford saw her scowling at her husband, he nudged her and she glanced down at her lap, her jaw twitching and her head bobbing. The Vaughans, sitting in the gallery next to Derek DeJong, watched the captain and shook their heads.

"Once, before our marriage," Ben said, "I walked into the kitchen and her mother told me, 'Why don't you just leave her alone?' Things were very uncomfortable and this was far more difficult for Jennifer than for me. Her parents didn't want her to leave Seattle but wanted her home for Sunday dinners."

Gentry stood for cross-examination and moved toward the witness. He stopped, made eye contact with each member of the jury, and then peeked over his shoulder for a quick mug at the gallery, as if telling everyone that he knew things about Ben Reali they would never believe.

"The anal sex," Gentry said. "That's just a figment of her imagination?"

"Yes," the captain answered glumly.

"Never came up between you?"

Ben cocked his head and looked ready to fight or cry. "No."

"Huh." Gentry pressed his lips together and stared at the witness, giving the curious impression that at any moment he might just turn around and leave the room. "Never?"

"No."

The lawyer frowned in disgust. "Are you—?"

Aspinwall rose to object.

Gentry cut him off and addressed the judge. "Mr. Reali's credibility is at issue here and I can explore impeaching this witness to show that he is biased and prejudiced. His attitudes bring all of his ideas on the matter of 'anal rape' into question."

Judge Looney hesitated, looking from one attorney to the next before telling Gentry to continue. Aspinwall slowly sat down.

"Did your career have an adverse impact on your marriage?" Gentry asked the captain.

"I don't believe so. I think, Elvin, if I'd been working for IBM or IT&T, the effect would have been the same."

The attorney grimaced, clearly displeased with being addressed in the courtroom by his first name.

"I think it's difficult," Ben went on, "for any wife when her husband goes away. I don't think Jennifer went through anything any military wife doesn't and there are quite a few, Elvin, that deal with these things quite well."

The attorney flinched and began another question.

Aspinwall stood and interrupted him. "The jury can hear the hostility in Mr. Gentry's voice."

"I do get upset," Gentry told the judge, "when witnesses change their testimony from things they've openly talked about in the past." He turned to face Ben. "Are you now distancing yourself from your wife so that you can maintain your top-security military clearance?"

"No. I still have that clearance but it comes up for review next year. I'm sick of all this, Elvin, and I'll be glad when it's over. I've recently met a woman and she's helping me with my children and when all this is finished, we'd like to get on with our lives. This has been a nightmare."

Jennifer was looking at the floor and had begun to cry.

"Do you think you're a victim of what's happened?" Gentry asked him.

"No," the captain said. "Dianne Hood is the victim and her kids."

He paused and looked out at the courtroom, speaking slowly and with emphasis, as if he wanted everyone to know that he did not blame his wife for everything that had gone wrong.

"Brian Hood," he said, "is the monster you've been looking for."

Twenty-four

Behind his goatee and glasses, Dr. Seymour Sundell, the medical director of the Department of Safety for the City and County of Denver, bore an unmistakable resemblance to Sigmund Freud (several courtroom observers said that he had come straight from central casting). He had interviewed Jennifer in January of 1991, had found her sane, and was now appearing as the prosecution's first rebuttal psychiatrist. "Her history," he testified, "was remarkable for its absence of psychological disorders. Perhaps she had some depressive tendencies but nothing more ... The desire to have Brian was the driving force for her, not some bizarre psychosis."

"Was she brainwashed?" Aspinwall said.

"No. There's a difference between being influenced and being brainwashed. She wasn't removed from her normal circumstances and isolated or altered psychologically with sleep deprivation and those kinds of things. There was none of that here."

"Do you find any reason to believe Dr. Morral's opinion that the defendant suffered from a delusion?"

"No. Those with delusions don't have the inner conflict that she had. Ms. Reali knows that there was a tremendous conflict going on inside of her about all of this, a true internal struggle. That's a normal response to what she was involved in."

As Dr. Sundell testified, Gentry drew sketches on his yellow legal pad. When Aspinwall had finished his direct examination of the man, the defense attorney approached him and said, "Did my client not tell you, Doctor, that she was now freer in prison than she'd ever been before? And that she was, in many ways, happier than she'd ever been?"

"I think," Sundell said, "she meant that she was happier and freer in prison because she was no longer in her marriage."

"Under your theory, she was willing to kill Dianne even though both of them were young mothers?"

"Yes."

"And willing to risk losing her own children to be with Brian Hood?"

"Yes."

"And those are the thoughts of a sane and rational person?"

"A tragic person, an uncomfortable person, but not a crazy one. This is something we often see in domestic circumstances."

"If people really believe that something is God's will, can they tell right from wrong?"

Dr. Sundell shifted in his chair. "There you move closer to the borderline."

Dr. Elissa Ball, chief of forensic psychiatry at the state mental hospital in Pueblo, had evaluated Jennifer during her six-day visit to that institution earlier in the year. Adult females, testified Dr. Ball, were twice as likely as adult males to have major depressions. In her opinion Jennifer was sane at the time of the crime and had no major mental illnesses but did have "dysthymia, which is a mild depression, and personality disorders with narcissistic features . . . She needed to be seen as the significant person in another's life. She had a more-than-normal need to be perfect and a more-than-normal fear of not being perfect. She told me that she'd stayed in her marriage because she didn't want to fail at something. I thought that was very important.

"When she confessed to the police, she focused on whether she could do the murder. It was a challenge to her.

She wanted to show that she could do what others wanted her to do and that she was more than adequate. She had to prove herself to her father and her boyfriends and to Brian Hood. It was not whether she would do it but whether she could meet the challenge, and that's how Brian hooked her in. Most women, even those who are unhappily married, if the subject of murder came up they would leave. She stayed because of her need for his approval and to hold his love and to show what an exceptional woman she was.

"I think Ms. Reali is a very likable and engaging young woman and that's important. It's difficult to meet with someone you actually like and would enjoy working with or socializing with and then have to render an opinion that she will not like at all. I believe that she was clearly coerced and persuaded to commit the crime. It was Brian's will that she kill Dianne, not God's will, but we're all coerced at different points in our lives. That doesn't change our ability to know right from wrong. We still have other information that we choose to ignore. She is not a psychopath or sociopath who has no moral sense. She does not believe that people should kill other people to get a new wife or husband. She did not throw her values away lightly or easily, but she did throw them away."

For the hearing's final arguments, spectators who could not find seats in the courtroom leaned against the back walls or milled in the hallway, hoping someone inside would leave. Bob Harward went first and in his brief remarks to the jury, he said that Brian was the "driving force behind the killing" and then nodded toward the Vaughans. "We sympathize with Ms. Reali's parents," he went on, "and we understand when they say this is not the little girl they raised. A lot of parents say this in court and they are right. This is not the same person they knew but that does not excuse her actions. I ask you to put aside your emotions and focus on the legal issues. It's crucial for you to separate those things that make Dianne Hood's death understandable from the legal definitions the state legislature has provided for you. With that in mind, I urge you to find her sane at the time of the murder."

As Gentry began his closing speech, his manner was shaky and his voice thin. He recounted much of the testimony in words that were not memorable but then he seemed to find himself and to talk from a place that hinted at how much he wanted to help—and to comprehend—Jennifer Reali and how puzzling she was to him. There was some courtroom ham in the lawyer but he spoke now without artifice, his voice growing firmer and deeper, reaching out for something he could not quite grasp. At the end, he was almost yelling.

"To believe," he said, "that she was doing God's will by putting Dianne out of her misery makes no sense unless she is insane. To believe that by killing a young mother she was seeking an Eden-like life with Brian Hood makes no sense unless she is insane. To believe that this would bring her happiness—to believe that she could be rescued from her marriage by such things—it makes no sense at all unless she is insane. Brian wasn't satisfied with killing one woman last summer but two. As she sits here today, Jennifer Reali is as dead as if she had followed through with his plans and committed suicide.

"Ladies and gentlemen, she does not deserve freedom and she will not have it. She will not walk out of here. She will not go home or back to her kids. She deserves to be inside the walls of a mental institution and she may be there yet. The need for approval and affection are the only important things in this case and to receive them she killed a woman—and that makes no sense unless she is insane.

"You, ladies and gentlemen of the jury, are the law. You are justice. You have the ability to do the right and merciful thing. Go out, elect your foreman, focus on the legal requirements, take your vote, find her not guilty by reason of insanity, and we can all go home at peace with your having made a wise and just decision. Thank you."

* * *

Bill Aspinwall walked over to a small wooden table in front of the bailiff, a table holding several pieces of evidence, and picked up Ben's long black Colt .45. He opened the gun's chamber and turned it with his thumb, one turn at a time, and each turn made a dull clicking sound that spread out through the room. With precise movements of his fingers, he showed how Jennifer had dropped the bullets into the chamber, all the while turning the pistol over and over in his hand so that everyone in the room could have a good long look at this small, fascinating piece of machinery. Then he aimed the gun right at the jury and made them stare down the barrel, as Dianne Hood had once done. He cocked the hammer, once, twice, three, four times—each cock echoing with another dull click—until the gun was ready to be fired.

"This is a big ugly weapon," he said. "You have to pull the hammer all the way back before you can shoot it. There's no way around this. The defendant had to do this before she could kill Dianne and then she had to hide the gun. This weapon is a piece of evidence you can hang on to. Hiding the gun tells you something. It tells you that the person wielding it knows that what she is doing is wrong."

Jennifer, as had happened each time the long Colt had been brought out in the courtroom, had started to weep. Gentry folded his hands in front of him and closed his eyes.

"Why does she wear a disguise on the night of the twelfth?" Aspinwall said. "Because she knows it's wrong. Why does she make it look like a robbery if killing Dianne is the good and godly thing to do? Because she knows it's wrong. This woman"—he turned and pointed at the defendant—"shoots her right in the back. Then she shoots her again, the fatal shot, from less than two feet away. Then she runs away real fast.

"Even after she admits doing the murder there is not one word to the police—not one—that she killed Dianne so she could be with Jesus. When Detective Wood brings up Brian, she starts finger-pointing right away and she's been doing it ever since. Brian was driving her nuts. Ben was too, and Derek and her father were dominating personalities. There's a little more finger-pointing there. And what about Willis Black, the boy who first got her pregnant? She points the finger at him too.

"She herself has said that adultery and murder are sins but we can be forgiven for our sins if we repent. She asked for forgiveness after all this because she knew it was wrong. She may be forgiven by God at some point but it's not up to you, ladies and gentlemen of the jury, to forgive her. Your job is to apply the law, even if it makes you sad. Unfortunately, for this defendant, every circumstance around this act tells you that what she did was for a purpose and that purpose was to not get caught. It was to disguise that she was going to kill Dianne, take her husband, and start a new life with some money, a little bit ahead of the game."

The lawyer looked at the jurors and shook his head. "Huh uh. She's sane and you should find her sane."

After two days of deliberation, the six men and six women on the jury agreed with Aspinwall and found Jennifer competent to stand trial for first-degree murder, scheduled for later in the year. Upon learning of the verdict, Gentry was disappointed with the outcome but liked the fact that the jurors had at least taken a while to reach their decision. It gave him hope for what lay ahead.

"I think we're getting near to finding that she has multiple personalities," he said. "There's Jenny Vaughan and there's Jennifer Reali. Jenny Vaughan is a nice person but Jennifer Reali can be a real bitch. You never know which one you're going to get. That's why I've been so reluctant to put her on the stand."

Would she be receiving any therapy in the interim before her trial?

"Oh, no," Gentry said. "I don't want to tamper with the evidence."

Over in the D.A.'s office, two blocks east of where

Gentry worked, Aspinwall was pleased with the verdict but felt that, despite this victory, things were about to become much more complicated.

"Now, in order to convict Brian Hood of first-degree murder," he said one morning not long after the sanity decision had come in, "I've got to turn around and essentially prove Gentry's case. I've got to show that Hood controlled her and programmed her to kill and is primarily responsible for what happened to his wife."

These were tricky steps, he acknowledged, even for a veteran ballroom dancer like himself. He looked around his office and curled his lips into a distasteful expression. Then he sighed.

part four

THE TRIALS

Twenty-five

Fort Morgan, a small town on the eastern plains of Colorado, smells like a rich combination of blood and sewage, but after three days you don't notice it too much. On brisk fall mornings, thick blasts of steam from the local sugar beet factory shoot high into the air and hang there, like unbreakable clouds. South of town is the Excel slaughterhouse, where truckloads of cattle are brought every day to be converted into food. Blood from the abattoir occasionally backs up into the local water supply and visitors find the drinking water troublesome. What Fort Morgan lacks in charm, it makes up for in friendliness. People say hello without prompting, they smile openly at you on the sidewalks, and act genuinely pleased to see new faces. It is the kind of place where the police will not tolerate speeding but the first time you are pulled over for doing thirty-three in a thirty-mile-per-hour zone, you might get a warning.

The town does have some charm, with its large frame houses and spacious downtown avenues. Fields of stubbled corn, and chevrons of geese flying overhead at dawn highlight the rich dark farmland that stretches out in every direction. It is an environment that produces or attracts people who are essentially practical and believe in following the rules. Frigid in the winter and burning in the summer, the place conjures up notions of long-suffering endurance.

Because of the great local publicity the Dianne Hood murder had received, Richard Tegtmeier fought hard to move Brian's trial, set to begin August 5, out of Colorado

Springs. Judge Looney finally granted him a change of venue, shifting the trial to Fort Morgan. Tegtmeier filed scores of other motions with the judge—on one day alone she considered forty-nine of them—and this inevitably created delays and postponements. The trial was originally rescheduled for September 3, but then in July something totally unexpected happened. The state Supreme Court overturned Colorado's 1988 death penalty statute, throwing everything into confusion. Tegtmeier and Pat Mika immediately put forward the motion that, because of this new ruling, all capital punishment crimes committed between 1988 and mid-1991 could not be subject to any death penalty legislation, for in that time period there were no workable laws on the books. Aspinwall and Harward countered by saying that an older capital punishment statute, passed in 1986, had been in effect all along and that Brian Hood, if convicted of first-degree murder, still faced lethal injection.

The defense asked for the trial to open as scheduled on September 3, while these issues were still unresolved, but the prosecution wanted a delay until after September 19, when the state legislature, in a special session in Denver, would vote on the validity of the 1986 law. Judge Joseph Weatherby, who would be presiding over the trial in Fort Morgan, granted the postponement. The legislature approved reinstatement of the older law and ten days later Judge Weatherby ruled that the 1986 death penalty statute would indeed apply to the Hood case. On September 30, the lawyers gathered in Fort Morgan and began the lengthy and tedious process of selecting a capital punishment jury.

One other event in the summer of 1991 deeply affected Brian's trial. After Jennifer had been found sane, Ben asked her to give him sole custody of their children and to grant him a quiet divorce, away from the courtroom and the media. He had made plans to remarry and transfer to Germany with the girls and his new wife. Jennifer said no—she would never give up her daughters without a fight, and in August, in a hearing in Colorado Springs, she beseeched a divorce court judge for joint custody of the girls. If there were many people at the sanity hearing who had believed that her rocking and weeping were an act, the result of coaching by her attorney or his body language expert, no one said that about her behavior at the divorce hearing. While pleading with the judge for the right to see her children in the future, she cried so hard that some reporters covering the event found it too painful to watch. On August 28, the judge gave Ben custody of Tineke and Natasha but also instructed the girls, through their father, to send cards and at least two pictures a year to their mother, who could mail them letters and talk with them by phone twice a week. Captain Reali had won this round but only after a bitter struggle that would not be forgotten anytime soon.

Following the divorce ruling, Jennifer regularly heard from her daughters for a while, but then her ex-husband took them off to Germany, where he joined a Warriors Preparation Center in order to ready himself for any future American military battles. The calls stopped completely.

While Tegtmeier had been laboring for weeks and months to get Brian's trial away from the media barrage and conservatism of Colorado Springs, he did not know that it would be shifted to an isolated rural setting that was perhaps even more conservative than the Springs itself. As the lawyers assembled in Fort Morgan, one could not help wondering if he had only succeeded in moving it to a place that would be thoroughly unforgiving of things like adultery, double indemnity insurance payments, and murder, things that in some communities were still referred to as sin.

"This town," said Pat Mika, after settling into Fort Morgan for jury selection, "is a hellhole."

The attorneys took six weeks to choose fifteen jurors, a phenomenally long time (most criminal trials complete this task within a few days). The first jury pool contained three hundred people who gathered at the local high school auditorium and were introduced to Brian, who sat before them and smiled like someone running for mayor. Many farmers immediately wanted out of the pool because they were in the midst of sugar beet harvest and were far more interested in getting their crops in than in earning the fifty dollars a day the state of Colorado would pay them to sit in a courtroom and listen to testimony. Before a single person was selected from this pool, the lawyers asked them thousands of questions about their values, their knowledge of the case, and many other subjects, and at times it seemed as if the trial would never start.

While this was taking place, Tegtmeier filed an extraordinary motion with the court requesting that Elvin Gentry turn over all his private correspondence with Jennifer to both Brian's defense team and to the prosecutors. Because she had cooperated so fully with the D.A.'s office and provided them with information leading to Brian's arrest, Tegtmeier contended, the details of that cooperation should now be made public. Gentry vigorously protested, saying that the request was a violation of a basic constitutional right, the attorney-client privilege, and whatever transpired between lawyer and defendant was supposed to remain confidential. The debate soon left Judge Weatherby's courtroom and was taken all the way to the Colorado Supreme Court. Tegtmeier won again. Everything that Jennifer had written from jail to her attorney or to his investigator, Jeanie Brooks, could now be presented at the trial. The ruling was precedent-setting for a murder trial but not the last unique thing that would happen in Fort Morgan.

Up in Seattle Keith and Gail Vaughan were following these legal maneuvers closely and paying dearly for Gentry's involvement in them (taking this issue to the state Supreme Court was very expensive for all concerned). If Jennifer's parents were not well-disposed toward Tegtmeier to begin with, his new motions did not soften any of their feelings. They were further angered when

Brian's lawyer subpoenaed them for this trial, although he had no intention of calling them as witnesses. His strategy was simple and effective: because those under subpoena in this particular case could not listen to testimony until after they had appeared at the proceedings, this was an excellent way of keeping the Vaughans from coming to the Fort Morgan courtroom and offering their daughter moral support while she was on the stand, something they had already made plans to do.

Just before the start of the trial, Jennifer's father, in a moment of complete exasperation, said, "If Tegtmeier calls me as a witness, I'll rip off his testicles."

Twenty-six

On the afternoon of November 12, a jury was finally seated and the trial could begin. The fifteen jurors (three were alternates) had a lot of rough palms and weathered faces. They had one modern haircut and fourteen others, including a beehive. One man never took off his sunglasses and looked as if he had been driving a rig cross-country for thirty-six hours straight. Another man wore overalls with red suspenders and got his crew cut trimmed whenever it reached three-quarters of an inch. Another one kept smiling out at the gallery and chuckling, as if he were high on dope. Another one listened to testimony with his eyes closed. The jury included a wastewater treatment specialist, a first-grade teacher, an electrical engineer, a feedlot hand, and a retired schoolteacher. Every one of the fifteen appeared familiar with hard work.

Judge Weatherby, who bore a passing resemblance to a leaner and much quieter Groucho Marx, was faced with an astoundingly entangled set of legal circumstances. On one side he had the prosecution team, which had made a deal with a young woman who was a confessed murderess and who, in the eyes of many, had a serious credibility problem. On the other side he had a defense attorney, in Tegtmeier, who would test, cajole, complain, object, and bitch for his client; in short, he was extremely good at his job. Tegtmeier had fought tenaciously to keep Brian's past sexual endeavors in Colorado Springs from being admitted as evidence and he had won on this ruling too.

Throughout the exhaustive jury selection process and the trial, all of which lasted nearly three months, there were many times when things veered in an uncomfortable direction for the defense, and each time this happened Tegtmeier would leap up and cry, "Mistrial!" It was absolutely the last word the judge wanted to hear after countless hours had already been invested in the proceedings to date. During those three months, there were numerous opportunities for things to go awry, but because of Judge Weatherby they never did. He was remarkably patient, intelligent, gracious, and fair. He treated everyone well and revealed only one courtroom flaw—his voice was almost below the threshold of hearing and he would not speak up. Like everyone else connected with the trial, he looked more and more weary as the weeks dragged on but he never snapped.

After a year in jail Brian's curly blondish hair was gone. It was much darker and shorter and flatter now that he could no longer get a permanent. He looked pale, deflated inside his courtroom attire of a modest tweed jacket, dark slacks, and brown loafers. He had sad, red, shocked eyes. He was thin and extraordinarily polite to everyone, not at all the cocky, flirtatious young man people had described him as being eighteen months earlier, when he was working out at the spa every day and interacting with women. He seemed humbled and vulnerable, more like the person who had written one very striking sentence on a 1987 "psychological test" given to him by Village 7 Church. It read, "I want my wife to touch me more." During the trial he cried almost as easily as Jennifer.

His parents, Suzanne and Andy Hood, and his older brother, John, the architect from California, were allowed into the courtroom to listen to the opening statements. The older Hoods looked intelligent and prosperous, like an advertisement for middle-aged couples who enjoy high-end casual attire. Suzanne, an attractive woman with blond-gray hair and a long, handsome jaw, conveyed the sense of someone with so much inner tension that it had slowly tightened all the lines of her mouth. She sat directly behind Brian, smiled at him whenever he glanced over his shoulder, and once, when the armed guards permitted closer contact, she leaned over the railing, hugging and kissing her son. Andy wore black—black pants, black suede shoes, black mock turtlenecks. He had a disarmingly pleasant smile, features that were nearly as good as his wife's, and a gentle way of speaking. On many occasions he roamed the halls of the courthouse or those of the north side Days Inn, where all of the attorneys were staying, telling everyone he met that his son had been terribly wronged by Jennifer Reali and this trial was going to prove that. Sometimes while doing this, Andy's shoulders collapsed, and he broke into tears that made him look twenty years older.

He and his wife had inherited the burden of raising Brian's three young children—Jarrod was now ten, Lesley was eight, and Joshua was three—in their high-rise apartment in Houston. "The two older kids understand some of what's happened," Andy said one morning in the courthouse, "but it's really hard because they have neither a mother nor a father. It's very, very sad. My wife and I have learned to listen and pay attention a lot better to the three kids we have now. When they say something, we don't just say, 'Get out of here.' We really listen."

On the afternoon the trial began, John Hood was standing in the Fort Morgan courthouse talking to reporters. He said, "For fourteen months, our family has kept silent and waited for the truth to come out. In the face of all these untruths, we've stood our ground. We've looked forward to this day because Brian is now one step closer to being free and home with his children. The authorities are just badge-shining here. They're just looking for any conviction they can get at the D.A.'s office."

"This sad case," Tegtmeier said in his opening statement, "is about a sad woman who was obsessed, a woman who would stop at nothing to get what she wanted. This is about what went on in the twisted mind of Jennifer Reali

in the summer of 1990. She is the master manipulator who
set this whole thing up. Brian Hood, no question about it,
had an affair with her, but that doesn't have anything to do
with why Dianne was murdered. One thing Brian wasn't
was faithful. That's the truth. He also ran off at the mouth
in ways that were inappropriate. He was a complainer who
griped about his golf game and his insurance sales. He became so depressed that he thought about pulling out in
front of traffic on I-25 with his wife in the car. Jennifer
Reali twisted these events into acts of guilt. This is a
woman who pleaded insane and tried to convince a jury
that she could not be held responsible for this murder. All
of the evidence against Brian comes from her lips. All of
the accusations come from her—and she is unbalanced."

Tegtmeier, with his aggressive courtroom manner and
bald head, would have looked perfectly natural wearing a
toga and playing Julius Caesar. In his mid-forties and a native of Carleton, Nebraska, a town of ninety-five people
(he told the press that going to Fort Morgan was just like
going home), he was the oldest of six children. When he
was four, his mother died and he went permanently blind
in his left eye. Nonetheless, in high school he played all
sports. And when he entered the University of Nebraska, a
national power in college football, he decided to be a
"walk-on" quarterback; walk-ons receive no scholarship
money and usually serve as scrimmage fodder for the good
players, until they get hurt or come to their senses and
quit. After the young man, who stood only five feet nine
inches and weighed 145 pounds, had been bloodied in one
especially rugged practice, Coach Bob Devaney took him
aside and graciously told him that he probably would not
make the squad because he had only one eye. Two decades
later, when Tegtmeier mentions this occasion and his deciding to leave the team, his voice is wistful, as if he still
believes that if Devaney had only shown a little more faith
in him, he might have made the varsity.

The attorney owned a Harley-Davidson motorcycle and
liked to drive it through downtown Colorado Springs on

the way to his office. In recent years he had taken part in a number of Forum seminars (formerly known as est) and on the right evening when he was in the right mood he would talk about how the experience had revealed to him his own emotional patterns and helped make him a better person and a better lawyer. In many ways Tegtmeier, the man, who was the father of five children, was more complex, unpredictable, and interesting than Tegtmeier, the attorney, but it was the latter who took charge in Fort Morgan.

"What Jennifer Reali got from the El Paso County D.A. in this case is worth more than money," he told the jury. "She got her life. She could never get the death penalty for committing the murder, if she would just give the D.A. Brian Hood. It is these prosecutors," he looked over at Harward and Aspinwall, who did not return his stare, "who have decided if she has been telling the truth. They should be going after the death penalty with her—a cold, calculating, vicious killer.

"Ladies and gentlemen, I want you to keep your eye on the ski mask and the gloves she wore when she shot Dianne. Jennifer knew that all of the physical evidence came from her. There wasn't a thing she could link to Brian. On September 14, 1990, the day of her arrest, she had seven hours—from the time the police came into her flower shop until her confession later that night—to think something up that would implicate Brian. First, she denied doing the murder. Then she said someone broke into her house and got the clothes and the gun that killed Dianne. Finally, she said, 'I did it, but Brian put me up to it.' She has a pattern of not being responsible for her actions and she's had it all her life. It's clear that Jennifer Reali lied about the ski mask and the gloves. She said Brian bought the mask but we'll show that he did not. She said that Brian gave her the gloves but they are Army issue gloves. She didn't think that Ben would ever say they were his but eventually he did. This woman is disturbed. She is sick and demented and doesn't live in the same world as yours and mine.

"I don't know if we will ever know why she did this, but what we do know is that Brian was withdrawing from her in August of 1990 and she sensed this. He gave her an identity, and the fear of losing him perhaps led her to such a crazy act. No one could have guessed she would have done this. If neither her parents nor her husband nor her friends could have predicted it, how could Brian have done so? She planned everything, every detail, and after shooting down a woman in cold blood, she went home and had sex with her husband. I ask you, What kind of a woman is this?"

He looked at the jury box, scanning all fifteen of them. "I'm not going to ask you to find Brian innocent of first-degree murder and guilty of any of the lesser charges of conspiracy or solicitation. I'm going to ask you to acquit him so that he can go home and be with his children for Christmas."

By now the defendant was also looking toward the jurors and weeping, his big torso rocking in his chair. His mother leaned over the wooden railing that separated the gallery from the rest of the courtroom, tapping her son on the back and passing him a tissue. He wiped his eyes and kept sobbing. Pat Mika, who was sitting next to Brian, placed his hand on the defendant's shoulder and patted him repeatedly, offering more comfort.

Twenty-seven

For a week the prosecution presented evidence of the murder scene, the autopsy and many other technical matters, but then it was time for Jennifer to face her accusers. Entering the courtroom, she wore white high heels, an off-white skirt, and the cream-colored sweater she had worn at the hearing. Her hair, which had been disappearing throughout the various legal proceedings, was now boyishly short. She looked skittery and uncertain. As she took the stand her eyes moved toward the defense table and she saw a quartet of determined, well-prepared, highly competitive men—Tegtmeier, Pat Mika, Brian, and the private investigator, Tony DiVirgilio. Her opposition contained two former football players, one ex-cop, and one former national judo champion. She glanced around a little frantically for Chaplain Cooperrider, who was sitting in the gallery and squeezing a Bible. The chaplain winked at her and Jennifer gave a weak smile in return.

"While she's on the stand, I'll be praying for her that God is her refuge," Cooperrider had said a few days earlier. She had promised the young woman that she would be in the courtroom throughout Jennifer's testimony, which would last a minimum of several days. "Some of the weapons they'll use against her are lies and hideous statements, but I'll pull down those strongholds through prayer. Jennifer's coming to terms with this murder. She's gonna make it. During that sanity hearing, she was near death but she has more light in her eyes now and is stronger. She psyched up for Tegtmeier. She's ready to play ball."

214

Jennifer also found Elvin Gentry in the courtroom—he was sitting next to the prosecutors—and nodded to him. After waiving Jennifer's attorney-client privilege, Judge Weatherby, in another rare move and over Tegtmeier's protests, had decided to let her lawyer be present for her testimony. Gentry looked up at the young woman and smiled grimly, then took out his legal pad and began doodling.

The gallery was standing room only this morning and the place was abuzz; Fort Morgan residents had waited decades for something this juicy to happen in their town. In the air was not just excitement but the potential for revelation. This was Jennifer's chance to speak out publicly (her testimony would be seen nationwide on Court TV) and her best opportunity to answer the lingering questions. The murder had occurred fourteen months earlier and she had had all that time to try to comprehend her own behavior and make sense of it. Had she really been programmed to kill Dianne Hood or had she and Brian, in the unique chemistry of homicide, formed something like a third person who was able to carry out the mission? What were the dynamics—emotional and erotic—between her and Brian? Were they master and slave, as she had long contended, or were they equally guilty partners in crime? And if she had been his robot, what had made her so susceptible? Why had she gone with him to the In & Out store at least a dozen times, according to her own testimony, as they had planned the execution? What was the rush for her, the seductive high in this powerful mixture of sex, religion, money, and bloodshed?

Despite all of the testimony that had been delivered thus far, a void remained at the heart of the murder, aching to be filled. The lawyers, judges, police detectives, witnesses, and others connected with the case had done their jobs properly yet something was missing, and that vacuum could be felt whenever people gathered in Judge Weatherby's courtroom. What had really happened between these two people in the summer of 1990? Because Brian would most likely not take the stand in his own be-

half, the responsibility for answering that inquiry fell on
her. The farther the murder had receded in time and the
more the legal system or the psychiatric experts had tried
to penetrate it, the more unreal everything had become. It
was enough to encourage a collective scream—or something else that would cut through the formal courtroom
routines, enliven the dead air, and bring at least a partial
sense of clarity to the crime.

An enormous amount was at stake in Jennifer's testimony. While neither she nor the prosecutors would acknowledge it, if she could help them convict Brian of
first-degree murder, there might be a reward for her later,
a plea bargain and a lesser sentence than the mandatory
life without parole she faced if she went to trial and was
convicted. Months earlier, Aspinwall had told Gentry that
he did not think his client had been fully honest with the
prosecution. Aspinwall was convinced that Jennifer had
lied about the ski mask and this one detail bothered him
deeply. If she had twisted these facts, what else had she
twisted? He told Gentry that in order to convict Brian in
a capital punishment case he needed the whole truth and
wanted to speak with the young woman himself. This request went nowhere. When Jennifer entered the Fort Morgan courtroom she had never exchanged a single private
word with either Aspinwall or Harward. The former
placed great importance on preparing witnesses, especially
the most critical ones, but all he could do now was hope
for the best. That had never been his style, and, although
he tried not to show it, he was beyond pessimistic.

No revelations came. During two exhausting days of direct examination by Harward, Jennifer repeated virtually
everything she had said in the past, using the phrases
"Brian told me to" and "I was supposed to" innumerable
times and never wavering from her position that she had
been brainwashed and manipulated. It was Brian who had
purchased the mask and given her the gloves she had worn
at Otis Park. He had made her kill.

* * *

For his cross-examination, Tegtmeier placed in front of the jury a 1985 photograph that was originally a three-inch-by-five-inch picture Ben had taken of Jennifer at a European firing range. Her finger was on the trigger of a German handgun known as a Broom-handled Mauser, a nasty-looking piece of equipment that conjured up neo-Nazis and Uzis. In the photo, Jennifer wore headphones to protect her ears from the gunfire, she was smiling and she looked very pretty, like a young wife who takes part in a lot of activities in order to find things in common with her husband. The picture was no longer three-by-five inches. Tegtmeier had blown it up to three-feet-by-two-feet and one could not glance at it without recalling Patty Hearst's bizarre stint in the early 1970s as Tanya with the Symbionese Liberation Army.

When it was time to begin his questioning, Tegtmeier stood and grinned at the witness, moving toward her like a fighter who answers the opening bell by rushing across the ring and throwing a flurry of punches. He advanced and advanced, standing in front of her and smirking.

"You had an intention to kill Dianne Hood, didn't you?" he said.

"I had my instructions," Jennifer replied.

"You were trying to kill her?"

"If the bullet hit her."

"You've practiced a combat shooting position before, haven't you?"

"No, not by name."

"But you've practiced holding a gun with both hands and aiming it, as you did on the night of September 12, 1990, at Otis Park?"

"I only know that position because my husband taught me how to shoot."

"Stand up," the attorney glanced over at the enlarged photograph, "and show us how to shoot a Broom-handled Mauser."

She hesitated and her voice grew smaller, childlike, until

it was nearly inaudible. "I can't remember, Mr. Tegtmeier. Every gun is different."

He walked over to a wooden cabinet and brought out Ben's long Colt .45, placing the murder weapon on the lip of the witness box, a foot away from her. He smiled at her again and Jennifer recoiled, shaking and glancing away from the .45. She started to cry.

"The gun is empty," Tegtmeier said. "Stand up and fire it."

Her head twitched to the side, as if he had slapped her.

"Just stand up and do it," he repeated.

She twitched again and cried harder. "I don't remember how. I'm sorry."

"You've fired this Colt .45 before, haven't you?"

"Yes."

"When did you last shoot it?"

She jerked to the right and gave him an incredulous stare, the look of a woman who had killed someone but not lost her ingrained sense of decorum. When this passed she sat quietly and did nothing, like a frightened child.

Elvin Gentry was staring at his lap and drawing pictures of his client on a legal pad, while the two prosecutors gazed into the distance, as if they knew what was coming and did not want to watch. Brian's face was blank, as it had been throughout her testimony, and Tony DiVirgilio was busy digging into one of the thirty-seven volumes of evidence he carried into the room each morning and aligned on makeshift shelves behind the defense table. Pat Mika looked up at Tegtmeier with an expression that resembled adoration. The chaplain rocked and prayed. "It is fear," Gentry had once said during the sanity hearing, "that motivates everyone in this courtroom."

"When did you last shoot this gun?" Tegtmeier asked Jennifer again.

"September 12," she fumbled over the words, "1990."

"When you murdered Dianne Hood?"

"Yes." Her voice grew smaller still.

"You had an intention to kill her, didn't you?"

"I had instructions."

"Pick up the gun."

Her eyes wide with terror, she gazed out at Gentry, who gave her a brief nod. She glanced at Aspinwall and Harward, who did nothing in return. She looked at the chaplain, who stared back and kept praying. She looked over at the judge, who was impassively studying some papers on his desk. Something crossed Jennifer's face, an expression of absolute loneliness, a recognition that there was no one who could help her now and she had to face whatever lay ahead by herself.

"I really don't want to touch it," she said.

Tegtmeier smiled at her broadly. "You didn't have any trouble touching it before, did you?"

She hesitated, leaned forward, and gently took the weapon in her hands, which looked very small and delicate and pale. She held it with only her fingertips, the .45 hanging flaccid in front of her. Her features crumbled into another wave of tears. Setting the gun down, she reached for the box of Kleenex on the stand and covered her eyes.

"You bought the ammunition on August 28, 1990, to kill Dianne with, didn't you?"

"No."

"No?"

"I don't remember the date."

"And you stood over her and heard her beg for her life, didn't you?"

"No, sir. I did not hear that."

"You took this gun and pointed it at her heart."

"No."

"You heard her say, 'No, don't shoot. Don't!' "

"No, I didn't hear that. I didn't. All I heard was Brian's voice say, 'Two shots. She's gotta be dead.' "

The lawyer turned and grinned contemptuously at the jury. Over at the defense table Mika wore exactly the same smile.

"Then you took off running," Tegtmeier said, "didn't you?"

"I was told to do that."

"You didn't want to run?"

"I didn't care."

"Did God tell you to run?"

"No."

"Did Brian?"

"Something like his voice. It was planted in my head. I knew my instructions. I knew what I was supposed to do."

Tegtmeier brought out the sweatshirt, the gloves, and the ski mask, meticulously draping them over the railing on the witness stand. At the sight of the mask, Jennifer again recoiled, squirming backward in her chair. While performing these tasks, the attorney never stopped smiling and was light on his feet, almost jaunty, moving about the courtroom with the focus of a man who knows exactly what he is doing and has waited a long time to do it. After watching his cross-examination of Jennifer, there were people in the gallery who said that they would never— ever—again consider breaking a serious law.

"Put on the mask," he told her.

She looked at him with another expression of disbelief and then at the judge, her eyes silently begging him to stop the man.

"What is the purpose of asking her to do that?" Judge Weatherby softly asked.

"To show how she killed Dianne."

The judge lowered his eyes. "What else?"

"Just that."

"I don't think that will be necessary."

Jennifer's whole body exhaled relief and she fell back in her chair.

"You've said," Tegtmeier addressed her, "that Brian told you to walk like a man."

"Yes, he did."

"Show us what that means."

"What?"

"Show us how you did it."

Once more she looked at the judge but this time he turned away and lowered his gaze.

"Will you stand up and walk like a man?" the attorney asked her again.

"I just hunched my shoulders."

"Show us, please."

"I was to make my shoulders square."

"Show us."

"Do you want me to take off my high heels so I'll look more like a man?"

"Whatever you like."

The witness's neck jerked and the chaplain swayed with her eyes now shut, clutching the Bible with both hands to her chest.

Jennifer got out of her chair and walked toward the center of the room, trembling and pausing like a schoolgirl being humiliated before her class. She awkwardly threw back her shoulders and took a couple of fast robotic steps. She glanced toward the jurors, as if they might offer her something, but they were quiet and blank, most of them staring down.

Tegtmeier smiled at the witness and thanked her for her demonstration.

Jennifer sat down and hid her face.

"That," someone in the gallery whispered, "was sadistic."

Twenty-eight

Tegtmeier was not finished with her. He paced so close to the witness stand that the judge suggested he move back, which he did, and then he said to Jennifer, "Now, you worked your deal with the prosecution in November of 1990, didn't you?"

Her attorney put down his legal pad and shot out of his seat. "My client," he addressed the court, "does not have to answer that."

Tegtmeier faced the judge. "Mr. Gentry is an intrusion here and should leave."

Jennifer's lawyer glared at Brian's and made a low, unfriendly sound.

Weatherby warned Gentry not to interrupt the proceedings again and instructed the young woman to answer the question. Gentry sat down, went back to drawing on his legal pad and on the corner of it he wrote some large black letters that read, "TEG IS PISSING EVERYBODY OFF."

But Tegtmeier went blithely on with his cross-examination. "So your deal depends on whether you do a good job and please the D.A.'s office, doesn't it?"

"I don't see it that way," Jennifer said. "I don't think the D.A. is going to turn around and do anything nice for me."

"You've been trying to avoid responsibility all your life, haven't you?"

"I'm very responsible for what I've done. I feel like I'm being used by everybody in this case, by you and by the legal system. I've been given this responsibility to convict Brian and it's not mine. It's the D.A.'s."

Gentry looked up from his legal pad, where he had been drawing an unflattering portrait of Tegtmeier.

"Your whole deal depends on your ability to convict my client, doesn't it?"

"That's not true."

"What's not true is that Brian purchased the ski mask, isn't that right?"

"No, it is true."

"The mask was purchased by you on August 31 at the Ski Haus, wasn't it?"

"No."

"All that is a lie, isn't it—about the gloves and the mask?"

"No."

"And once you made up a lie you had to stand by it, didn't you?"

"No."

"You told Dr. Arthur Roberts, a psychiatrist in Colorado Springs, that Ben raped you vaginally and rectally, didn't you?"

Her face tightened and she squirmed again. "He tried to do that vaginally and wanted to rectally but I wouldn't let him."

"And none of that was true, was it?"

"Yes, it was true," she spit out the words.

"And you said he spanked you with a belt?"

"Yes, he liked that."

"And that wasn't true, was it?"

"Yes, it was."

"And you said he put things on your nipples?"

"He wanted to."

"And that wasn't true, was it?"

"Yes, it was true."

"You didn't go to that shed behind the convenience store to plan the murder with Brian. You went there to have sex with him, didn't you?"

She laughed, a forced stunned sound. "No. We had

many other places to have sex. We didn't have to go there."

Brian stared up at her, a flat stiff-jawed stare. She never looked at him.

"You thought you were losing Brian in August and September, didn't you?"

"No."

"When you're not getting the attention you want, you do something bad, don't you, just like you did when you were a child?"

"I was young back then."

"You knew Brian wasn't going to leave his wife, didn't you?"

"I knew he wanted his wife dead."

The lawyer switched directions and asked about an Oriental rug she and Ben had apparently lost in the summer of 1989, after they had moved from Arizona to Colorado Springs. As Tegtmeier described it, the couple had filed an insurance claim on the carpet, an heirloom in Jennifer's family, and received $4,400 but later discovered it folded up under a stairway at their Briargate address.

"What happened," the attorney asked her, "after you found the rug?"

"I asked Ben what to do and he said to keep the money so we did. I always took his advice on everything like this."

"Who spent the $4,400?"

"He did, on a gun."

"And he told you what to do?"

"Yes."

"And you did it?"

"Yes."

"So it was all his doing?"

"Yes."

Tegtmeier grinned at her one last time, a full-faced grin that made it seem as if his whole body were smiling at her.

"Thank you," he said. "That's all I have."

* * *

Walking into the courtroom, Ben looked squarer than ever: square face, square shoulders, square crew cut, square chest, square neck, forearms, and chin. He moved, acted, and spoke like a soldier, drawing obvious pleasure from the military jargon—"in garrison," "brigade-level exercises," "NTC"—that most civilians could not understand. As he sat down in the witness box and glanced around, his eyes came to rest on Brian and he gave the defendant a friendly nod, a very surprising gesture in light of the fact that the man had lately cuckolded him and that Ben, during the sanity hearing, had called Brian a monster. The defendant nodded back and smiled. Ben had been called to Fort Morgan as a prosecution witness—his round-trip flight from Europe was paid for by the state of Colorado—and this was the first indication that he was about to disappoint Harward and Aspinwall severely. The second indication came when he interrupted his direct examination and sharply asked Harward to refer to Jennifer not as his wife but as his "ex-wife."

"I kind of regret," the soldier testified, "that I ever told her I would stand by her one hundred percent right after all this happened and she was arrested. My feelings have changed markedly toward her. I'm angry now. I despise what she did. I'm ashamed that I was married to her. She asked me to hold off divorcing her until her trial was over so she could have a husband when she was in the courtroom. She thought that might help her. The divorce upset her and her parents. I just wanted to have my daughters with me and to put together a semblance of a normal life but she didn't agree with that."

He spoke of a warm midsummer day in 1990 when his wife and children were laughing and playing with a hose in the backyard, having a wonderful time. Jennifer was in the dog kennel when Ben sprayed her with cold water and she suddenly charged out at him, her features distorted by what he called "the rage on her face." She grabbed his arm and cut his skin with her nails. "I was speechless," he told the court. In Italy, he recalled, during her first pregnancy she had tossed a large cheeseball at him and on another occasion she threw a steak knife in his direction.

What he did not reveal on the witness stand was that a few days earlier, when he had arrived in Fort Morgan to await his courtroom appearance, Pat Mika had invited him to dinner, they had gone out and had a couple of drinks together, and the young lawyer had explained Brian's trial from the defense's point of view. If Jennifer's testimony succeeded in convicting the defendant of first-degree murder, the El Paso County D.A. would offer her a plea bargain, perhaps second-degree murder, perhaps even manslaughter, and she would be out of prison in a few years. As soon as she was released, she would come looking for Ben and her children. Why didn't Captain Reali join forces with Tegtmeier and Brian against her, just to protect himself and his own future? Were there any stories about her that he had not yet exposed in court? Anything that would make her look worse?

While being cross-examined by Mika, Ben denied ever abusing his wife sexually or hitting her. Then Mika brought up the Oriental rug.

"It was old and ratty," Ben said, "and was given to Jennifer by her parents. I once suggested that we cut it into pieces and lay them in the doghouse but she wouldn't hear of it. After we unpacked the carpet in Colorado Springs, I went down range and when I returned she said it was missing. I searched for it everywhere and was ready to forget about it but Jennifer demanded we file a claim on it.

"She did all the research on this with the insurance company. We got $4,400 and I bought a $650 hunting rifle, after asking her permission. The rest of the money went. It was gone. I found the rug later in a crawl space. I didn't put it there. I was upset and told Jennifer we had a problem. She said we didn't have the money anymore. I was seriously concerned about it but she said, 'Don't worry about it, they won't find out.' "

Following her arrest, Ben went back to the insurance company and offered to return the $4,400 but they took the rug in lieu of payment. One of their employees appraised the carpet at $75.

"Would it surprise you," Mika asked the witness, "to learn that, in this courtroom, your ex-wife blamed you for this insurance situation?"

"No, it wouldn't," the captain said. "She did a fair amount of blaming me during the sanity hearing."

"She blamed you for not being a good husband?"

"Yes."

"And blamed your work?"

"Yes. I thought she was fairly manipulative, blaming me for our marriage. Everything in the summer of 1990 was directed at me."

"She wanted a husband at her trial but not because she cared about you?"

"She wanted an image."

"And she used the children for this image too?"

Ben hesitated, as if reluctant to bring the issue of the girls into the courtroom. "Her concern for the kids, when she went through with the murder, was not a high priority."

"She used you to become a better shot so she could kill Dianne?"

"I'd say that's correct."

"She used your clothes and your gloves?"

"Yes."

"She used a weapon to shoot Dianne that was given to you by your father?"

"Yes. And she used me the next morning to get the gun out of the house."

"And she used you to have sex right after the murder so it would look like you were together that night?"

Ben hesitated again, as if he had never thought of that. "Yes, possibly."

After a few more questions, the judge called a recess and Mika and Tony DiVirgilio escorted the captain into a small conference room out in the hallway. There they laughed with him, gave him coffee from their own private source—there was no public coffee machine in the courthouse—and prepared him for their next round of inquiries.

During Harward's redirect examination of him, Ben conceded that he still believed Jennifer had been telling the truth the night of her confession, when she had poured out the story to Detective Wood. But ever since then, the captain indicated, he felt that she had just been looking for a good murder defense.

In an impromptu speech delivered from the stand, he said, "Jennifer blames Brian Hood for where she is now. I will state for the record that, based upon the garbage I heard in the past and what I think now that—"

Harward leaped up, waving his arms and cutting the man off, as certain as everyone else in the courtroom where Ben was heading—straight into a declaration that Brian was innocent of all the charges.

Twenty-nine

The recently constructed $5,700,000 Morgan County Courthouse had no coffee machine and exactly one pay phone. It was hard to say what the media covering the story were more anxious about—the lack of caffeine in the morning or the difficulty of reaching their editors without leaving the premises. Worse still, the town had no nightlife to speak of, and the funky smell of Fort Morgan occasionally slipped into the courtroom and pervaded the air. Just behind where the gallery sat was a small enclosed space holding the television cameras and crews of both Court TV and several Colorado news stations. A thick glass window inside this space gave onto the courtroom, so reporters could sit in there, behind its cement walls, and watch the TV monitors showing live coverage of the trial, all the while bantering irreverently about the proceedings. Comic relief centered on Brian ("Give me a close-up of the wife killer") or on Jennifer ("Who dresses that woman?") or on the lawyers' anatomies. Every now and then a blast of joyful laughter would penetrate the glass and shoot out into the courtroom, causing Judge Weatherby to look up and frown.

Aspinwall and Harward called some of Brian's Christian friends—Mark Ramey, William Bramley, and David Blue—but they proved to be as hostile to the prosecution as Ben had been. They portrayed the defendant as an excellent family man, a superb father and an outstanding Christian, well above average at quoting Scripture. They all said that in the late summer of 1990, following the

229

Hoods' trip to Sun Valley, Brian and Dianne were definitely reconciling their marriage and going forward together. If he had had an affair earlier with Jennifer Reali, it was over by September. If he had been with her on the morning of the shooting, embracing her on a mountain road when a policeman discovered them, it must have been their final good-bye. If Brian had occasionally complained about his wife, he had certainly never intended her any harm. The testimony of these men came out in fits and starts, with some obvious embarrassment and discomfort. They stuttered, blushed, wriggled on the stand and claimed they had forgotten certain talks they had had with Brian about his marital problems, the same talks they had had no trouble recalling the previous spring at Jennifer's sanity hearing. During recesses, Mika and DiVirgilio whisked the trio into the small conference room, giving them coffee and encouragement.

"These people," said one aging female observer after watching Ramey, Bramley, and Blue testify, "are scary."

The prosecutors called Jeanne DeBoe, an attractive woman with a pale face, redness in her hair, and a tinge of sadness or regret around her mouth. The twenty-seven-year-old was now a receptionist in Colorado Springs, but she had met Brian in 1987 while working in a video rental store and they had been intimate for about a year. He had told her that he had never been in love with Dianne, had married her only because she was pregnant, and that he had wanted to leave her for years but his religion did not permit divorce and he did not want to lose his children. In January of 1990, he had gone to Jeanne's house and said that he had been thinking about pulling into traffic on I-25 with Dianne in the passenger's seat. On another visit he had asked Jeanne to run into his wife with her car or to run the Hoods off the road, but she had adamantly said no, and he stopped making these requests.

The prosecution also called Dallas Salladay. Six days after the murder, the police had found a .45 automatic in the trunk of Brian's Honda Accord and the gun was traced to Salladay, who owned a junk shop called Bargains Galore in Fountain, a small town just south of Colorado Springs. Salladay, a hulking shaggy fellow who resembled a wary sheepdog, had known Brian from his days as a liquor salesman. In 1989 Brian had introduced Jeanne to Dallas and she had sold the dealer some silver. A year later, in August of 1990, Brian called Jeanne, said he was interested in buying a gun from Dallas, and thought he could get a better price if she were involved in the transaction. On August 23, the two men drove over to Jeanne's house, where Salladay looked through a box of coins and offered her $300 for the lot of them, agreeing to pay her in the near future. The next week Brian gave her a check from Dallas for $225, plus another check from himself for $75—a clever way for him to purchase the .45 from Dallas without any money or documents changing hands between the men.

In early September Brian went to Fountain with his oldest son, Jarrod, to pick up the .45 automatic at Bargains Galore. While there, the insurance salesman asked Salladay if he had any ski masks in stock.

"No," Dallas replied.

"Got any Halloween masks?" Brian said.

"It's too early for those. What are you gonna do—rob a bank?"

Brian laughed at him. "Do you sell .45 ammunition?"

Salladay shook his head.

Michael Maher testified that in the spring of 1990 he had contacted Brian, an ex-colleague from his days as a beer distributor. Maher was recently divorced and wanted to obtain a new insurance policy. The men took a camping trip to the Lost Creek Wilderness, outside of Colorado Springs, and during the excursion Brian spoke at length about his wife's illness and having to work all day in the office and then come home at night and take care of the kids, clean the house, and prepare dinner—all without the benefit of an intimate life with Dianne. "He more or less said his wife was just a bitch," Maher told the court. "That was his word." When they returned to the Springs, Brian came to Maher's home to close the insurance deal and they sat together on a davenport, the salesman again speaking of his wife, this time with even more intensity.

"Before I knew it," Maher testified, "he said that she was so miserable with the lupus and in so much pain that her life wasn't fulfilling now and she would be better off dead. He talked about how he would kill her but he couldn't because he couldn't collect the insurance if he did. He said if she committed suicide the insurance policy wouldn't work. He talked about turning left into traffic and hitting her side of the car and killing her. He said he needed a third person."

Maher, a pale, soft-spoken man with short brown hair and a quiet voice, looked profoundly uncomfortable in the courtroom, staring down much of the time and unable to meet the defendant's gaze.

"I told Brian that he needed to get help," he said. "I suggested he go to the Christian organization that he belonged to, a group he met with on Tuesdays and Fridays, and he could find the answers there. He didn't reply to that. He didn't hear what I was saying. He talked about staging a robbery at a convenience store and finding a third person to pull the trigger. That might be the way to go. He said he needed someone to do this. I told him that he needed counseling and this was over my head. He said, 'No, she needs to die.' His tone was matter-of-fact. He'd thought about it a lot and he was serious. I laughed at him, a kind of hysterical laughter, because my point wasn't being made. He said, 'I need a trigger.' "

When the trial recessed during Maher's testimony, Aspinwall stood right next to the witness and would not leave his side, so that when Pat Mika tried to herd him into the small room and offer him coffee, the prosecutor warded him off.

* * *

Terry Wenzlaff, a Prudential employee in the Colorado Springs office, told the jury that in June of 1990, he and Brian had had two prolonged discussions in which the defendant said that all sins were equal and that he could do anything he wanted to now—including commit a murder—and this would have no effect whatsoever on his spiritual life because he had been saved. After learning of Dianne's death, Wenzlaff, a Christian himself, went to the police and informed them of this conversation. Emilia Vargas, another Prudential employee and a woman who suffered from lupus, testified that in the week before the shooting Brian asked her three times where the upcoming lupus meeting would be held on the night of September 12. He wrote down the community center's address and also wanted to know when these gatherings adjourned.

"Brian came in on the Friday before Labor Day and talked to me about Dianne's new permanent," Vargas said. "I told him that because of the chemicals in perms they can be dangerous for people with lupus. He said, 'That's just it. There's always a problem. She can get sick from anything. I'm gettin' tired of it. I'm just gonna get rid of her.' "

John Williams, who lived near the In & Out Mart at the corner of Platte and Institute, told the court that in mid-August of 1990 he had noticed a broad-shouldered man driving a green Honda Accord around and around his block. The man was talking on a car phone.

The fourth time the Honda went past his house, Williams, a bearded, long-haired truck driver, ran out his front door, stopped the car, and asked the driver if he could help him with something.

"What fucking business is it of yours?" the man said.

"It's my neighborhood," Williams replied, "so it's my business."

The prosecutors showed the jury telephone records proving that Brian had made five long-distance calls to his relatives on the night of September 12, 1990, all of them between 8:08 and 8:15 P.M., exactly as Jennifer had told Detective Wood that Brian had done on the night of her arrest. The records also revealed that on the afternoon of September 10, a Monday and two days before the murder, Brian had made his longest recorded call ever on his car phone, twenty-seven minutes worth. It came at precisely the time that Jennifer had told Wood that the young man was riding around Otis Park giving her a detailed account of the layout of the community center, the grounds, and the nearby alleys.

Thirty

On Friday, December 13, one month after the first witness had been sworn in, Andy Hood arose early and walked into the coffee shop at the Days Inn, preparing himself for his 9:00 A.M. courtroom appearance. He was still well dressed in black but he looked nervous and exhausted, like a man in unraveling health. Seeing a familiar face across the room he attempted to smile but it came out looking more like a wince. He sat alone at a table, dabbling at his food, and one could only imagine what he had endured trying to explain to three small children why their mother was dead and their father was absent. As he stared at the walls of the motel restaurant, there were tears behind his glasses.

As Tegtmeier prepared to open his defense of Brian, the courtroom was again standing room only. Sitting in the gallery next to Suzanne Hood, who looked grave and dignified this morning, was the town eccentric, a middle-aged Fort Morgan pianist who lived with his mother and came to the trial wearing a sparkling red-and-gold Christmas tie over a green-and-charcoal flannel shirt. He had recently baked fudge and shared it with the defense team. He giggled at odd moments and local people said he was a genius.

Out in the hallway Andy paced and talked to reporters about Brian's athletic triumphs as a youngster, saying many of the things that he would soon repeat under oath on the witness stand. His son, he emphasized, was the type of person who made serious commitments and then complained about them endlessly, but he also held to those commitments for the duration of whatever he was involved in—playing on the football team, working at a tedious job, washing his parents' car as a boy, or staying in a marriage that was not always smooth.

"Brian's football coaches would hit him upside the head to get his attention," Andy testified a few minutes later. "Once, he told me that he hated football. He'd get mad and say, 'I quit,' but then he'd think about it, go back, and be a star player. He says what he thinks immediately. He's always moaning, always groaning. He's constantly unhappy and he expresses it and then he goes on and does what he has to do."

Tegtmeier wanted Andy to tell the jury his opinion of Jennifer Reali.

"I'm very angry at her," the man said. "She trapped Brian into this. She's taken him down to the bottom and killed the kids' mother and these children will be damaged for life. She killed Dianne and now she's trying to take away their father through her lies. She's falsified many statements against my son. This,"—he looked around the courtroom—"is absolutely ridiculous. Brian Hood does not have the heart to engage in the terrible lies that Jennifer Reali has imposed on this family."

He left the stand weeping and hugged Brian on his way out. A few people in the gallery were also crying, but the jury was dry-eyed.

David Moore was Dianne's older brother and someone the defense had long considered a critical witness for their side. An attorney in civil law in San Antonio, Moore had come to Colorado Springs for his sister's funeral in September of 1990, and while there he had attempted to discover what evidence the El Paso County D.A. had against his brother-in-law. Bill Aspinwall had curtly told him that his job was not to prove anything to the Texas lawyer, but to a jury of Brian's peers. Moore had taken offense at this remark, concluding that Brian was innocent and the victim of the local district attorney (although in private, if pushed, he would concede that he had struggled to reach this opinion and still wrestled with some doubts).

Pale-skinned and dark-browed, the usually composed and nice-looking Moore changed dramatically on the witness stand. His head bobbed, his cheek developed a tic, and he looked like someone who was trying to convince himself that a disaster was not about to occur. He told the jury about his difficult upbringing in Texas, with a father who had left him and Dianne early, and with a mother, engulfed by economic hardships, who tried to raise her children alone. As he spoke one could not help but wonder if he had found in the successful and attractive Hoods the family he had always wanted.

"Dianne had done some modeling on TV in San Angelo," he testified, "and it was devastating to her that she couldn't keep her appearance because of the lupus. She fought to get to where she was and she wasn't gonna let anyone, including Brian, steamroll her. His affair with Jennifer Reali was unfortunate but I don't think he was involved in the murder."

When Harward rose from his chair for the cross-examination and approached the witness, Moore stared at him so hard that his eyebrows arched. Ever since he had taken the stand, his face had been twitching and one could feel the tension gathering in him, just waiting to explode, but he had managed to hold it back. As the prosecutor stood before him and commenced asking his questions, Moore could no longer contain himself and burst into a monologue.

"I can't figure out why," he nearly shouted, "the D.A. has said in the past that this might not go under first-degree murder for Jennifer Reali. He's said that it could be second-degree murder or even manslaughter. This infuriates me and it's all so senseless. In my wildest nightmares, I never imagined this would happen. This woman took my sister away from me."

He began to sob.

Harward attempted to pose another question but Moore was not finished.

"Now she's trying to take Brian away from me!" he said through the tears. "It's ridiculous! I don't think the people of Colorado want a confessed murderer back on the streets. It's crazy! How can you do this?" he yelled at Harward. "How can you do this to Brian?"

The prosecutor made no response and for several moments the only sounds in the courtroom were those of the witness, the defendant, and the Hood family crying.

Moore was soon escorted down from the stand and departed the room, trembling and weaving as he walked past his brother-in-law and touched him on the back. Tegtmeier, Mika, and DiVirgilio had all stood and were huddling over their client, the three men forming a circle so that only Brian's shoulders were visible, moving up and down as he wept in his chair.

After a moment, Judge Weatherby said quietly, "Does the defense have another witness?"

The circle held its shape and a number of seconds passed, filled in with nothing but the gasps of this large man who was on trial for his life.

Then the circle broke and Brian gingerly stood, searching for his balance, like an old man who'd been sitting in one place for too long.

"I want to testify," he told the judge, "but I'm going to take the advice of my counsel and not do it."

He sat down and there was another pause, which seemed to last a long time. Tegtmeier finally looked at the judge and said, "The defense rests."

Afterward, when the proceedings had been adjourned for the day, the courthouse cleared very slowly, folks lingering in the hallway and then lingering some more in the parking lot, talking among themselves and speculating on what would happen next, telling themselves how lucky they were not to be on the jury. No one in Fort Morgan, it seemed, wanted all this to end and the people to go away.

Thirty-one

For their deliberations, which would be long and extremely difficult, the jury was not sequestered. They began on the morning of December 18, one week before Christmas, a bad omen according to the prosecution. "Never try anyone around the holiday season," Aspinwall said. "People are always more sentimental this time of year."

In preparing to reach a verdict, the jurors had been given a number of options: they could find Brian guilty or innocent on any combination of three counts of solicitation, one count of conspiracy, and one count of first-degree murder. He could be set free by their decision or placed on Colorado's death row. For three full days the six men and six women on the final jury argued in a small room behind Judge Weatherby's chambers and at the end of each day, as they filed back into the courtroom to announce the results of their labors, Suzanne Hood stood behind her son and held her breath. Three times Ron Shaver, the jury foreman, told the judge that a verdict had not been reached and on each occasion Suzanne loudly exhaled, leaning over the wooden railing and hugging Brian in full view of those who were deciding his fate. By now the jurors looked as if they had been engaged in a marathon self-help seminar—worn, frayed, unhappy, and stuck together in a small room they could not escape—and they were, it was becoming clear, seriously divided about what to do with the young man. Some would later talk about the terrible sense of pressure in the deliberation room, about shouting matches that erupted and about being "tattered and torn."

Others would say that even though they were allowed to go home at night, they could not sleep. Others, who had been only passing acquaintances for years in Fort Morgan, became friends during the ordeal. After a while they lost count of how many times they took a vote that resulted in another deadlock. While they deliberated, the defense lawyers jogged and the prosecutors played the card game, hearts, at the Days Inn.

Near the end of the fourth day, December 23, the jury came back and Ron Shaver announced that a verdict had been reached. Within minutes the lawyers, the journalists covering the event, the Hood family, and most of the regular gallery members began arriving at the courthouse and rushing to find seats. By now, Tegtmeier had grown exceedingly pale, his cheeks showing creases not there the previous summer. The more nervous Pat Mika became, the softer he spoke. His voice had become a whisper. Aspinwall and Harward appeared resigned to the outcome; neither would say how much he wanted to win, but both admitted they hated to lose. The Hoods arrived in court wearing jittery smiles and an air of hopeful expectation—Suzanne had nearly fainted when Tegtmeier told her that the verdict was in. Andy carried a photo album of his grandkids, showing it to anyone who was interested, and he spoke of boarding an airplane with Brian soon and all of them flying back to Houston for a Christmas reunion with the children. When everyone was finally assembled and the jurors were in their box, the judge entered the courtroom and cleared his throat, telling the defendant to stand. Brian complied, with the quick polite movements he had used throughout the proceedings. He looked as pale as his lawyer.

Since the trial had begun six weeks earlier, one thing had not changed at all. The faces of the jury were as inscrutable at this moment as they had been on opening day. There was no possible way of knowing how they had received the enormous amount of information they had taken in since mid-November, and their expressions revealed only that they were exhausted and had found no joy in their endeavor.

"Charge of murder in the first degree," Judge Weatherby read from the piece of paper the foreman had given him. "Jury finds the defendant not guilty."

Suzanne shut her eyes and gave a long relieved sigh, Andy bending down next to her, as if he were collapsing from a great release of tension. Brian remained motionless.

"Charge of solicitation of Jeanne DeBoe for murder," the judge said. "The jury finds the defendant not guilty."

The men at the defense table and the Hoods looked at one another and started to smile with the hope of victory.

"Charge of solicitation of Michael Maher for murder. The jury finds the defendant guilty."

The smiles were just as quickly gone and all of them stiffened.

"Charge of solicitation of Jennifer Reali. The jury finds the defendant guilty."

Brian slumped over, his hands rolling into fists at his sides, his face suddenly red.

"Charge of conspiracy to commit murder. The jury finds the defendant guilty. Sentencing will be on February 18."

With that the judge stood and walked out of the courtroom through the large oak door behind the bench.

Brian turned around and grabbed his parents, hugging them once more, a long deep embrace for his mother and an even longer one for his father, all of them brushing at tears. Then he was led away by a guard.

The lawyers stood around talking among themselves and looking rather stunned, as if they were still trying to understand exactly what the jury had done. The only thing that was clear was that none of them was pleased with the outcome. Then they quickly disbanded, wanting to escape the media and avoid all of the questions, but a reporter caught up with Aspinwall in the hallway and asked him for a response. For the first time since arriving in Fort

Morgan, the man let slip just how much he had wanted a first-degree murder conviction.

"Fuck," he said, "and you can quote me."

And then after a pause, he said, "Have you ever seen such an amoral group of people?"

Brian's parents did not vanish from the courthouse but stayed on, talking to journalists and TV cameras, Suzanne finally breaking her silent vigil.

"Because of Jennifer Reali," she said, "my grandchildren have no mother."

"My son's human rights," Andy said, "have been violated by Jennifer Reali and by the D.A.'s office in El Paso County and something really smells in Colorado Springs. The investigation was mishandled from the beginning and the police stacked the deck against my son. It's just unbelievable the pain and suffering we've gone through. It goes so deep, especially for our grandchildren, who do not have a mother. Now it appears that their father is gone too."

Up in Seattle, when Keith Vaughan was informed of the verdict he said that Brian did not have to be found guilty of first-degree murder to satisfy him because he felt no personal vengeance toward the man.

In her cell in Colorado Springs, where she was awaiting her own trial, Jennifer was pleased when she received the news.

"I can live with that," she said, "because it's accurate."

Two months later, on a warm sunny day in late February, the Hoods and David Moore gathered one last time in Fort Morgan for the sentencing. Solicitation and conspiracy are Class 2 felonies in Colorado, punishable by eight to twenty-four years in prison. If Judge Weatherby found enough mitigating factors in Brian's case, he could give him nothing more than probation. If he found enough aggravating factors, and if he decided to run the sentences consecutively rather than concurrently, he could give him 144 years. In the eight weeks since the verdict had been rendered, the defense had been as aggressive as ever, collecting more than fifty letters and sending them along to the judge, each of them speaking highly of the defendant and asking Weatherby to give him probation so that he could be with his children and reenter the community as a reformed man. The letters came from friends, family members, from those who shared Brian's religious convictions, and from Brian himself.

From post-trial media reports Tegtmeier and Mika had noticed that Ron Shaver, the jury foreman, had been quite outspoken about the jurors' difficulty in reaching a verdict. Only four of the twelve people had wanted to convict Brian of first-degree murder, and many said that Jennifer's testimony had left them more confused than enlightened. The defense attorneys wanted Shaver to appear at the sentencing and ask the judge to give Brian probation—an unprecedented step for a jury foreman to take. Shaver did appear and told the court that his views on the case had caused some fellow townspeople to make harassing late-night calls to his number, to send him anonymous threatening letters, and to throw eggs at his house. Dorothy Geist, another jury member who had come to the sentencing on her own, listened to Shaver's testimony and was appalled. The other jurors, she said privately, totally disagreed with what Shaver was doing on Brian's behalf.

Tegtmeier brought in a Denver psychiatrist, Dr. James Selkin, an extraordinary-looking man with a bald bullet-shaped head, a goatee, and histrionic eyebrows. He could have passed for a professional wrestler. From his examination of the defendant, Dr. Selkin told the judge, Brian was "deeply remorseful" about the past and "his whole view of human relationships has changed dramatically. He's a much more human person now. He's become a sensitive, caring human being. He's a good candidate for probation and leading a law-abiding life."

"Did Brian," Aspinwall asked the doctor on cross-examination, "conspire to kill his wife?"

"I don't know."

"But you're recommending that he get probation?"

"Yes."

"And you don't know if he solicited Jennifer Reali to kill his wife?"

"Yes, that's correct."

"Have you considered the effect on the Hood children of having the person who coconspired with the woman who killed their mother receive no punishment?"

"The process I'm recommending is to help them deal with this."

"Have the children even been told that their father is guilty of a crime or have they been told that he's a victim of the legal system?"

Unruffled, Dr. Selkin looked directly at the prosecutor and said, "They're dealing with the loss of both of their parents."

Tegtmeier, in his closing speech at the sentencing, said this was the most unusual case he'd seen in twenty years of practicing criminal law. "Is it greater punishment," he asked the judge, "to have Brian sitting in jail or out dealing with the anger of his children since their mother has died? The greater punishment is out there facing his parents and his family and the community and dealing with the damage that he's done. This case is a tragedy from every viewpoint, but especially that of the children. The court, if it metes out punishment, must show some mercy . . . Brian will suffer for his moral improprieties for the rest of his life. His children are angry about that and he will deal with that in his own heart and soul forever. That is punishment enough."

Brian was also given the chance to speak and for the first time since his arrest he made a public statement.

"It's amazing," he said, "how when you're in prison and things are taken away from you—your wife, your kids, and your freedom—then life becomes crystal clear. I can control my actions now and want the opportunity to do that. I desperately want to be the father of my children, to be there financially and emotionally and in all ways for them, and what I really want is leniency and to be able to be a part of the community. I want to donate my time now to support groups that would benefit others. No matter what happens, I'm gonna do the very best I can wherever I am. Thank you."

Aspinwall spoke last, slowly walking to the rostrum and facing the judge in silence for several moments. The lawyer's fervor had been suppressed almost the entire time he had been in Fort Morgan, but at the end he decided to release it or perhaps it just came out on its own.

"This defendant," he said, glancing over at Brian, "hasn't taken any responsibility for soliciting the death of his wife. Not one word of that from him or his attorneys. He's said only that he had an affair. The court knows that this man's character was such that when his wife had lupus he was out having sex with another woman. In one breath he talks about being saved through Jesus Christ and in the next he's talking about killing his wife by shooting her or running her over or turning left into traffic. That's his character, Your Honor. This is an abomination of the Christian religion. That's what you've seen on display throughout this trial and you should consider this when you make your decision.

"The reason his children are having a hard time today is because of the actions of this man. This fellow," and his voice shook as he pointed at the defendant, "never once thought about Dianne or his children. He thought only about himself. I don't think a killer who conspired to kill their mother should be returned to his children. That should never happen. Nothing goes in this defendant's favor for granting probation."

Andy Hood had been sitting in the gallery but now he stood and left the courtroom.

"Dianne Hood," the lawyer went on, "was a pretty girl and had three kids she loved very, very much. When she had lupus and needed all the help she could get there was somebody sneaking around the back alleys of Colorado

Springs taking her very life away from her. That precious life."

Aspinwall stopped, lowered his head and, to the amazement of everyone in the room, when he raised it again he was crying. He drew in a long breath, then another, holding the sides of the rostrum with both hands. "This defendant told Michael Maher that Dianne was a bitch and needed to die. Maher said, 'You need help.' He ignored this and went on and solicited Jennifer Reali to kill Dianne. That makes the first solicitation aggravated. Then he goes on to conspire to kill her. He takes away the kids' mother and she will never see them grow up. When they get cuts on their hands or legs, she won't be there to bandage them. When they play sports, she won't be there to see them. When they graduate from high school, she will miss that and they will miss her being there too. That pain's gonna go on forever and ever.

"When I see these attorneys,"—he looked at the defense table and then back at the judge—"hiding behind these children, it's awful. If you grant him probation, he will have accomplished his purpose just one year later than he'd planned. At the very least, the court should find the murder of Dianne Hood an aggravating factor. We don't want to send a message that you can solicit and conspire to have your wife murdered and get probation. I ask the court to sentence him to the high end of these charges and to run his sentences consecutively. Thank you."

The judge, remaining gracious to the last moment, thanked everyone for participating in the trial and apologized for having spoken so softly throughout the proceedings. Then his tone shifted to a deeper and louder register and he told the courtroom that much thought and many hours had gone into his sentencing decision.

"Mr. Hood," he said, "I've considered your letter and the letters of your friends and family. Your letter acknowledges your sinful nature, in terms of adultery, but not your criminal involvement. I'm not here to punish you for your sins but for your crimes. You solicited two people to kill your wife and you planned with Jennifer Reali the death of Dianne Hood. The main purpose of sentencing in our society, whether we believe it or not, is to punish people. What occurred that night in Otis Park was tragic and violent and must be controlled.

"You were the instrument that planted the seed that led to your wife's death. You did it twice and were successful once. The sentence I'm about to impose will affect your children's lives and their children's and your parents' lives. I'm sorry about that but I have to deal with the crimes committed. A sentence is not just words out of a book. It means a lot. I sentence you to fifteen years for your solicitation of Michael Maher, twenty-two years for your solicitation of Jennifer Reali and twenty-two years for your conspiracy to commit murder with Jennifer Reali. The first two sentences will run concurrently."

Within moments the judge had disappeared and Brian, facing thirty-seven years in prison, was silently escorted away. After serving roughly a third of this time in one of the state penitentiaries, he would have a chance at parole. The defendant's parents left the courthouse quickly on this occasion, but David Moore stayed behind and told reporters there would definitely be an appeal.

Thirty-two

Glenwood Springs, Colorado, three hours west of Denver and sitting in the bottom of a mountain valley, is known for its naturally heated outdoor steam pools that shoot fog into the air and create an odor that is fainter than Fort Morgan's but pungent at close range. People say the smell is good for you and has a healing power. Jennifer's trial, moved from Colorado Springs because of the publicity, began a week after Brian's sentencing (the El Paso County D.A.'s office never offered her a plea bargain). The trial, held in the Garfield County Courthouse, was to determine, once and for all, if she were mentally impaired and should be sent to the state hospital for an indeterminate stay or if she were guilty of first-degree murder and should now be incarcerated for life. The proceeding, which was presided over by Judge Mary Jane Looney of Colorado Springs, lasted seven weeks and was every bit as exhausting as the Fort Morgan trial. One afternoon during a recess, Bob Harward was seen walking outside the courthouse in a heavy snowstorm, wearing no coat or hat, moving his arms and arguing aloud with himself, a lonely figure obsessed with this seemingly endless legal monstrosity.

Ben's last courtroom appearance came in early March and he finally got an all-out war to fight in but it was one he could never have anticipated. The combat training he had received to prepare himself for not cracking under pressure served him well in these circumstances—because pressure might be defined as facing a murder defense that says you abused your wife so severely you caused her to kill someone outside your marriage; and pressure is having an attorney, Elvin Gentry, accuse your new wife of child abuse (after word had come back to Jennifer that Ben's new spouse had slapped one of the girls); and pressure is having that same lawyer accuse you, in public and on television and on the front page of newspapers, of violating your ex-wife sexually with the barrel of a loaded revolver.

Ben denied everything, never lost his self-control on the witness stand, and seemed more amazed than ever by all the accusations.

Pressure is answering numerous charges aimed at you by a nationally known Denver-based psychiatrist, Dr. Lenore Walker, who had written nine books on abused women and counseled many females who had committed homicide. According to Dr. Walker, Ben had put a scarf in his wife's mouth during sex, thrown her to the floor, choked her, smothered her, blindfolded her, and forced her to make love in front of the children. His constant abuse, Walker testified, had left Jennifer programmed to become Brian's instrument, ready to sit passively in his car while the man played Christian tape recordings in the background and asked her to murder his wife.

The case had moved to another level entirely. Who could ever know which of the charges were true and which were false? Wandering through the utterly gray area of sexual behavior between adults, one felt, more than anything, simply lost.

On the stand Keith Vaughan broke down as he recounted his daughter calling him from jail and telling him that she wanted to kill herself. Suicide would be easier than confronting the future, he had told her, but it would also be "a betrayal of our love." After he finished testifying, Keith walked into the hallway and on into a small conference room, where he could be away from the crowd of onlookers who gathered every day at the courthouse to see what would happen next. The Seattle architect with the white hair, the glasses, the quick smile, and the look of deep inquisitiveness that had settled into his features, sat down and began to talk, speaking openly and without regard for the outcome of the legal process and perhaps without even the hope of being understood. He talked for a long time and when he said that his daughter was insane and badly needed psychiatric help, he cried once more.

"Most of the time," he said, "when Jenny talks about all this with me, she's very childlike and naive. She can't yet articulate what happened to her. But at other times, it's different. I know this sounds strange but I think I've actually spoken with her unconscious mind. Occasionally, I reach a depth with her, a place where there is no more distortion in what she's saying, and I get a sense of what really happened. We've gone that far together. The legal system doesn't tell you the why of anything. It's just concerned with the good guys and the bad buys, but I'm interested in knowing what went on beyond that. I want to know why."

He paused and glanced around, as if he might stop talking because he had already said too much, but then he continued, almost as if he could not help himself and this was his way of confronting great pain. "When I say this, my wife gets very upset with me. I say it with all my sympathy for Dianne Hood and for what her family has suffered. I say it because I mean it. What has happened to Gail and me is about the worst thing that can happen to you if you're a parent, the absolute worst. And yet, I wouldn't have missed it for anything. It has taught me that I have the strongest wife in the world and the strongest daughter, in Jenny. It has taught me more about love and about my own inner resources than anything that has ever happened to me. And it's so fascinating and so important to try to penetrate the mystery of what goes on inside a human being and how we operate.

"My wife and children tell me not to pursue these thoughts. They say I get carried away in my desire to understand. They think I'll go out there too far and not come back. But I want to know more. We're only going to learn more about these things by asking questions and opening the debate and talking about them. I've spent $300,000 on Jenny's defense and I still don't know the answers. My wife and I are hundreds of thousands of dollars in debt but I'll keep looking. If we win the lottery, I told Gail to take her half of the money and save it because I'm going to spend my half searching for the truth.

"The most phony things in this case were the four psychiatrists who testified at her sanity hearing. None of them went far enough with her. None of them would take the necessary time to get some answers. When I asked them why, they indicated that I didn't have enough money for them to do the work it would take to get there. I don't have any money left but I would raise some for that. I have friends who would help me. I could get more. I'm not qualified to deal with these questions but there are people out there who are and we need to find those people and use them so we can learn more about the nature of violence. What happened to Jenny is something psychiatry doesn't have a name for yet. She doesn't process information the way you and I do. She's crazy. It hurts me to say that but it's true. I can't stop asking questions, no matter what my wife and children say. I have to do this."

He paused again but had more to say. "Jenny would call us and give hints about the abusive things Ben was doing to her but she never really told us the truth. Ever. When all of the legal things are resolved, she's going to have to go back to when she was younger—maybe twelve or thirteen—and find out where all of this began and start over from there. That's where she stopped. She has to do this for herself."

Keith was asked what he had heard from his daughter when he had spoken to what he believed was her unconscious.

He did not respond quickly, as if he were thinking about his answer. "It happens after she's slept for a long time, maybe twenty hours straight. She does that sometimes in the prison. When she's just awakened and gets on the phone, I hear her telling me that she has to do things for others but she cannot yet do things for herself. She sounds childlike and sleepy. Her voice has a tone of survival in it—pure survival—either she does these things for someone else or she will die. That's where Jenny got stuck. We don't know how it happened. We don't understand it. We never even knew about it until all this occurred. When she speaks from her unconscious, that's what comes out. It's fear, total fear, the sound of someone trying to survive. A child who feels she has no choice. It goes all the way back."

He was asked what would happen if she took the stand and tried to explain these feelings to the jury.

"Aspinwall," Keith replied at once. "Aspinwall would tear her to shreds. He would make her angry and she would fight back. Nothing good can come out of this trial. Nothing at all. Prison won't help her and she wouldn't get the treatment she needs at the state hospital. If she's convicted, we've just got to try to keep her alive for the next eighteen months, until we can file an appeal. Her mother and I would like for her to be able to come home with us. We think we could help her now."

After five days of deliberation, six men and six women found Jennifer guilty of first-degree murder and conspiracy. Several jurors cried as the verdict was read and only one would talk about his decision afterward. The forty hours of deliberating, he said, had been "very, very difficult. This experience will echo through my mind forever."

David Moore, who had attended parts of the trial, reacted to the verdict by saying, "Jennifer Reali is the embodiment of evil."

Elvin Gentry, when asked to describe his client, said, "She's probably every bit as sweet as she seems."

Lenore Walker said that Bill Aspinwall and Bob Harward "were as guilty of using and abusing Jennifer as were her husband and Brian Hood."

Richard Tegtmeier refused to comment.

When Ben was reached by telephone in Germany,

where it was 1:00 A.M., he was so happy with the verdict that he said he planned to celebrate with a fine dinner and a bottle of champagne.

As Jennifer left the Garfield County Courthouse for the last time, to be returned to her cell in Colorado Springs, she refused to speak to reporters. And leaning her head against the rear seat of the patrol car, she smiled when the vehicle pulled away, as if she were relieved. She would be given life imprisonment at Canon City's state penitentiary, which has a flower garden that she may one day tend. After being transferred to Canon City, she was reunited with her old friend, Robin Krisak, and the two of them once again began singing the gospels that Jennifer had written. She also composed a few new hymns, including one for Dianne and one that mentioned Brian. The latter went,

> *"The enemy was big and strong*
> *He hid behind deception . . ."*

Harmonizing with Robin, Jennifer looked nothing at all like the young woman who had once traveled alone through Europe and dreamed of living there, but like someone who had slipped into a whole new identity, a place of refuge, and had no intention of coming back.

She was sentenced in Colorado Springs by Judge Looney, who said, "I find the disparity between your sentence and Mr. Hood's intellectually unfair and emotionally unfair. There is no question in my mind that you were carrying out Mr. Hood's plan . . . He took what we hold most sacred as a society, love and religion, and used those repeatedly to influence you . . . It seems to me this is almost a Greek tragedy. We have a person, you, who is otherwise really decent but with some fatal flaw. I suspect that had you not become involved with Mr. Hood chances are you wouldn't have had anything more serious than a traffic ticket or two the rest of your life."

EPILOGUE

On a cold winter's day the wind blew across Otis Park and sent a chill straight to the bone. Pikes Peak rose to the west, high and wild and bald, sunlight and long fingers of snow lying across its face. The mountain seemed very close this morning, swelling right above the community center. Murder locales are usually smaller than one expects them to be and hold a special resonance—perhaps because one brings his own particular fear or curiosity into such a place or because one has seen this patch of earth or cement depicted so many times in photographs or on TV that one cannot look at it without reliving the notorious scene. Or perhaps it is because something really is left behind, not ghosts but feelings or traces of energy—powerful things that exist on the other side of language.

Sarah Troup and Marty Wood, two lupus support group officers who were at the park on September 12, 1990, walked out of the center and into the wind, wrapping their coats tighter around them. They looked reasonably healthy but their features were not entirely discernible on their puffy faces. Their eyes, mouths, bones, and even their noses appeared to be hiding within the flesh they had put on since contracting lupus and taking many disease-fighting drugs. They looked warily at a stranger and spoke with hesitation of their illness, as if they feared they might be judged harshly for having become sick or gaining weight. As they talked one glimpsed what they had looked like before the lupus and one saw them leading different lives with different bodies, an eerie sensation but somehow appropriate at Otis Park.

"Sarah and I know what it's like to have lupus and to need the support and understanding of your husband," Marty said, her red-orange hair stretched by the breeze, until it was upright. "That's when you need someone to stand by you the most. I wish Brian had gotten more time."

"He better not ever come around here again," Sarah said, turning her back to the wind.

Dirt swirled and stung the eyes. The air made the blood shiver. Branches near the center rattled, scraping against one another, and the empty swing set on the playground flew up into the sky, twisting its chains.

"Yeah, he better not show up here," Marty said. "A lot of women are waiting for him."

In prison Brian looked very different from in the courtroom—harder, tougher, his hair longer, his face sporting a mustache, his torso bigger and bulging at the shoulders, as if he had been lifting weights. He wore a green jumpsuit and heavy shoes and, dressed like a convict, he looked like a convict, the polite smile now gone. His new home was in Limon, Colorado, a small town on the high plains between Denver and the Kansas border. The pastel-colored penitentiary resembled a huge plastic toy that had been stuck on a hillside on the edge of Limon, but a toy surrounded by metal fences topped with coils of glistening barbed wire, a toy that would grow paler and paler in the terrible heat of July and August. In his first days of incarceration, Brian was taunted by other prisoners and guards for being "a media celebrity." One inmate offered him sexual favors, another wanted to fight. He dodged both options.

As he sat at a table in the small visiting room he was reticent at first and kept glancing at his attorney, who had insisted on being present at the meeting. Tegtmeier had driven up from Colorado Springs in his red convertible and was still representing the young man on appeal. The lawyer looked much better than he had in Fort Morgan, his skin having regained its tan and the strain no longer narrowing his eyes. In time Brian began to relax a little, drinking soda from a can and letting out a few more words, belying the notion, put forward so often at his trial, that he was a big dumb inarticulate jock who could not have spoken for himself on the witness stand. For more than an hour he talked freely, denying absolutely any involvement in his wife's death and referring bitterly to Jennifer, his language a combination of religious rhetoric and profanity. Tegtmeier barely intruded at all, listening and watching with a deeply curious expression, as if he too wondered what the inmate would say now that the legal dust had settled.

At one point, Brian said, "Justice has finally been served. At last that little fucker Aspinwall did something right by getting a life sentence for Reali. If he can convict an innocent man, he shouldn't have had any problem convicting a guilty woman."

Tegtmeier gradually stirred and got out of his chair, either ready to leave or simply restless because he was hearing the same story told once again. Brian looked at him and said that he wished he had been tried by a judge instead of a jury because a judge would surely have acquitted him of all the charges. The attorney smiled back at him, rolling his eyes and grabbing his own throat in a mock gesture of someone being hanged.

"Brian," he laughed. "No, Brian. You don't mean that."

The prisoner showed no signs that he was joking and resumed talking.

After a while, the room fell silent and for the first time there was a small opening. Tegtmeier had begun to pace in short strides from one wall to the other and Brian tapped his empty soda can on the tabletop, a hollow clanking sound that grew louder with each tap.

A visitor who was sitting with them cautiously suggested a different scenario for the murder—that Brian and Jennifer had played a kind of intricate game of dare with one another, a contest in which each of them had pushed the other forward, each one making suggestions and asking the other to take small steps toward the crime, each one riding a wave of passion and deceit and searching for a way to escape the lives they had created, each one excited by the new possibilities. Had it suddenly stopped being a game and turned monstrously real on that evening of the twelfth? Had Brian never really intended for his wife to be killed but engaged in a push-pull dance that had somehow ended in murder?

Absorbing this information, perhaps considering it, the young man's eyes changed, flicked inward, as if something unusual had just passed through him and he wanted to look at it, to talk about it, to see what it was. His face twitched and his eyes winced. The soda can was silent and the opening in the air hung wider. Tegtmeier had stopped pacing and was staring at the man, his lips parted in anticipation. He leaned toward his client and for several seconds the room was utterly still.

Brian blinked and glanced around, as if returning from someplace else. His large body shifted in the chair and the wince was gone.

"No," he said. "That's not what happened. There wasn't any game. That's Reali's story. That's what she said. That's what she made up to take away my wife and children. If you believe her, then . . ."

As Tegtmeier was leaving the penitentiary, he walked across the parking lot and stood next to his car, studying the prison with an intense penetrating gaze. "A lot of people will just lie to you and know they're doing it and not care," he said. "Brian isn't like that. He thinks he's telling you the truth. He really believes that what he says is what happened. It's been that way with him since the day we met."

On a gray summer's day the wet branches overhanging Evergreen Cemetery made everything seem dark and enclosed, like a tunnel composed of leaves. At the office near the front gate a visitor stopped to ask for directions, was given a map and told to go to section 22. The walk was brief but the grass was so cool and damp that one's shoes were quickly soaked. Fog covered the far end of the cemetery and the deeper one ventured into the field of headstones, the larger Evergreen became, stretching in every direction and onto a distant mound. Some of the markers were old and whitened; some were of shiny new marble. The place was quiet except for some workmen in a nearby section, excavating a fresh plot. After searching unsuccessfully for a while, the visitor approached one of the gravediggers and asked if he had any recollection of where Dianne Hood was buried.

"I know exactly where she is," the young man said, laying aside his shovel and raising himself out of the shallow hole he had been expanding. He brushed some mud off his blue jeans and wiped at his mustache. Despite the cool morning, he was sweating.

"I remember her funeral," he said, walking across the cemetery. "There were a lot of people out here for that."

He stopped near a rectangular piece of ground wedged in between a number of large carved headstones. Dianne had been dead nearly two years but nothing marked her final resting place except a vague patch of new grass, lighter than the rest.

"I guess they didn't do anything for her," he said. "Thousands and thousands of dollars for defenses and lawyers but nothing to show that she ever lived."

He stared down for several moments, as if trying to think of something appropriate to say. "That's where she is," he said, turning away and moving slowly through the thick wet grass, going back to work and throwing more dirt over his shoulder.

Her grave was too small and silent, the way graves always are. One wanted to hear something other than raindrops striking the face of a nearby headstone or the wind soughing in the trees, but there was only the faraway chatter of the workers and the sound of a shovel biting the earth. Unmarked graves are so unsettling because they feel unfinished and the strange worry creeps in that one doesn't know exactly the shape of the plot and one may be standing on it and that feels very disrespectful. The visitor took a step backward, stared into the thick web of grass, said good-bye, and walked away quickly, wondering what Dianne's children were doing this morning.

Bill Aspinwall came awake with a start and looked around in the midnight darkness of his bedroom. He rolled over and sat up. His heart was racing and he pulled in a few long breaths to calm himself, to bring himself back into his familiar reality. His wife was sleeping next to him, his house was quiet, and the dream was beginning to fade, at least for now. Three months had passed since Jennifer's conviction but some old feelings and images still came rushing in through the blackness, disrupting the small hours and clanging his nerves, images of her in the courtroom, images of her right after her arrest. He thought about the ski mask and about Brian serving all those years up in Limon and he wondered to himself, What if he were innocent? What if she'd fooled everyone? What if her story had been a lie? Aspinwall lay back down, annoyed with himself for rehashing these issues—he was prosecuting another murder now and had other things to think about—but he had had trouble shaking the Hood case.

Maybe we should have worked it differently, the lawyer told himself as he gazed at the dark ceiling and tried to go back to sleep. Maybe there was a better way. Maybe we should have tried Jennifer first, without promising her that she would get her life in return for testifying against him. Maybe she would have told us more without any deals and then it would have been easier to convict Hood, Aspinwall thought. *He was guilty but I couldn't prove it without the full story. I couldn't. There was no way. If she'd just told me the truth, I might have been able to change things but she made me doubt her and there was nothing I could do. I couldn't get him for first-degree but I know he was guilty. They both were. I know it.*

Compelling True Crime Thrillers
From Avon Books

THE BLUEGRASS CONSPIRACY
by Sally Denton

71441-8/ $5.50 US/ $6.50 Can

FREED TO KILL
by Gera-Lind Kolarik with Wayne Klatt

71546-5/ $5.50 US/ $6.50 Can

TIN FOR SALE
by John Manca and Vincent Cosgrove

71034-X/ $4.99 US/ $5.99 Can

"I AM CAIN"
by Gera-Lind Kolarik and Wayne Klatt

76624-8/ $4.99 US/ $5.99 Can

GOOMBATA:
THE IMPROBABLE RISE AND FALL OF
JOHN GOTTI AND HIS GANG
by John Cummings and Ernest Volkman

71487-6/ $5.99 US/ $6.99 Can

The Best in Biographies from Avon Books

IT'S ALWAYS SOMETHING
by Gilda Radner   71072-2/$5.95 US/$6.95 Can

RUSH!
by Michael Arkush
                                 77539-5/$4.99 US/$5.99 Can

STILL TALKING
by Joan Rivers   71992-4/$5.99 US/$6.99 Can

CARY GRANT: THE LONELY HEART
by Charles Higham and Roy Moseley
                                 71099-9/$5.99 US/$6.99 Can

I, TINA
by Tina Turner with Kurt Loder
                                 70097-2/$5.50 US/$6.50 Can

ONE MORE TIME
by Carol Burnett   70449-8/$4.95 US/$5.95 Can

PATTY HEARST: HER OWN STORY
by Patricia Campbell Hearst with Alvin Moscow
                                 70651-2/$5.99 US/$6.99 Can

SPIKE LEE
by Alex Patterson   76994-8/$4.99 US/$5.99 Can

COMPREHENSIVE, AUTHORITATIVE REFERENCE WORKS FROM AVON TRADE BOOKS

THE OXFORD AMERICAN DICTIONARY
Edited by Stuart Berg Flexner, Eugene Ehrlich and
Gordon Carruth   51052-9/$9.95 US/$12.95 Can

THE CONCISE COLUMBIA DICTIONARY OF QUOTATIONS
Robert Andrews   70932-5/$9.95 US/$11.95 Can

THE CONCISE COLUMBIA ENCYCLOPEDIA
Edited by Judith S. Levey and Agnes Greenhall

63396-5/$14.95 US

THE NEW COMPREHENSIVE AMERICAN RHYMING DICTIONARY
Sue Young   71392-6/$12.00 US/$15.00 Can

KIND WORDS: A THESAURUS OF EUPHEMISMS
Judith S. Neaman and Carole G. Silver

71247-4/$10.95 US/$12.95 Can

THE WORLD ALMANAC GUIDE TO GOOD WORD USAGE
Edited by Martin Manser with Jeffrey McQuain

71449-3/$8.95 US